"I've spent four long years getting you out of my system, Mike," Sandra whispered hoarsely, her eyes glistening with tears. **"I don't want you back. I can't afford to have you back."**

"Why not?" he rasped, the taste of her still on his lips. "You felt it, too—"

"Of course I felt it! Passion was never our problem, Mike. You could look at me and I'd burst into flames. But what about outside the bedroom? What about real life?"

"Sandra, what do you want from me?"

"I don't know. I…just… I want you to go home."

"Fine," he said savagely. Blood was still pounding in his veins. He was angry. And confused. Then he looked at Sandra, and desire took over again.

He took a step forward. She cut him off.

"You walked away  Mike," she said. "I it now.…"

Dear Reader,

Happy New Year! Silhouette Intimate Moments is starting the year off with a bang—not to mention six great books. Why not begin with the latest of THE PROTECTORS, Beverly Barton's miniseries about men no woman can resist? In *Murdock's Last Stand,* a well-muscled mercenary meets his match in a woman who suddenly has him thinking of forever.

Alicia Scott returns with *Marrying Mike... Again,* an intense reunion story featuring a couple who are both police officers with old hurts to heal before their happy ending. Try Terese Ramin's *A Drive-By Wedding* when you're in the mood for suspense, an undercover agent hero, an irresistible child and a carjacked heroine who ends up glad to go along for the ride. Already known for her compelling storytelling abilities, Eileen Wilks lives up to her reputation with *Midnight Promises,* a marriage-of-convenience story unlike any other you've ever read. Virginia Kantra brings you the next of the irresistible MacNeills in *The Comeback of Con MacNeill,* and Kate Stevenson returns after a long time away, with *Witness... and Wife?*

All six books live up to Intimate Moments' reputation for excitement and passion mixed together in just the right proportions, so I hope you enjoy them all.

Yours,

Leslie J. Wainger
Executive Senior Editor

Please address questions and book requests to:
Silhouette Reader Service
U.S.: 3010 Walden Ave., P.O. Box 1325, Buffalo, NY 14269
Canadian: P.O. Box 609, Fort Erie, Ont. L2A 5X3

MARRYING
MIKE... AGAIN
ALICIA SCOTT

INTIMATE™ MOMENTS®
Published by Silhouette Books
America's Publisher of Contemporary Romance

To my grandfather,
Virgil Chadwick, for all the rides in the red pickup truck.
I miss you, Grandpa.

 SILHOUETTE BOOKS

ISBN 0-373-07980-X

MARRYING MIKE... AGAIN

Copyright © 2000 by Lisa Baumgartner

This edition published by arrangement with Harlequin Books S.A.

Visit us at www.romance.net

Printed in U.S.A.

ALICIA SCOTT

recently escaped the corporate world to pursue her writing full-time. According to the former consultant, "I've always been a writer. It's the perfect job, and you just can't beat the dress code." Born in Hawaii, she grew up in Oregon before moving to New England. Winner of *Romantic Times Magazine*'s award for Career Achievement in Series Romantic Suspense, she also writes *New York Times* bestselling mainstream suspense thrillers as Lisa Gardner.

Alicia is also proud to announce that she finally met the man of her dreams. She and her hubby have settled down in Rhode Island, where they are raising one cat and a bunny.

Alicia loves to hear from readers. You can reach her c/o Silhouette Books, 300 E. 42nd St., New York, NY 10017.

IT'S OUR 20th ANNIVERSARY!
We'll be celebrating all year,
starting with these fabulous titles,
on sale in January 2000.

Prologue

Letter to the Editor
April 18

Editor's Note: This letter arrived at the Citizen's Post *last week. After much deliberation we made the determination to print the letter in the interest of freedom of speech. We have printed it in its original form, all language stands as the author intended. Please note "The Man" is slang for law enforcement while O.G.B. is the acronym for Original Ghetto Blood. Also, according to our city beat editor, "picnics" is generally used to describe gang members congregating in a parking lot to, indeed, picnic. Unfortunately, such gatherings are often an invitation for drive-by shootings by rivals.*

Responses to the letter can be sent to us. If you have any information on who might have sent the letter, please contact Sandra Aikens, Chief of Police, Alexandria County.

Members of the Man:

I had me a dad once. Not a real dad, but an alright one. Respected my mama. Bought me and my brother smokes. He went out one night. Cops caught him. Shot him in the back. I heard one say, Shhht, they gotta teach these boys how to run.

I had me a sister once. Pretty. Other boys, they be lookin' at her, but my mama not dumb. She tell her to play it straight, keep her inside most nights. We don't argue with my mama. She work hard. My sister be by the window. Sun nice and bright. She comb her hair for the boys grinning on the sidewalk. Banger open fire. My sister don't got a cheek now. Just a big, brown hole. Look like a snail live in her face.

I had me a brother once. Big O.G.B. Man of respect. Push me around, make me tough. Make sure I know the score. My brother went to a picnic one day. He ain't ever come back.

I had me a mother once. Now, she sit in a big, ripped up chair. Stuffin stuck in her hair. Hold pictures and cry for things that ain't gonna exist no more. Beg me, plead me, tell me to be better when we both no I wont.

I gotta live on these streets. I gotta get through these halls and they be long and hard. Ain't nothing she can do. Ain't nothing I can do. You give us this world and y'all don't care.

You took my father. You took my sister you took my brother. Y'all broke my mama's heart.

Now you listen to me Man. I be tired of brother killin' brother, homey takin' homey. I'm gonna start my own war, and I got you in my sight. If a Man enters this neighborhood, I'll take him down. Drive my streets, I'll blow off your damn head. It be startin' now. It be startin' and its gonna be big.

I be a straight killer since I wuz ten. Now I be thirteen and I ain't got no need to grow no older.

Call me Vee.

That'll do.

Chapter 1

First day on the job and Sandra Aikens had already violated Playing with the Big Boys rule number one—never let them see you sweat. In fact, on this bright and sunny morning the brand-new police chief was fighting not to violate the next rule—never let them see you cry. There was probably some fine print about never let them see you swear or break small objects, as well. She had a feeling that rule would be gone the moment she stepped into her office, where the twenty-four-hour-old brass nameplate had already been blacked out and overwritten with *Bitch*.

She'd never thought her appointment to chief of police would be well received, particularly by a male-dominated police force under attack for corruption, racism and all-around bad behavior. The nameplate vandalism, however, she thought was crude and unnecessary. As if she didn't know she was trespassing into their precious clubhouse world. As if they didn't know that from day one, she was going to turn their boys-will-be-boys culture upside down. That was her job, and Sandra Aikens never backed down from a challenge—not even on a worse-than-average Monday.

Now her low-slung heels sounded like tiny machine guns rat-tat-tatting their way down the marble halls of a nearly deserted city hall. Her plum-colored pantsuit was sleek, smart and already in a state of disarray. She'd unbuttoned her blazer for air, loosened her brocade vest out of frustration, and was now hard at work dismantling the tight knot holding her wild, chestnut-colored hair.

To hell with appearance. Sandra figured she had exactly ten seconds before she reached the front doors of city hall and was ambushed by the press. At this point, she was simply trying to salvage peace of mind.

"You gotta stand tough, Sandra," Mayor Charles Peterson had barked at 0600 this morning. "This city is in a state of crisis. Did you see that letter in the Sunday *Citizen's Post?* Do you know what that means? We need an image of strength! Competence! People need to feel we have the department and the city under control. *You* need to appear in control."

Sandra had smiled wryly. She'd understood what he was saying. As with many local governments, Mayor Peterson had been forced to recruit a civilian to be the new chief of police because the current department was too bogged down with allegations of fiscal mismanagement, corruption and police brutality to provide a credible leader.

In theory, Sandra's background as a former security company vice president would enable her to provide better management and budgeting sense than the typical chief of police, who probably had more experience as a good cop than as a good boss. She also entered with a clean slate—with no allegiances to old buddies or political factions. She could look at her staff with the cold, frank gaze of impartiality. She could assess their actions honestly as she launched an intensive in-house investigation into numerous complaints.

Of course, she would also enter without any support from the police officers and with a great deal of skepticism from the D.A.

Six months, Mayor Peterson had given her—the limited time span before the next election—to take over the beleaguered police force, turn it around and make both her and the mayor look like heroes. Right. Piece of cake.

Once upon a time, Alexandria had been the quaint small town where people moved to escape crime, pollution and poverty. Streets had been clean, lawns mowed, citizens well-off. Main Street had beautiful old storefronts run by the well-off families in the third generation of ownership. People trusted the police and people trusted one another. People thought the textile mills along the river would last forever.

It had been a long time since the 1950s and *West Side Story* had taken on new meaning in Alexandria, Massachusetts, where one-half of the town drove home to white picket fences while the rest walked through crumbling streets of bullet-ridden projects. Where the white, west-side leadership said they knew what they were doing, while the minority, east-side civilians claimed they were grossly out of touch. Where the police force said they were in control of the situation while the taxpayers accused them of breaking half of the city's laws.

And now a thirteen-year-old kid had written a letter to the editor, threatening to shoot the next cop that drove into his neighborhood.

At Sandra's weakest moment, around four-thirty this morning, when her alarm clock went off before the sun had even gotten out of bed, she was afraid her parents might be right.

"For heaven's sake, you don't know the first thing about law enforcement, Sandra. What are you thinking?"

"It's not money is it? I thought you had managed your trust fund quite well."

Then that wonderful moment when full horror had struck her mother's fine patrician face. *"It's not…it's not…him, is it? Good Lord, you've been divorced four years. Surely you've realized what a mistake…surely you've gotten him out of your system. Sandra, really!"*

Sandra really, she thought with a sigh, and picked up her footsteps.

The huge brass doors loomed ahead of her, the last barrier between her and the press. She could hear the dull roar of news vans and screeching microphones. This was it.

Sandra took a deep breath. She'd run dozens of meetings more important than this; she'd handled situations more critical. She was capable, she was efficient. She would get the job done. And yet her hand was shaking on the large brass handle and, for just one moment, she was picturing her ex-husband.

The way he'd looked at her that first day, those bright, amused eyes, that strong, massive chest. The way he'd drawled her name with a slight Cajun accent, sending shivers down her spine.

It was interesting how many things Sandra had learned to forgive over the past four years. And it was even more interesting how many things she didn't know how to forget.

Sandra pushed open the yawning brass doors, and the lightbulbs exploded in her face.

* * *

"Chief Aikens, Chief Aikens. Is it true you're establishing an independent council to look into corruption—"

"Chief Aikens, what is it we hear about requiring all police officers to attend 'race sensitivity' training—"

"Did you see the Sunday *Citizen's Post*—"

"Will there be layoffs?"

"What about community policing—"

Sandra raised her hand to signal silence. More lightbulbs flashed, then the hordes settled down. She surveyed her audience. Half-a-dozen print reporters plus the four local news affiliates. But no Mike, she thought, and she was immediately irritated by a sense of disappointment.

"I'm planning a formal news conference at four o'clock tomorrow afternoon," she announced crisply. "Until then, you have ten minutes."

Groans, then a surge forward as the reporters fought for their questions to come first.

"What about community policing?"

"Community policing has proved highly effective nationwide and I think it's a model we should look into. For too long the police force has stood outside of the people. It's time to get everyone back together, working together."

"Are you serious about a racial sensitivity course?"

She looked at the two police officers in the back—both white, both middle-aged, both stoney-faced. "I'm *very* serious about a class in racial relations. Alexandria's track record in this department is appalling. There will be changes."

The tough talk earned her a moment of silence, but it lasted only a moment. While the reporters hastily scribbled her reply, Sandra watched the two officers in the back turn away. She wondered if it was their job to report back to the locker room everything she had just said.

"What about the kid? What about the one who calls himself Vee?"

"I am aware of the situation," Sandra said carefully. "We encourage anyone who knows the letter writer to come forward. This is obviously an angry child and we'd like to do everything we can to help him. He does have choices. If he'll come forward, we'll help him identify those choices and get the support he needs. There is no reason for this to lead to violence."

"Are you going to send officers into the east side, even with that kind of threat?"

"A police officer's life is always under threat. That goes with the job."

"There were three lieutenants who thought they deserved being promoted to chief. Now they have to answer to an 'outsider.' How do you think they'll handle that?"

She smiled thinly. *With lots of hugs and kisses.* "We are all professional."

"What about your husband?"

"Wh-what?" For the first time she faltered, not prepared for this line of questioning. The reporter appeared pleased with himself.

"Isn't it true you were married to Detective Mike Rawlins, aka 'Big Mike'?"

"*Were* is the key word there. I don't see how that's relevant—"

"Well, you have to have feelings for this man, good or otherwise. I mean, you were his wife, right?"

Sandra gave the young reporter a steady look that hid just how much she resented this line of questioning. She said without one iota of hesitation, "Detective Rawlins and I have been divorced four years. It is not an issue."

She looked at her watch. It had been only eight minutes, not ten, but she ruled it close enough. With a last wave, she descended the steps and headed straight to her sedan. The cameramen crushed in, snapping away and forcing her to turn sideways to cut a clean line.

Finally her police officers intervened and grudgingly held back the tide.

"Thank you," she murmured.

The men did not answer back.

"So what's she like? Come on, Rawlins, you were married to the chick."

Leaning against the back wall of the police department's sadly worn debriefing room, Detective Mike Rawlins arched a brow, while, in front of him, the bony police officer everyone called Weasel flushed.

"Now, Weasel," Mike drawled, "might I recommend that you don't start your interactions with our new chief by using the word *chick*. She might take offense. And for the record, an Aikens who takes offense...well, you might as well dig your own grave now."

Standing next to Mike, Rusty Koontz snickered. Mike's partner for the past eight years, Koontz dressed like a pimp and maintained the coldest eyes on the force. He liked to crack off-color jokes, chase women, and torment rookies until they broke.

Local legend had it he'd bet his last partner he could make Big Mike blow a fuse by the end of the day. Koontz had followed the former college football player for eight hours. He'd brought up Mike's weak knee, his failed football plays. He'd attacked his faint Southern drawl, a legacy from his Cajun father who'd left New Orleans forty years ago to play pro football for the Jets. He'd even taken on Mike's spitfire mom.

At the end of the day, the huge rookie who could've taken out tall, thin Koontz with a single punch had merely shaken his head and said, "You need a therapist, man. A real *good* therapist."

Koontz had been impressed. He'd become Big Mike's partner, and there wasn't a pair more mismatched—or more effective—in the whole department.

Now Koontz made a show of studying his neatly pared fingernails. "Come on, Weasel. You know Big Mike isn't the kind to kiss and tell. He considers himself to be a Southern boy. They have rules."

"Yeah, but I still hang out with the likes of you, so that can't explain everything." Mike winked and the rest of the room burst out laughing, fifty cops finally getting to dispel some of the tension that had been growing as they waited for their new chief of police. The laughter ended uneasily. It was now seven-thirty in the morning. Chief Sandra Aikens was due to arrive any minute and no one was sure what that meant. Some officers paced the cheap industrial floor. Two detectives appeared to be counting water stains on the drop ceiling. One of the older cops, Higgins, who was two years from retirement and anxious about the rumored layoffs, was downing coffee and Tums in equal measure.

Up front, Lieutenants Banks, Hopkins, and Thoron sat in the cheap plastic chairs, keeping their faces straight ahead. They looked stiff and uncomfortable. Hopkins had been the most vocal about his certainty that he would be the next chief of police. Now, no one would meet his eye.

Men had a rule about letting other men eat crow in peace.

The sound of ringing heels finally echoed down the hall. To a man, they stiffened, exchanged looks. Weasel cracked a nervous joke. It promptly fizzled.

Seconds later, Police Chief Sandra Aikens appeared in the doorway, looking sharp and totally out of their league in a well-tailored silk pantsuit that probably cost more than any of them made in a week. She gave the room one long, measuring look, then headed for the podium with a take-no-prisoners stride.

"Holy—" Koontz muttered under his breath and, beside him, Mike finally faltered.

Four years, he thought. Four years since he'd last seen his wife. And sweet Lord, even after all this time, cool Sandy Aikens walked into his life like a punch in the gut.

She didn't just enter a room, she *entered* a room. Maybe that's what it meant to inherit your daddy's yacht-club world and million-dollar corporation. Mike had never fully understood it, but when Sandra appeared, the planets stopped spinning and the stars started aligning. She had the look, that certain carriage that stated she knew exactly who she was and she didn't really care if you liked it. She was going to do it her way, so put up or shut up.

Damn, he'd always liked that about her. Not just a woman, but a grade-A challenge. *Ah, ma chère…*

Sandra Aikens with the crazy, curly, red-brown hair. Sandra Aikens, with those direct blue eyes that used to make him want to crawl inside her head just so he could finally learn everything she was thinking. Sandra Aikens, with those sleek pantsuits that hid the best damn collection of French lingerie ever to walk this earth. Sandy Aikens, who'd always driven him wild.

Mike could have had any woman he wanted, but from the minute he'd responded to a report of a mugging and met Sandy Aikens, he'd only wanted her. She'd run down her own mugger with her Mercedes that day, pinning the gangly kid against a brick building. Mike hadn't known whether to laugh at the terrified look on the young mugger's face or lecture Sandra thoroughly. He'd ended up asking her out to dinner. He'd plied her with wine. He'd watched her relax and grow a little silly from good food and good company. And his poor stupid heart had simply flip-flopped in his chest—he'd become hooked on fierce, haughty Sandra Aikens.

That's because men don't do any thinking with the appendage above their necks, his mama had told him later. Looking at how everything had turned out, he'd had no argument there.

Sandra tapped the microphone. Koontz, who had never liked Sandra, not even when he was the best man at her and Mike's wedding, lit up a cigarette and pointedly exhaled toward the No Smoking sign. Like most of the men, he was ticked off by her appointment to chief. Mike just found the whole thing twisted and amusing. But then, that was his way.

Sandra didn't say a word about Koontz's smoking. She just flashed him the same tight, annoyed look most people reserved for gnats. Then her gaze swept the whole room, meeting everyone's gaze but Mike's. That made him grin. Maybe he wasn't the only one feeling their meeting in places down deep. Maybe she was also thinking about how they ended their first date—on the floor, on the kitchen island, on the sofa, the dining room table…

"All right," his ex-wife said crisply, her gaze locking on the front row, "let's get on with it. I'll start with the good news and work my way down."

"There's good news?" Koontz murmured, and a few officers tittered.

"There will be no layoffs," Sandra stated, and that quickly caught them all by surprise. "In fact, as of last Friday, I got Mayor Peterson to agree to allocate an additional two million dollars to the police department's budget, the first increase in five years. There will be no layoffs. You have my word."

The room buzzed, even Koontz looked unnerved. For years officers had been griping about being underpaid, unappreciated, and unloved. The new chief of police couldn't have started the show better if she'd just doubled their pensions. Mike crossed his ankles. Knowing his brilliant ex-wife, he waited for the other shoe to drop.

"Of course," she continued smoothly, "nothing is free. Let's not mince words. This department is in shambles. I know it, you know it, the public knows it. The mayor has appropriated funds for us, but in return, we *must* deliver results. I'm talking firearms training, pursuit and capture training, interrogation techniques. I'm also talking community relations training, basic PR, and yes, the dreaded rumor you have already heard—racial sensitivity training. We will learn to be a kinder, gentler police department."

"Great," Koontz muttered. "Ebonics in the police force."

Sandra arched a brow. "Do you have a comment, Detective, or are you merely suffocating on your own secondhand smoke?"

More nervous laughter, then abrupt coughing sounds as the men realized they were rooting for the wrong side. Koontz flicked a shower of sparks onto the already burntup floor and said calmly, "I'm just wondering when we're going to do all this training. You know, we have so much free time around here. Or—" his eyes narrowed "—did we finally get money for OT?"

"No OT," Sandra said, and the whole room groaned. She rapped the podium sharply. "Look, I know compensation is a big concern around here, but we're going to have to take this one step at a time. Right now, this department does not have the public equity it takes to negotiate higher pay or more OT dollars. But if everyone pitches in, if taxpayers begin to think we're doing our jobs again, then next year, we can go after the additional compensation. Rome was not built in a day.''

More grumbling. If they all had a nickel for each time some bureaucrat had told them that, they'd finally have that pension they'd been yearning for.

Sandy got back to her speech. Mike found himself wondering if she still practiced the night before in front of the mirror. He used to watch her rehearse for big meetings, going over each word, analyzing every syllable, until everything was exactly right. He had his own way of helping out—he'd wait until she was in the middle of the important part, then he'd come up behind her and slowly peel away the first layer of silk...

''That brings me to my next point,'' she was saying. ''We have received part of a federal grant to start a community policing program. Basically, you will all be assigned neighborhoods where you will form community task forces, then teach community members how to monitor for illegal activities and conduct basic patrols on their own. In addition to building community pride, this is one way of freeing up some of our manpower to focus on more serious crimes. It's also going to help us reclaim our city.''

''Hallelujah and praise the Lord,'' Koontz muttered dubiously. ''Let's train a granny patrol to chase off drug dealers. Now that makes me proud to wear a badge.''

Sandy got a tight look around her mouth. She gripped the podium harder, and Mike knew she was working hard to control her temper. Sandra had quite a temper. Of course, one advantage of all those fights had been the making up....

''Finally, as of next month, we're refurbishing this police station. New pipes, new wiring, and for heaven's sake—'' she glanced up at the ancient collection of yellow stains ''—new ceilings. Not only are we going to have a new attitude, but a new look. So get used to being shaken up. It's going to be a long time before you consider your job to be business as usual. Any questions?''

"Yo, I got a question." Koontz shook out his double-breasted suit. "Are we getting new uniforms, too? 'Cause you know, last time I went to make an arrest, I just didn't feel that I looked like the 'real me.' I mean, am I a warm tone or a cool tone? I just don't know and it's really keeping me up late at night."

Sandra cut him a narrow glance through the fresh burst of laughter. "Make your point, Detective, or stand down."

That was it. Mike shook his head. He'd seen this interplay between his ex-wife and his partner too many times before. Koontz always rattled her chains and she always responded by upping the ante. Already the men were looking away, the air getting tense. They'd seen Koontz in action.

"My point is," Koontz said slowly, "that we're finally getting money and you're sending us back to *school?* Lady, have you been on the streets lately? Those 'kids' are carrying AK-47s. What do you want us to do, read them Dickens?"

"No, Detective, I'd hate for you to stumble over all the big words. As a matter of record, studies have shown that proper training in violent confrontation leads to more effective handling of the situation and fewer police shoot-outs. And this department certainly needs something. Last year, officers were involved in five high-speed pursuits that resulted in only one capture but four critically injured civilians, plus thousands of dollars in damage. This department also suffered six major shoot-outs, killing five suspects—a statistic totally out of proportion for a department this size—"

"Oh, well, then I take it all back. I mean, if the *studies* say I'll be safer…'' Koontz shook his head in disgust. "Have you even been out there, *Chief* Aikens? Can you make it one block on the east side without some kid showing a piece or flashing a sign? All those teenagers loitering on the corners, watching every move we make. Even the eight-year-olds have thousand-yard stares and we *know* it's not toy pistols they're carrying in their pockets. Fact is, we're outmanned *and* outgunned by the dear old public. We don't need education, we need assault rifles.''

"Here, here,'' a few men muttered.

Sandra pursed her lips. "Well, as long as we're on the subject, I'm sure you've all heard about the letter that appeared in the Sunday *Post*. At the moment, I think it's too soon to know whether it's a hoax or not, but in the interest of safety, I want all officers patrolling the east side to wear vests.''

"'Cause kids never take a head shot,'' Koontz snapped sarcastically.

Sandra frowned. "Let's not lose perspective here. We're talking about a confused thirteen-year-old boy. Not a professional assassin.''

Koontz immediately jumped at the comment, but Mike finally took pity on his ex-wife and put a silencing hand on his partner's shoulder. He said calmly, "Actually, he is.''

His ex-wife rewarded his interruption with an annoyed look. He returned her glare with his most charming grin and kicked himself away from the wall.

"The kid called himself a straight shooter,'' he explained. "That's gang lingo for *assassin*. Used to be that the sixteen-year-olds were in charge of shootings, but now the state will try them as adults and these kids aren't dumb. Gangs lowered the bar, as well, training their shooters younger. Hell, a thirteen-year-old is just plain ancient in the east side. Soon we'll be facing off with toddlers.''

"It's a war out there," Koontz murmured fiercely. "A damn jungle, where they don't have any rules and we're bound by all of them. This Vee is not a kid. He's a killer, a cold-blooded killer and we ought to be going after him with everything we have. To hell with kinder or gentler.''

"No, Detective, you're wrong. Declaring war on the community is exactly what's gotten the department into this situation. Alexandria must stop thinking in terms of 'us' and 'them' and that change will start right here, right now. We're not going to barrel into the east side with guns blazing. We're going to work to find this child. Furthermore, we're going to work with this community so other children won't grow up with this level of rage and alienation. That's what community policing is about, and that's what this department will become about.''

"And then we'll skip through fields of daisies," Koontz said.

She smiled grimly. "If that's what it takes.''

"Come on, *Chief*. You live in a half-a-million dollar house and drive a sixty-thousand-dollar car. You don't know a damn thing about police work and you certainly don't know what it's like out there. Save your little speeches for the press. They're the only ones buying it. I for one am telling you that if I see a kid with a gun in the east side, I'm gonna respond to that and I'm gonna respond *hard*. You know what they say—'it's better to be tried by twelve than buried by six.' ''

"And I'm telling you," Sandra said evenly, "that the next shooting experienced by this department will be investigated with every resource I have available, and if there is the *slightest* indication, Detective, that the situation could have been handled without force, I will personally take that officer's badge. We will be playing by new rules. Are we clear?''

The room was silent and way too tense.

Sandra's gaze went man to man. Most looked away. But Koontz didn't, and neither did a handful of others. Her next comments were directed at them.

''I'm going to say this once and once only, and then I consider this matter behind us. You don't have to like me. You can hate me because I'm a woman. You can hate me because I'm a civilian. You can hate me because I'm a Virgo if you like, and you only play with Geminis. Regardless, things around here are going to change because, whether you like it or not, I'm not the enemy.

''You are.''

Her gaze came to rest on Koontz. ''As a department, you have betrayed the trust of your community. People do not respect the Alexandria police force, they fear it. They do not consider you part of the solution, they consider you part of the problem. You have ended up with a civilian chief of police because taxpayers did not trust one of your own to clean up shop. So you can argue with me all you like. You can write *bitch* on my nameplate if it will make you feel better. But I'm not going anywhere. I'm going to turn this department upside down, inside out, and front to back. By the time I'm done, I'm honestly not sure how many of you will still be part of this force. But I promise you this, those of you who do remain will finally have a job and a police department to be proud of. *That* is what this is all about.''

She snapped off the mike. ''Lieutenants, in my office. Rawlins, Koontz, plan on meeting at eleven. That will be all.''

She strode out of the room. It took about another minute

more for everyone to recover. Guys were rattled. Koontz looked fit to kill.

"I still can't believe you married her," he muttered to Mike. "I tried to tell you better. Holy Hillary Rodham Clinton."

Mike simply smiled, his gaze still on the doorway, where Sandy had vanished with a flourish. For a minute, he was thinking of that last day, when she had looked at him so calmly, without even a tear marring her face, and had told him their marriage was over. That last moment when she had simply walked out of his life and stolen all the breath from his lungs. There just wasn't a woman in the world like Sandra Aikens, he thought wryly, bitterly, hopelessly.

Never should've married her? *Mon Dieu*, Koontz didn't know the half of it.

Chapter 2

Sandra made it back to her office just before her nerves gave out. Well, that meeting had gone about as well as she'd expected. Anger, distrust, resentment. Kind of reminded her of the good old days of crashing Mike's family picnics.

Oh, God, and that whole business with thirteen-year-old "straight shooters." She hadn't known that meant *assassin*. She simply hadn't had the time to debrief on the current street-gang situation in Alexandria. She'd get to it, but Koontz's point still stood. She was a thirty-four-year-old blue blood. What did she really know about kids like Vee? Or for that matter, the men she was supposed to lead?

Eight-thirty. Her lieutenants would be walking in at any moment. And once she was done with that barrel of fun, she'd get to meet with Koontz and Mike. Big Mike. Big sexy Mike Rawlins.

He'd looked good. She wasn't sure what she'd expected—her ex-husband had always been unbelievably attractive, tall, dark and handsome to a T. She supposed she'd thought time would dull the edges. Or maybe because they weren't married anymore, she'd look at him more objectively.

No such luck. Lounging in the back of the room with his arms crossed over his massive chest, his dark features carrying his easy Cajun grin, he'd looked irresistible. A man who could stop a woman's pulse with a single wink. A man comfortable enough in his own skin to spend a whole Sunday buck naked. A man who'd once devoted two hours to worshiping the curve at the small of her back.

Sandra had spent four years purging all thoughts of Mike Rawlins from her head. Now, just minutes after seeing him in the back of a room, she was once more overwhelmed. The scent of him, the feel of him, the sound of his low, rumbling voice.

She still remembered their first date vividly. Her nervous giddiness at having a bona fide hunk ask her out to dinner. Her growing admiration over pasta primavera when she realized the former-football-hero-turned-cop had a brain. And a wicked sense of humor. And a slow, easy-spreading smile that caused an equally slow spreading fire deep in her belly. One glass of wine leading to three. The growing astonishment that she was enjoying herself. In fact, she was having the most fun she'd had in ages.

Then he'd turned to her with that dark, sinful gaze, whispering sweet words in French, and she'd started fantasizing about moving straight from dinner to dessert. At her house. She'd wanted the Cajun's shirt off. She'd wanted his pants off. She'd wanted to strip the man naked and lap him up like a bowl of cream. She, the woman who had a rule about no necking until date three.

She'd taken Mike home after dinner. She'd broken every rule she'd ever had about men, and he'd made it so much fun, she'd broken them all again the next morning. On the sofa, in the hallway, somewhere halfway inside the bedroom, the marble countertop of the master bath.

When she'd finally made it to work the next day, she'd been so flushed and happy, she'd moved the board meeting outside and had a picnic lunch with her secretary. Maria had told her whatever she'd done, she should do it again and often.

So Sandra had. Mike showed up with flowers just to say hi. They made love on a sea of rose petals in the front hall. Mike swore the next night he'd actually take her out to dinner. They coupled like wild animals in his truck still parked in her driveway. They decided they would have to go out in public if they wanted to have a conversation. They ended up horizontal in an elevator Mike conveniently knew how to jam between floors.

Sandra lost five pounds that first week alone. Her friends remarked on how radiant she looked. Her mother wanted to know what spa she'd discovered. She told them nothing. Mike was hers in a way nothing had ever been hers before. He was magical, romantic, tender. He was whimsical, physical, and sexy as hell. He brought out parts of her she hadn't known existed. He made her whole.

And sometimes, when just the sound of his voice on the phone brightened her day and brought a silly little grin to her lips, he frightened her. She'd never wanted anyone the way she wanted him. She'd never spent an entire Saturday waiting for a phone call, then feeling deliriously happy when it came. A Friday-night date would have her glowing all week. An unexpected Wednesday dinner left her flying.

He consumed her world with terrifying speed, and even when the sensible part of her mind told her they were too different to last, the rest of her simply wanted more.

Then, six months later, on a warm sultry night, he took

her out to an especially fine French restaurant, her favorite. Afterward they strolled around, enjoying the fading days of August and the scent of petunias in the air. Mike was quiet, which she thought was odd. But then she was feeling strangely quiet herself.

Wordlessly they went back to her place. And there, he cradled her against his chest and told her that he loved her. He peeled off her clothes piece by piece. He played with her wild chestnut hair. He worshiped her body until she begged. And when he finally entered her body, hot and panting from the strain, they both kept their eyes wide-open. They shared the wonder, the slow-building heaviness, the driving need. They shared the climax, and for reasons Sandra had never fully understood, she'd wept.

Mike kissed away her tears. He gazed at her with a dark intensity she'd never seen in his face before. He asked her to be his wife.

Sandra never hesitated to say yes.

It had been one of the happiest moments of her life.

Now, alone in her office five years later, Sandra did her best not to think about the rest.

Her lieutenants were sullen. Sandra tried to compliment them on some aspect of their leadership, but it wasn't enough and they all knew it. They'd been good cops and they'd assumed being good cops would make them good lieutenants, which would make them good chiefs of police. That they practiced nepotism and received kickbacks shouldn't matter. Hell, everyone did that.

Sandra understood that all three of them thought she would fail. Outsiders, after all, couldn't get cooperation, and it was hard to run a law enforcement department without help. The first time she had a high-profile case—say a shooting by a thirteen-year-old gang member—one of them would call in an old favor and the Crime Scene Unit, the CSU, would magically lose a shell casing. The Medical Examiner's Office would suddenly need four weeks to run fingerprints, and heaven help her if she wanted an autopsy performed fast. Need a search warrant? The ADA would be busy. Need a cross-reference with an old case file from Gang Task Force or robbery homicide or Vice? What old case file? Never let it be said that middle-aged law enforcement bureaucrats weren't passive-aggressive.

Sandra wasn't worried. For one thing, she had the mayor firmly behind her. Also, Sandra Aikens hadn't doubled the family security business without learning a few things. What did all cops worry about? Retirement. What did all retired cops do to supplement their pensions? Work for security companies. What did Sandra's family own and Sandra formerly work at? Ahh. She spelled it out for her lieutenants, and they looked as if they might be ill.

Mess with the new chief, they garnered, screw your future. Maybe she'd have it made into a bumper sticker. She could hang it outside her office, underneath the hastily scrawled nameplate, Bitch.

One of the lieutenants, Hopkins, would have to go in the end—he'd been too vocal about his desire to be chief and too humiliated by her subsequent appointment to ever play nice. As for Banks and Thoron, the jury was still out. Lieutenant Banks, in her opinion, was a genuinely good cop. She would go out of her way to make him feel valued in the new organization. Whether that would be enough for him remained to be seen. Lieutenant Thoron, on the other hand, was a mixed bag. He had a strong following in the department, but was also rumored to be involved in some of the "extracurricular" activities. Sandra hoped that it wasn't true. Alexandria honestly couldn't afford to lose two lieutenants at once; they didn't have the replacement pool for it. Especially now, when a threat had been issued against the police department and everyone was wound tight.

Would a thirteen-year-old really open fire on a cop? How in the world would men like Koontz respond if he did?

She'd have a war. A full-scale war. Good Lord.

Rapping on the door. Sandra looked up and there stood Mike.

He was well dressed today. In honor of her first day? She didn't know. But he was wearing navy-blue pants that caressed his powerful legs. Blue pin-striped dress shirt sharply pressed and stretching over his barrel chest. His tie appeared to be silk and had a dark blue backdrop with little gold daisies. Very daring for Mike. She wondered immediately what woman had picked it out for him and wished she'd stop thinking that way.

His face still looked exactly as she remembered. Solid square jaw already covered with a five-o'clock shadow at eleven in the morning. Full lips, curling up in one corner as if he was sharing a friendly joke. Dark, gleaming eyes framed by ungodly thick lashes and deeply etched laugh lines. The face of a man who smiled easily and often.

His black hair was beginning to gray at the temples. She hadn't realized that before and waited for it to make him look old. It didn't. His dark eyes were still bright, his body powerful and strong. Age would be kind to Mike Rawlins. She suddenly wanted to cup his face with her hand, to see if he would turn his lips against her palm the way he used to, and it shamed her.

Four years was such a long time. Why did it suddenly seem not long enough?

Sandra took a deep breath. Then she said, "Thank you for coming, Detective. Please have a seat."

"Detective, huh?" Mike raised a brow as he strode into the room. "I suppose I've been called worse."

She managed a smile. "I know you have."

He chuckled, taking the lone wooden chair, turning it around and straddling the seat. Then he met her gaze as if debriefing with his ex-wife was something he did every day. She appreciated his professionalism, but then Mike's job had always been the one thing he'd taken seriously.

"I imagine Koontz will join us shortly?"

"Uh...well, you see, he had something come up."

"Something come up?" It was her turn to raise a brow. "And what, pray tell, could be more important than meeting with his boss?"

"Well, pray tell, I don't know."

Sandra planted her hands on her desk, no longer amused. "He's boycotting this meeting on purpose, isn't he, Mike?"

"I'm just his partner, *ma chère*, not his baby-sitter. Koontz is a big boy and can speak for himself."

She'd opened her mouth for a sharp retort, when she caught herself and gritted her teeth. The Koontz argument was old. And bitter. And something she and Mike wouldn't resolve in the next five minutes, let alone the next five years.

She said more levelly, "Fine. I'll debrief with you now and you can inform your partner of our discussion. Please pass along as well that I'm sorry he couldn't be with us this morning—and if he makes me any sorrier, he'll be spending the rest of his days writing parking tickets."

"He'll be delighted to hear it," Mike assured her. "Rusty responds well to authority, you know."

"Trust me, I know. Let's get down to business. I have a case for you and Koontz that I'd like you to make top priority."

Mike looked mildly surprised. "Someone's died and I haven't heard about it?"

"No one's died. That's the point of this case. I want you to keep it that way. I want you to find the boy who wrote the letter to the paper. This Vee."

"*Huh?*"

Mike was genuinely startled. She'd expected that. He and Koontz were homicide detectives; they only got involved with kids like Vee when one turned up dead. But the Gang Task Force had a lot on its plate right now. And the Gang Task Force contained the majority of the men Internal Affairs was about to begin investigating for police brutality. Not that Sandra could tell Mike that.

"Hey, *ma chère*—"

"Chief. Chief Aikens. Not *ma chère.*"

"Hey, *Chief,* maybe I should explain the different departments to you. Homicide, Vice, White Collar, Gang—"

"Mike, I know the departments. Listen to me. You were at the meeting this morning, you know the mood around here. We have tensions between blacks and whites, tensions between civilians and policemen, tensions between the haves and the have-nots. And now we have a thirteen-year-old boy sitting in the middle of this storm. He's angry, he's resentful, and he's disenfranchised. According to you, he's also experienced. So what do you think will happen if he makes good on this threat?"

Mike conceded her point with a nod. "War. A big war. Which I suppose would then be homicide. Lots of homicides."

Sandra gave them both a minute to absorb that thought. Then she said quietly, "This case is very serious, Mike. I need the best men in the department on it—that's you and Rusty. I know you both have the time and the ability, so what do you say? Help me out on this one?"

He appeared to consider it, leaning back, crossing his arms over his chest and giving her his famous slow appraisal. Sandra didn't really doubt his answer—Mike was too good a cop to say no—but she understood his need to drag it out. It wasn't often she asked for anything from him. And having your ex-wife at your mercy had to have some perks.

"I suppose we could check the gang database," Mike drawled shortly. "It has all the known gang monikers cross-referenced with the kids' legal names. Even if he isn't known, you gotta figure he's already in the system somewhere. Been picked up for loitering or possession, maybe burglary or assault. Not too many thirteen-year-olds in the east side who don't already have a record. NCIC might spit him out for us." He nodded. "So say I can punch a few buttons and find the kid. Then what? We pick him up and bring him in?"

"No, I don't want him brought in, at least not right away."

"*Chief,* the kid threatened to shoot cops. You don't let that kind of thing go unanswered. Particularly when you're the *new* chief of police."

"Hear me out. This kid already feels cops are the enemy. In his own words, they shot his father in the back and are hardly a symbol of security. Right now, he's angry, but he hasn't done anything yet. Two cops standing on his front door, however, may decide matters for him."

"The kid wrote a letter declaring war, honey. I don't think he's undecided."

"Yes, *sweetie,* but that's the point. He wrote a letter. He didn't simply open fire. He wrote." Sandra leaned forward, all sarcasm aside, and looked at her ex-husband earnestly. "Think, Mike. You say he's probably had experience in killings, that he's not an innocent. If he really wanted violence, why wouldn't he just wait for the night patrol and open fire? We don't generally wear vests. We wouldn't be expecting it. He could have easily taken out two good men before they would've had the chance to blink. Instead of doing that, however, this kid wrote a letter and sent it to the paper. That's reaching out.''

''Or building a rep.''

''What, is it standard practice for gang members to notify the newspapers of their intended targets?''

''Not yet, but maybe the kid is starting a trend.''

''Mike, he's just thirteen—''

''Nah, nah, don't go saying that.'' Mike threw his hands up in the air. ''Now see, this is where you get yourself in trouble. You're looking at Vee as a kid, as an age range for you to fit into some standard mold of other thirteen-year-olds you've seen at your parents' parties. Cute, maybe a little awkward, still kind of on the small side. *Mon Dieu,* Sandy, he's nothing like that, and what the hell are you doing having two detectives waste valuable time hunting him down for a chat?''

''I don't know! You want the truth, Mike? *I don't know.* But I'm betting two officers on the front porch will lead to war. So I'm going for option number two. Identify who he is. Learn about his life. See if we can pinpoint people who are important to him, say an adult he trusts. Clergyman, teacher, parent, what the hell, his parole officer. Then we can approach this person and, hopefully, through them, get some kind of dialogue going. Outreach. Communication. Work him through his rage.''

''And if he opens fire first?''

''We hope that doesn't happen. We move *fast* to help insure that it doesn't happen. You and Koontz move fast.''

Mike rolled his eyes, but at least he'd stopped shaking his head. Sandra was thankful for that. She didn't want to have to force the issue. She didn't want to have to confess to her ex-husband that he had to take this case because he was the only person in the department she could trust.

"Yeah," he said abruptly. "What the hell. We'll track the kid down and do a full background report. If he's in the system, we could have it to you by the end of the day. Then you can approach him to your heart's content. Outreach away."

"Thank you."

He shrugged. "It's the job."

"Sure it is."

"No, honey, it's the job."

"Mike, it's been four years. We're divorced. I *know* you don't owe me anything, okay. I got it."

The outburst was too defensive, and shamed them both into silence. Mike's gaze dropped to the floor. Sandra felt simply humiliated. Fifteen minutes into her first conversation with Mike, and she already sounded angry and hurt. She had to bite her bottom lip to keep from sighing heavily.

Mike said abruptly, "Nice meeting this morning."

"Yeah? You think I alienated everyone? I was trying very hard to."

"I think you can consider yourself a success." His gaze came up; he wore a reluctant grin. "You always did have style, *ma chère.*"

"Thanks." She bounced her pen against the desk. "So what's the pool at?"

"The pool?"

"You know, the 'how many weeks until I run screaming from the office' pool."

"Oh *ma chère,* we're not counting weeks."

"Days?"

"Hours, honey. Hours."

"Ah, hence the new nameplate." While she'd been meeting with the lieutenants, someone had thoughtfully taken down the *Bitch* plate. Someone else had thoughtfully replaced it with a new four-letter word. One that was far worse.

Mike looked troubled again. "I'll take that down on my way out."

"Don't bother. They'll just put up another."

"Well, maybe I could pass the word around—"

"Not your war to fight."

Mike's jaw clenched. "No," he said after a second. "I suppose it isn't. You know, *Chief,* maybe it shouldn't be war. Maybe going head to head only guarantees that you'll lose. So some of these boys are rough around the edges. So Rusty likes to mouth off. He's still a good cop. Give him a little ground now, maybe you'll get it back later."

"You're blind to Rusty, Mike. He doesn't just mouth off. He believes what he says."

"He's a good cop—"

"He's a racist, sexist, egotistical pig, and I'm not just speaking from past experience. For God's sake, he's carrying a gun in the name of the law, not selling life insurance."

"Is that really why you hate him, Sandy, or is it simply 'cause he's my partner?"

She drew up short. So did Mike. He exhaled first. "Sorry," he acknowledged. "Shouldn't have gone there."

"I think we have to agree to disagree on that subject," she said stiffly.

"Yeah. Maybe we should make a list, all the things we aren't allowed to talk about during these meetings."

"Then the meeting would be too short."

"Yeah, yeah." His lips twisted. "Ah, hell."

He drifted into silence, and Sandra understood how he

felt. She was trying her best, too, and it was still hard not
to hit old buttons. Or escape old memories and emotions.
Everything had always been so tangled between them.
Love and war, passion and pain. So unbelievably good
inside the bedroom. So completely incapable of carrying
on a simple conversation outside of it.

Sandra had hoped four years would be enough time to
put things behind them. She'd been wrong.

"Sandy, how are you? I mean, *how are you?*"

"I'm—I'm okay. And you?"

"Fine." He shrugged, smiled wryly. "You know me.
Always fine."

She smiled. Yes, *fine* was definitely Mike's favorite
word. "And your family?"

"Good. Chris is getting married. The last Rawlins to go.
He found himself a naval pilot if you can believe that. The
woman can not only outthrow him on the football field,
but she can also fly rings around him. So far we're threatening to accept her into the family and kick him out."

"I can imagine." Mike's family had threatened to kick
her out, too. Definitely no love lost there. Belatedly Mike
seemed to realize he'd touched a nerve, and he moved
hastily to a fresh subject.

"And your family?"

"Same as usual. Mom has her bridge club and new in-
terior decorator. She's happy. The firm's still growing, so
dad's happy." *They're relieved we're divorced,* but no
need to say that. Mike knew her parents loved him about
as much as his parents had loved her.

"What'd they think of you getting into law enforcement?"

"That I'm nuts."

"Same old, huh?"

"Yeah, same old. I imagine your parents had a few choice words about you getting to work for me."

"They're still rolling on the ground laughing."

"It is ironic, isn't it?"

"Hey, you know me. All water under the bayou."

"Yeah," she said softly, and had to look away. "Yeah."

Mike finally rose to his feet. He turned the chair around and placed it back in front of the desk. He kept studying her with dark, unreadable eyes. "So are you seeing anyone, Sandy?"

She hesitated, caught off guard by this line of questioning. "No. You?"

"Nah, nothing serious."

"With you, I didn't think they ever were serious."

"It had been with you, *ma chère*. It had been with you."

He strode for the door. It was just as well. Sandra's heart was beating too fast in her chest now and she couldn't think of a thing to say.

At the last minute, however, his hand on the knob, Mike turned around. That look was back in his eyes. Dark, somber, searching.

"It wasn't so bad," he said softly. "You and me. Our marriage wasn't so—"

"Mike, look me in the eye and tell me you were happy. Look me in the eye and tell me our marriage was the best year of your life."

He couldn't do it. And they both knew it.

After a moment, he turned around. He ripped open the door with more force than necessary. He slammed it shut behind him. He stormed down the hall.

And that made Sandra think back to other days, to the last day. The day she announced with a pounding heart and sweating hands that their marriage was over. And in-

stead of saying no, instead of finally fighting for her or at
least taking her in his arms and telling her it would be all
right, Mike had simply said, "Fine."

Fine. Mike Rawlins's signature word. *Fine.*

That had been the day Sandra had finally stopped loving
her husband and had learned to hate him instead.

"What the hell kind of assignment is this?"

"The easy kind."

"Let me see if I got this straight. We identify who this
Vee kid is. We track him down. We talk to his family and
friends. And then we just walk away? We turn our backs
on some cop-threatening punk and write up a report on the
subject instead? This," Koontz said seriously, "is what
happens when you put a woman in charge."

"Welcome to the nineties," Mike told him, and re-
sumed tapping on the keyboard. "She does have a good
point about him writing the letter, though."

"Conjecture. We're risking our necks for conjecture."

"When has it ever been any other way?"

Koontz scowled. He always got annoyed when Mike
was right. He hunkered down by the computer, where
Mike was perusing the gang database for Vee's name.
Koontz was actually the more computer literate of the two,
but he hated to work the keyboard when other cops were
around. Looked too clerical.

"You were in her office for a long time," Koontz said.

"It's called a debriefing, man. You should try showing
up for one sometime."

Koontz wasn't fazed. "That was some suit she was
wearing," he observed next. "Showed off just enough
curves and class to intimidate us poor working stiffs. Except for you, of course. You always did go for the uptown
type."

Mike kept his eyes glued to the computer screen. Koontz shook his head in disgust.

"Ah, man, I'm right, aren't I? You're going soft on her again. One look and you're like a junkie desperate for a fix. Didn't you listen to what I told you? When you go into her office, stick to business. Say nothing more, nothing less. In and out quick."

"The meeting was quick."

"Liar. You were in there for over half an hour. Debriefings for idiot cases never take more than ten, fifteen minutes. You made small talk. You got *personal*."

Koontz spat out the word as if it were a communicable disease. Mike didn't comment. He'd learned long ago that responding to Rusty's tirades just added fuel to the fire. It was easier to let him burn out on his own.

"Mike! I was there the first time, remember? I watched the whole thing unfold like a damn train wreck. I *know* what I'm talking about."

"Look," Mike said, "Three monikers that start with *V*. Write them down."

Koontz growled at him. Mike ignored the look and grabbed a pen. He didn't want to talk about Sandra right now. He wanted to work, he wanted to escape from all the confusion a simple thirty-minute meeting could bring. Besides, he had a rule: He never discussed Sandra with Rusty, and he never discussed Rusty with Sandra. Their mutual dislike was their problem, not his.

"One V-dubb," Mike read off to his partner, "one Vavoom, and one V-Vex. Vavoom is really Cheryl, so we'll count her out."

Koontz finally looked at the names. "Vavoom, huh? Wanna bet what her occupation is?"

"She's fourteen. Maybe not."

"Hah. Fourteen is prime age out there. I double my bet that she is."

Mike shrugged. Koontz was probably right.

A long time ago, Mike had figured out that the trick to understanding Rusty was that for him, the world was actually a simple place. There were good people—cops—and bad people—everyone else. Which meant that, despite Sandra's claims, Rusty was an equal-opportunity cynic. There wasn't a person he met whom he didn't assume the worst about, and not a man, woman or child whom he didn't suspect. If he ever met Sandy's well-groomed dad, Koontz would assume money laundering. If he ever met Sandy's pristine mother, Koontz would assume plastic surgery and Valium. That was just his way.

"Try known associates," Koontz said.

"I'm gettin' there." Mike typed in the search field and the ancient database whirled. The computer made an unhealthy sound, then coughed up an answer.

"Criminy," Koontz said. "We gotta get some new hardware around here."

"We did. White Collar grabbed them. Said they needed them more. All good fraud these days is on computer."

"Ha, more likely all good computer games. What kind of caseload does WC have these days anyway? I say we wait until dark, then steal the computers back."

Mike glanced over at his partner. It was always hard to tell when Koontz was joking.

"Zero matches found," he said. "Your turn. On to NCIC."

Koontz grudgingly traded places with Mike. Rusty was the most familiar with NCIC and already had the national crime database whirling as Mike rolled the first kink out of his neck.

"It's odd that Vee doesn't even appear as a known moniker," Koontz grumbled.

"Unless he doesn't actually belong to a gang."

"The kid is thirteen. You don't get to be thirteen on the east side without someone jumping you in."

"A holdout? Maybe outta respect for his brother."

"Do we got a name for the brother?"

"Nope."

"Damn. Dead end here, too." Koontz pushed back from the computer, frowning harder. "He's gotta be in the system."

Mike agreed. "Known family associations with gangs. Street name, claims of being a straight shooter. You'd think we'd find a record."

"Maybe it's fake. Whole letter's just a hoax to yank our chains. Someone out there likes toying with the men in blue."

"Or maybe Vee's a new moniker. Vee for vengeance."

"Huh. It's possible. Don't know why these kids have to make up new names, though. It's not like anyone in the east side is naming their son Bob anymore."

"What about the Crime Scene Unit? They get any prints off the letter?"

"Wrecked," Koontz told him. "Seems everybody at the newspaper touched it, so prints are impossible. Letter was hand-delivered, so no postage. Envelope not sealed so no saliva. Get this, the letter was actually typed. Old manual typewriter with Wite-Out for corrections. Not a neat job, but still means no handwriting analysis. Of course, we could probably match the letter to a particular typewriter, but that assumes we know enough to find the typewriter. Case is getting easier all the time, isn't it?"

Mike sighed and picked up his jacket. "Only one thing left to do."

"No…"

"We gotta find the kid somehow. Newspaper office sits on a major bus line."

Koontz groaned louder. "Ah, nuts, I hate this kind of grunt work."

"It's not just a job," Mike assured him. "It's an adventure."

Chapter 3

Driving to the bus station, Mike started thinking about his ex-wife again.

He didn't want to. After the divorce, he'd adopted a strict policy of not looking back. He'd been raised with a certain philosophy about the world. Roll with the punches, live life easy. So he'd gotten a divorce. That's the hand life had dealt him. Move on.

Besides, if he thought about it too much—remembered Sandra's smile, her scent, the way she'd sigh right after he kissed her—he got angry. Angry that she was gone. Angry she hadn't given them more of a chance. Angry that he was *divorced,* dammit, and he'd never wanted to be divorced. Would someone please tell him what the hell he was supposed to have done differently?

Mike didn't like getting angry. So he made the rule about not looking back. Easygoing Rawlins. Rolling with the punches. Living life fine. Yeah, that was him.

Until today. Today was doing him in.

Sandra striding into the morning meeting, looking even better than he remembered. God, he loved it when she had her chin up and her eyes sparkling for a fight. Koontz had it all wrong. Mike had never minded that his wife could be bossy or tough. Hell, he'd *loved* that about her. Sandra was the first woman he'd ever met who couldn't be swayed just by his grin. She gave as good as she got. She made him work for things. She made him feel alive. That was his wife.

And he knew the rest of her, too, the softer side she'd never show someone like Koontz. The late nights when she'd compulsively rub the back of her neck where her muscles knotted from carrying the weight of the world around with her all day. The next morning when she'd drag herself out of bed with the worst migraine rather than let her father's company down. Then along the way to work, she'd stop and watch the little kids run through the park, because Sandy really wanted to have children and worried that she was too driven and career oriented to be a good mother.

Rainy days dragged her down. Sunny days perked her up. Her favorite treat was undercooked brownies eaten hot and gooey straight from the pan. And her favorite way of spending Sundays used to be in his arms.

Mike didn't want to know how she was spending her Sundays now. That would make him angry. So he thought about their wedding, instead.

It had been in Boston, some huge stone church where all Aikenses had tied the knot since time immemorial. Sandy's mom had hired a fancy florist to deck the place out in satin bows and white roses, and they'd triggered a pollen attack so bad Mike's brother had to be led out of the church. Mike hadn't really noticed.

His mother was still injured about the reception menu,

he remembered that vaguely. She'd wanted to bring her special potato salad and Mrs. Aikens hadn't taken that well. The event was being catered. Caterers didn't need help. What were they thinking? Then his mom had offered Sandy her wedding headpiece, passed down for three generations, and that had also been refused. Instead Sandra had had some designer dress and veil custom-made for her on Newbury Street.

Mike hadn't paid much attention to those things, either, though maybe he should have. At the time, none of it had mattered to him. Not Rusty's dire predictions, nor his mother's stiff stance, or his future in-laws' condescending stares. So their parents didn't get along, so they came from different worlds. Sandy drove herself hard. He lived life easy. She believed in fine dining, he loved a good barbecue. She played bridge with her family, he played coed tackle football with his.

Diversity was the spice of life. Love would get you through. If there was a platitude, he must have believed it back then. Because mostly, he'd believed so badly that he'd wanted Sandy.

And then, there she was. Standing at the head of the aisle. Framed by white roses with golden light from the stained-glass window pouring in behind her. He'd stopped breathing. His chest had gone so tight it hurt. *Mon Dieu,* she was lovely. *Mon Dieu,* she was his *wife.*

The rest of the world had ended for him then. If he hadn't already fallen in love with her that first day, he fell twice as hard for her at that moment. He loved the strong, proud line of her shoulders. He loved the way she walked down the aisle, looking him right in the eye and never missing a step. He loved the way she clung to him after their first man-and-wife kiss and he loved the way a single tear had trickled down her cheek. *"I love you, Mike Rawlins. And I'm so happy to be your wife."*

Later, much later, finally alone in their honeymoon suite, they'd both been curiously shy. Sandy had a confession to make. She'd been reading magazines on the subject. Lots of brides and grooms end up too exhausted by the end of the big day to have a traditional "wedding night." So, if he was tired…they didn't have to…she meant, if he didn't want to…

Hell, there was nothing Mike had ever wanted more.

But it was funny, he'd taken it slow. He'd made love to a dozen women in his life. He'd made love to this woman over a dozen times. Sweet Lord, for the first month they hadn't been able to keep their hands off each other. Still, this was their wedding night. She was his wife. It did something to him, made him feel the moment way down deep. He'd never spent so much time carefully slipping little pearl buttons free as he did that night. He'd never lingered for so long over each piece of clothing, peeling away satin and silk and froths of lace to reveal smooth, creamy skin and firm, ripe curves.

He hadn't made love to Sandra that night; he'd devoured her. Slowly, carefully, exquisitely. Until he felt her soft, urgent sighs burn across his skin. Until her perfectly manicured nails dug into his back. Until the sweat was a fresh sheen across their bodies and she was wild beneath him.

And even then, some part of him didn't want it to end. Some part of him would have dragged it out forever if only he'd known how. Maybe even back then, some part of him had known it could never last. She hadn't even taken his name. How long before she decided she didn't need the rest of him, either?

Still he had tried. Still he remembered those first days

of marriage, when fierce, haughty Sandra Aikens had loved him and said she was proud to be his wife.

"What are you thinking about?" Koontz asked from the driver's seat.

"Nothing."

"Nothing," Koontz observed, "doesn't wear hundred-dollar perfume."

They struck out at the bus station. The city bus passed the newspaper office every half hour, making it hard to narrow down the time the letter was delivered, let alone by whom.

The station manager fetched the bus driver of the route for them, but when Koontz asked him if he'd carried a thirteen-year-old black kid lately, the man burst out laughing. He ran the east-west metro. About all he had on his buses were teenage black kids.

Next they tried the newspaper office. Surely they had people in all night, finishing stories, running presses. Newspapers never sleep, right?

Well, maybe in big cities. Alexandria's *Citizen's Post,* on the other hand, went to bed at eight each night. The presses ran all night long but, thanks to automation, took only six people to run. When the delivery crews arrived at five in the morning, they pulled up to the back, so no one noticed a letter in the front mail drop until offices opened at eight o'clock.

"Come on, don't you guys at least have a janitor?" Koontz wanted to know.

"You mean Hank?"

"Sure, Hank. Let's all go talk to Hank."

They all went and talked to Hank. He was seventy-five years old and deaf as a doornail. Mike wasn't sure, but he believed they finally established that Hank hadn't seen anything. The security guard was worse. Mike and Rusty knew him from his former days as a cop. He'd been a drunkard then and apparently hadn't done a thing to clean up his act. The editor-in-chief was sorry, but what more could he say? If they did learn anything, they'd pass it along, right? After all, *Citizen's Post* had cooperated with them....

Koontz said, "Sure," without blinking an eye, but Mike knew his partner was lying. Koontz held reporters in even greater contempt than defense attorneys.

Three-thirty in the afternoon, they descended the steps of the newspaper building.

"These kids are like ghosts," Koontz muttered. "Who really pays attention to a lone thirteen-year-old anyway? Maybe we are safer when they're traveling in packs."

"Vee's gotta be a new alias."

"I don't like it." Koontz shook his head. He had a good instinct about these things, so if he was troubled, Mike was troubled.

He glanced at his watch again. "Three-thirty," he commented.

"Afternoon patrol is probably in the east side...."

"And now school's out."

"Wonderful. Freakin' wonderful."

They headed for their car.

"What now?" Koontz asked a few minutes later. Mike gave it some thought. He'd told Sandra they'd have an ID by the end of the day. There had to be something more they could do.

"We got a copy of the letter. Let's take it to the junior high and see if a teacher recognizes the writing style. Maybe some word or phrase will ring some bells."

"Oh, so now *we* head into the east side?"

"Great plan, isn't it? Body armor's in the back. I'll fasten yours, you fasten mine."

Koontz grudgingly got out of the car and popped the trunk. "We are not being paid enough for this," he said as he fetched two Kevlar vests.

Mike was more philosophical. "Yeah, but think of how much the city will spend on our funerals."

The ride from Alexandria's city center to the east side took less than fifteen minutes, and was as dramatic as crossing from one country into the next. From wide, tree-lined streets, to narrow, cracking asphalt. From quaint brick storefronts and grand stone facades to boarded-up row houses and crumbling old mills. The streets were darker here and it wasn't just in Mike's head—as fast as the city installed new street lamps, the dealers sent their runners to shoot them out. Light was bad for business.

Deeper in, old textile mills, once the lifeblood of the town, sagged on their foundations, condemned, but still inhabited by vagrants sporting crack pipes. A group of teens loitered on one corner, smoking cigarettes and giving Mike and Koontz's unmarked car a baleful stare. More kids on the next block and now some working girls. The east side was never empty.

Koontz turned the corner and they were on Main Street, where a few family businesses did their best to survive. There was the local convenience store, known for its hot coffee and good conversation. Smithy Jones ran it with his wife, Bess, and was on good terms with the police. Smithy had been a decorated marine in Vietnam, and the last dope-head stupid enough to stick him up had gone straight from the store to the morgue. Nothing happened on Main Street during Smithy's watch. In addition to Smithy, the Santiagos maintained a liquor store guarded by reinforced steel bars, while the Chen family ran a small café-grocery. Mrs. Chen had been held up twice, but still persevered.

Koontz turned off Main street and graffiti promptly exploded over the landscape. The artwork, Mike knew, was not random, but represented markers dividing the area into four distinct gang turfs—the Hispanic Latin Kings; the Black Guerrilla Family; another black gang, the Crips; and the Brotherhood, white trash or white supremacists, depending on who you asked. The gangs ruled the streets and the rule of the gangs was simple and carved in stone.

Sometime between the age of five and eight, you got jumped into a gang. You didn't choose it, it chose you. That gang became your family. They were your protection, your buddies, and your employers. They came first in your life and if that meant stealing your mama's car, you stole your mama's car. If that meant killing your boyhood friend because he got jumped in by a rival gang or a rival sect of the same gang, then that was just business.

Here, survival mattered, and the difference between life and death could be as simple as being caught on the wrong city block at the wrong time of day. Five years ago, Mike and Koontz had gotten called in to investigate the death of a twelve-year-old black male. He'd been found with his hands tied behind his back, mauled to death by some sort of animal later identified as a pit bull. Further investigation revealed the kid belonged to the Black Guerrilla Family, a relatively new gang to Massachusetts. Unfortunately for him, the BGF didn't own much turf yet, so the boy had to cross four blocks of rival territory to make it to school each day. Apparently, the kid got to be a really good sprinter. One day, however, he didn't run fast enough.

The Crips caught him. They were angry at the BGF. Someone had stolen someone's car and stripped it down for parts, the ultimate insult. So this boy got to pay. They tied him up. They stuck him in a backyard. They brought out a full-grown pit bull one of the Crips's Original Ghetto Blood used as a breeding stud. They worked the hard-muscled dog into a frenzy, then turned it loose. They had left the twelve-year-old's legs untied, and he did run very fast, so things took a while.

Mike and Koontz learned this story from an informant named 3-Trey, picked up by Vice for dealing crack cocaine and now wanting to skip a trip to juvie. Three-Trey was fourteen. He had witnessed the murder firsthand. More than the details, Mike remembered the way the boy told the story, his eyes flat and his voice emotionless. Just another day in the hood.

Koontz had shrugged it off. Three-Trey named names, they picked the boys up, identified the crime scene and put together the case. Open and shut as far as Koontz was concerned. The only thing that kept Rusty awake at nights was an unclosed case, which he always took as a personal insult.

For Mike, however, it had been one of those days when he'd gone home unable to talk about his job. He'd needed to hold Sandy close, inhaling the scent of her perfume and concentrating on the feel of her skin. He'd wanted to bury his face in the crook of her neck until the picture of the mauled kid finally faded from his mind. Sometimes he couldn't get the job to roll off his back. Sometimes, in spite of his family's preaching, life leeched into his head, left him feeling weary. Those times he *needed* his wife to be soft and feminine and removed from the job. He needed her to be a reminder of the good things in life.

Most likely though, they had wound up in a fight. Because, as Mike had learned the hard way, love did not conquer all. It demanded your all. And somehow, he and Sandra had not been equal to the task.

Koontz pulled up to the junior high and they got out of their sedan. Dusk was starting to settle over the small, shrunken building and Koontz was looking over his shoulder. Mike felt it, too. The parking lot was exposed. The shadows had eyes. A lot of them.

"Kid's just a punk," Koontz muttered. "Can't believe we're letting a thirteen-year-old spook us."

But he unsnapped his shoulder holster as they both moved inside quickly.

"I honestly don't know if I can help you," Mrs. Kennedy was saying five minutes later as she started erasing the huge blackboard. "I have a hundred and twenty students. It's hard to get to know each of them personally."

"But you gotta give them homework, right?" Koontz countered reasonably. "Essays, reports, whatever the hell they're doing in English these days. Maybe you don't know each kid, but you gotta have a sense of their writing."

Mrs. Kennedy stopped erasing long enough to give Koontz a wry expression. She was a pretty black woman, younger than Mike would have expected, and speaking in a refined accent that didn't come from living in Massachusetts. He was guessing she came from affluence and now saw teaching underprivileged children as her mission. He also noticed she carried pepper spray in her desk drawer. A woman of experience.

"You're assuming they turn in their homework assignments, Detective. Frankly, most of my seventh graders don't. What makes you think he's in seventh grade, anyway?"

"In the letter. Kid says he's thirteen."

"Around here, that means he could be in any grade from third on up. The school district likes to run a tight ship.

Miss so many days and you automatically get to repeat the grade. We were hoping it would encourage attendance. Unfortunately, it's mostly made our kids permanent students.''

"But if this Vee kid has been making an effort..."

"Sure, he'd be in seventh grade. I haven't heard of anyone named Vee, though. Do you have a real name?"

"No ma'am, that's what we came to you for."

"I saw the letter, but show it to me again." She took the photocopy from Mike and glanced at it a second time, lines deepening in her brow. "So he's a thirteen-year-old who lost an older brother. Sorry, that doesn't narrow it down much."

"What about the sister?" Mike pressed. "A young girl with a bullet hole in her cheek? That's gotta be uncommon, even for around here."

Mrs. Kennedy conceded that point with a nod. "Any idea how old she is? Younger? Older?"

Mike shook his head.

"I can't think of any girl in junior high who fits that description," Mrs. Kennedy said after a moment. "But you could try the high school. It's much bigger and someone with a scar should stand out."

"Yeah, we'll do that," Koontz assured her. "But what about the letter? We don't got a lot of time here, so we'd love to learn the kid's name sooner versus later. Sure the writing doesn't ring any bells?"

"No, I'm afraid not." She handed the note back to Mike apologetically. "I just have too many students...."

"You keep it," Mike told her. "It's just a copy and some night when you're going through assignments, who knows. Maybe some phrase will catch your eye, or maybe you'll hear talk of something in the school halls. You never know."

"You think this kid, this Vee, is serious?"

Mike shrugged. "You have more experience with these kids than we do. You tell us."

Mrs. Kennedy hesitated for a moment, then she simply looked sad. "This part here, 'I gotta get through these halls and they be long and hard.' I've seen that. A child goes into gym class, then emerges beaten within an inch of his life. No one says anything, but you know he was just initiated into a gang. Suddenly the boy won't talk to his best friend anymore. He moves his seat to the back of the class. He hangs out with only the upperclassmen. It's as if he grew up overnight. And now, every time I walk by his desk, I get the stare. The flat, hard stare. I hate that look more than anything. The angry expressions, the hurt gaze, those are real emotions of a real child. But that stare, that cold, flat stare…those are the eyes of a person who no longer feels he has choices. They've just been made for him and now he's simply going through the motions.

"These kids do such unbelievable things to one another. It hurts me more that we let them."

"Well, we're not going to let this one do anything," Koontz assured her. "We're going to lock this one up and throw away the key."

Mrs. Kennedy looked up at him curiously. "And what do you think that will accomplish?"

"It'll get him off the street, that's what!"

"Detective, you have read this letter, but you are not listening. This child isn't angry because he was born that way. He is angry because we *made* him that way. And we're *still* making them that way. Half of my class could be Vee. And half of next year's class and half of the class after that. I've been here five years, Detective, and the only thing I know for certain is that we are failing these children. You want to make a difference, work on that."

Koontz took a step back, affronted by the attack. Mike immediately placed a hand on his partner's arm, subtly turning him to the door. Koontz hated being lectured and hated even more to feel like the bad guy.

"One last question," Mike said quickly, curiously. "Suppose this kid is angry enough to do what he writes. What do you recommend that we do? We can't keep him running around loose, and I for one would prefer not to be in a shoot-out with a child."

Mrs. Kennedy frowned. She looked down at the letter again. "The fact that he wrote a letter is encouraging," she mused out loud. "Shows a desire to communicate, to talk about what he's going through. It's a shame that his brother is dead. A lot of these children look up to their older siblings. Then again, it sounds as if he cares about his mother. Maybe if you can find her, she can speak to him. I hate to think of a thirteen-year-old as a lost cause, particularly one who wrote such a moving letter."

Koontz bristled again. "*Moving letter?* The kid threatened cops! Lady, maybe you should send a little bit of that compassion our way. We're the ones with our lives on the line."

Mrs. Kennedy returned his look levelly. "I do care about you, Detective. But you chose your path in life. This boy didn't, and that's the difference."

"Freaking liberals," Koontz said. "Freaking, feminist, Nazi liberals." They weren't even back in the car yet, and he'd worked himself into a frenzy. "Kids aren't born angry. Kids are made angry. I'll tell you what we have to show for that line of thinking—the crime wave of the eighties and nineties. All these murderers walking free because they were abused, or orphaned, or looked at the wrong way. Poor little them, *forced* by society to do bad things. So let's turn them back out on the street because those pathetic, tormented souls can't possibly be what's causing all the violence in the news. I mean, heaven forbid!''

"You don't really think people are born bad,'' Mike said, looking around again at the gathering gloom of the parking lot, holding his gun closer to his side.

"I don't think it matters. Who cares what makes people violent. Truth is, we still don't know how to fix them. The courts send them to the hospital, the hospital turns them loose, and we get to pick them up again. Court sends them to rehab, rehab turns them loose, and we get to pick them up again. Seems to me there's a theme.''

"So we lock them up and throw away the key?''

"Read the news,'' Koontz said seriously, also giving the parking lot a last once-over before crawling into the car. "I know you think I'm illiterate, but I follow the papers, my man. And all of them are talking about how violent crime is finally going down for the first time in years. You wanna know why? Because we've gotten tougher about sentencing and we've expanded the prisons. All the articles agree—rehab sounds nice, but prison works.''

"Even for thirteen-year-olds?''

"People don't change, Mike. What the hell do you think went so wrong with you and Sandy?''

"Koontz,'' Mike said seriously, "I could kill you for that.''

"Yeah, but you won't. Because you know me, man, and you know I'm simply saying the truth. People like to pretend there are no barriers in life. Blacks can marry whites, rich can marry poor, a backwater kid can become president of the United States. Hell, no. We are born into our worlds. We understand our world. We cross into someone else's world, we get burned. There is no such thing as a classless society. Just look at Alexandria.''

"You are a sick, cynical bastard, Koontz.''

"Yep, and you never try to change me, which goes back to my first point. Guys let each other be, the way nature intended. It's women, forever trying to 'fix things,' who mess things up.''

"Maybe guys just settle, while women are trying to make life better.''

"Was life better with Sandy?''

"Not your business, Koontz.''

Rusty smiled. "I think that's answer enough.''

They didn't get back to the station until after six and that was late enough to call it a day. Mike was still sore with Koontz and not much into talking anyway. Sometimes his partner's view of the world—and Mike's marriage—made him angry. Particularly when it contained a kernel of truth.

They determined they'd try the high school first thing in the morning. Koontz grumbled that the whole thing was probably a hoax anyway, but Mike didn't think his heart was in it.

Mike offered to stay late to write up their report. From where he was standing, he could see down the hall, where the light was still burning in Sandra's office. Long first day for the new chief of police. He wondered if she was rubbing the back of her neck yet. He wondered if seeing him for the first time in four years had been as hard for her as it had been for him. She'd been cool during their meeting, but then Sandra would appear cool having dinner with the Devil outside the Pearly Gates. It was part of her charm.

Of course, it also made it doubly fun to melt her into hot and bothered. Damn, he missed that.

Did she ever think of those times? Did she have any happy memories of their marriage? He realized he didn't know, and that left him feeling a little sad.

"Meet here at seven tomorrow?" Koontz wanted to know.

"Sure. Drive home safe."

"Yeah, yeah. Don't get misty—"

Koontz didn't get a chance to finish. Shouting erupted down the hall. Mike could only pick out the words *shots, shots,* before Weasel came tearing into the office space, his eyes wild.

"Oh, my God!" Weasel yelled. "Someone's opened fire in the east side. Officers down, officers down!"

"Vee," Koontz spit out, "I knew it!"

Then they were all running down the halls, and Mike was hoping desperately that his partner was wrong. Don't let it be Vee. Alexandria wasn't ready for such a crisis. And neither, he feared, was Sandy.

Chapter 4

In the locker room, patrol officers and narcotic detectives suited up and locked down. Weasel was still yelling details from the main radio. Shots exchanged. Patrol 32 down. Emergency vehicles en route. Backup vehicles en route. *Move, move, move.* Officers under fire was everyone's business in Alexandria.

Farther down the hall, Mike could hear a phone ringing violently, then a short burst of female cursing. Sandra, he thought, and unconsciously moved faster.

"Shotgun?" barked Rusty.

"Got it."

"Vest?"

"Still on. Yours?"

"Ditto. Come on. Move your butt, Rawlins, or we'll miss the party."

"Hang on." Rushing out of the locker room with a Remington 12-gauge shotgun in his hand, Mike made an unexpected left-hand turn—toward Sandy's office.

Rusty saw the motion and drew up short. "No," he said forcibly.

"Can't let the chief enter a violent area alone," Mike countered reasonably.

"Like hell. If she wants to prove she's tough, let her. Dammit, Mike. I'm your *partner*."

There was a lot of emphasis on the last word, and it made them both tense. The conversation of this afternoon had been leading up to this. Hell, Mike and Sandra's marriage had been all about this. Rusty wanted to come first. Rusty believed the brotherhood of cops should *always* come first. And Sandy, crazy her, had thought that a wife should be more important than a partner.

Mike didn't have an answer back then, and he didn't have one now. How was someone supposed to choose between their right hand and their left? Four years ago, he'd simply waited patiently—futilely, it turned out—for one of them to stop pushing the issue. Now, he realized, it was even more complicated. Sandra was no longer his right hand, but had become, like Rusty, his left.

"She's the chief," he repeated softly. "We have an obligation—"

Koontz didn't want to hear it. He turned away in disgust. "Do what you got to do, Rawlins. I'll see you downtown, where the *real* cops are waiting."

He stalked toward the garage. Mike watched Weasel go running up behind him, looking scared as he always did, but made anxious enough by the shooting to bum a ride. Mike would have to pay for that later, too: Rusty hated Weasel.

Rusty, however, could take care of himself, and Mike wasn't so sure about Sandra. Knowing her, she'd want to personally attend the scene. An Aikens never backed down from a fight.

Mike headed toward her office, where he discovered Sandra trying to put on her coat and hang up the phone at the same time. Her features were ashen, her lips pressed thin. She glanced at him once, then seemed to draw in on herself even more tightly. She suddenly hurtled the uncooperative phone to the floor.

"Incompetent...damn...incompetent..."

Mike retrieved the receiver. He replaced it gently on the base. "It's not your fault," he said quietly. "Whatever just happened over there, it's not your fault."

"I am the chief of police! I sent men into the east side."

"Which you had to do. Believe it or not, we'd all rather be shot at than labeled scared. Besides, you assigned your two best men to the case. We just..." Mike shrugged miserably. "Sorry, *ma chère.* We couldn't find Vee in the system, so we're having to do it the old-fashioned way. That takes time."

"I should've come up with a game plan until then," Sandra said relentlessly. "Dammit, I'd *read* the letter—"

"So did the rest of us."

"Yes, but you took it seriously, and Koontz was right, *I* didn't. I didn't really believe he'd open fire. I didn't honestly think a thirteen-year-old...dammit." Then more vehemently. *"Dammit!"*

Mike took her coat from her and helped her put it on. Her hands were shaking. She gathered up her clipboard briskly, however, and with a last composing nod—almost to herself—she headed for the door.

"Well, are you just going to stand there all day," she said, "or are you coming with me to the scene?"

"I'm driving you to the scene."

"I don't need a driver—"

"Sandy. Shut up."

Mike turned off the light behind them. He noticed that

the nameplate had once again been replaced, this time by a picture. It was even more graphic than the names. Sandy didn't look at it. She had her chin up, her shoulders square, and she was heading like hell on wheels for her car.

You never could keep her down, Mike thought. And just like always, he felt admiration tighten his chest. But then he felt something else. Something softer, sadder, lurking beneath respect and making him shift uncomfortably.

For a moment, he found himself wishing she wouldn't always be so strong. He wished that his fierce, independent ex-wife would allow him to hold her instead. But Sandra had never needed much. And he had discovered the hard way that the worse things got, the better she became at pushing him away.

Mike followed her to the car.

"Helluva first day," he remarked finally, and wasn't surprised when Sandy said nothing at all.

It took fifteen minutes to get from the central station to the shooting scene, and Sandy needed every second to pull herself together. The sick feeling in her stomach had started with the first news of shots being fired. It had grown with the information that officers were down. It had turned positively leaden when she considered that investigating Vee's case had most certainly brought Mike and Koontz into the east side.

The world had tilted on her. She'd had a crazy image of Mike and Koontz pinned down behind an unmarked police car. She'd seen her ex-husband's big, strong body covered in blood, Koontz screaming that it was all her fault, she didn't have enough experience for the job. Now look at what she'd done.

Then the sudden, jarring news that it was not Mike and Rusty, but two patrol officers answering a routine burglary call. The relief that had hit her had been out of proportion for what one should feel for her ex-husband, and that had left her secretly ashamed. She was Alexandria's chief of police. All officers were her responsibility, not just Detective Mike Rawlins.

And yet...

Mike was Mike. Warm, grinning, barrel-chested, exasperating, sexy, arrogant, maddening Mike. She'd been married to the man, she'd spent a year worrying about him night after night like a good cop's wife. She'd been nervous every time she kissed him goodbye and secretly triumphant every time he returned home.

Old habits died hard. Or was there more to it than that?

She risked a glance at him. His dark eyes were intent on the road, his square features set but calm. He had the siren going on the dashboard, and was weaving in and out of traffic at eighty miles per hour. But his broad hands were fluid on the steering wheel, his hard-muscled shoulders relaxed. Driving fast and hard to assist fellow officers, Big Mike Rawlins was in his element. He was in control.

And abruptly the tension dissolved in the pit of Sandra's stomach. Her fists slowly unclenched, her breathing came more easily. She watched Mike, strong and adept at the wheel, and she was comforted.

He would get them to the east side. He would guide her through her first crime scene in his smooth, easygoing way. He would take care of her, while taking great pains not to appear as if he was taking care of her, because that was his style. He let people be themselves, a trait she personally had never been able to master.

Funny how long it had been since she'd thought of that and how much she'd admired that about him. After a lifetime in a driven corporate culture, Mike had been the first man she'd ever met who didn't go around trying to force the world to fit his vision. He didn't demand, overpower or overwhelm. He simply enjoyed the ride, and in doing so, made you feel good about yourself. You could always depend on Mike.

She'd waited for him tonight. The minute she'd heard the news, some part of her had known he would come to check on her, so she'd waited. In all honesty, Sandra was afraid. She'd never been to a shooting before. She wasn't sure how she'd handle it and didn't really want to face it alone. She'd definitely been grateful when Mike appeared. Very, very grateful.

Sandra turned away from him. She didn't want to think these things about her ex-husband. The day had already been long; this night would be longer, and all of the eyes of the city were upon her. She needed to be strong now. She needed to be tough.

She needed to remember that she was not the woman who loved Mike Rawlins.

She was the woman who had realized they were killing each other with that love, and had left him instead.

Mike turned the corner and suddenly a thick black column of smoke came into view. They were there.

Yellow crime-scene tape had been hurriedly strewn across Main Street. Two ambulances and a fire engine had managed to get through, but now the street was choked off by a gathering mob attracted by roiling smoke pouring out of the charred police cruiser. Mike came to a careening stop at the edge of the crowd. Two youngsters threw the car a disinterested stare, then went back to watching the wrecked patrol car burn.

Mike popped open his door quickly, and Sandra was right behind him.

She was immediately assaulted by the smell. Gasoline, harsh and astringent. Gunpowder, dark and oily. Then she noticed the sounds. Sirens wailing in the distance, sharp male voices adding a staccato beat as officers yelled for assistance and crime-scene technicians, while four other patrol officers kept shouting at the crowd to move back, move back, *move back*. Finally a slow-building bass of rumbles and grumbles as the crowd murmured their discontent. The east-side civilians were not amused by the show, Sandra realized. They were resentful, suffering the presence of so many uniforms the way other people might suffer an invasion of a foreign army.

This situation would need to be handled with extreme care.

Sandra looked at Mike, nodded wordlessly, and let him tuck her into the protective curve of his body. Moments later, he delivered them both to the heart of the yellow tape, where one officer was already loaded into the ambulance and his partner sat pale and shaken on the bumper.

Immediately, Sandra went to the seated officer. Officer Johnson's face was streaked with soot. Moisture beaded his upper lip and tracked down his cheeks. Sandra didn't know if he'd been crying and knew better than to ask. Instead, she took his hand. After a moment, he returned the grip tightly.

Sandra turned to the EMT standing nearby. She learned that Officer Fletcher had been wounded in the lower leg. Nothing serious, but they had him on oxygen to help with the shock, so he was not available for questioning. Once the crowds thinned, they would transport him to the hospital, where he would most likely be treated and released. All in all, the EMT assured her, the only thing terminal at the scene was the patrol car.

They had responded to a call of an attempted robbery at the liquor store, Officer Johnson reported after a bit, finally releasing Sandra's hand. They'd pulled up to the curb, lights out, stepped from their car, and *boom!* Shots fired from above. They'd flattened behind their cruiser and fumbled with their side arms. The moment they peeked out again, *boom!* More freakin' shots. Then suddenly, Fletcher had yelled that he smelled something, and Johnson realized he smelled it, too. Gasoline.

Their damn car had been hit. Next shot...

They had no choice. They set their sight on Smithy Jones's convenience store and started running.

Boom, boom, boom, boom. The longest fifteen feet of Johnson's life. Hell, when he got home tonight, he was parking half a mile away from his house because that would still seem like a stroll through a field of daisies after the last fifteen feet.

Then suddenly, *whoosh!*

Shot must've finally got the gas tank and it seemed to them the whole world went up in smoke. The next he knew Smithy Jones was screaming down at him, "Are you all right, are you all right?" It took about four times before Johnson could hear through the ringing in his ears.

"And Officer Fletcher?" Sandra inquired quietly.

Johnson flushed, glanced at Mike, then turned away. "Ricochet," he muttered. "Maybe shrapnel or something."

Confused, Sandra looked at Mike, too, then the EMTs. "Ricochet? From what?"

"I don't know. A building, a car. It doesn't matter. It was *ricochet.*"

Dumbly Sandra nodded, though she didn't understand the vehemence behind Officer Johnson's words. Mike, however, was looking at her with an expression she'd seen before—*drop it,* his face read. Having learned her lesson this morning, she took her ex-husband's advice.

"Did you see who was firing at you?" she asked Officer Johnson.

"Hell, no."

"Did you see the direction the shots were coming from?"

"Across the street, high. I don't know. One moment we're getting out of our car, the next it's just *boom!* Huntin' time at the range and we're the endangered species." Johnson shuddered again.

"Ma'am?"

Sandra turned around and a large, bearded black man stepped in front of her. He was wearing a thin T-shirt with the sleeves ripped off to reveal thick-muscled arms covered in dark-blue tattoos. On his T-shirt, he sported a picture of a round yellow happy face—with a bullet hole between its eyes. Sandra was taken aback, but once again it was Mike's reaction that caught her attention. He was beaming at the aging biker as if they were long-lost pals.

"I'm Smithy Jones," the man said, and held out a heavily callused palm. "Pleasure to meet the new chief of police. Read your comments on community policing. Can't wait to be of help. Hell, I pretty much run this block already—well, tonight's little brouhaha excluded."

"Pleasure to meet you, too, then, Mr. Jones. Thank you for assisting our officers." Sandra returned the handshake with both surprise and gratitude.

"And you saw the shooting?" she asked, after introducing herself.

"Yes, ma'am. Shots were coming from the third window of that warehouse right there. Not a rifle, though. Sounded more like a 9 mm."

"Could you see who was firing?"

"No ma'am."

"Did you see anyone entering the building earlier, or fleeing afterward?"

"With all due respect, ma'am, it's a pretty busy street."

Sandra nodded absently. She was not an expert marksman herself, but she'd been shooting enough times to be comfortable and competent with handguns. And from what she could tell, that window had a clean line of sight onto the smoking patrol car. What had the officer said? *It was like being hunted....*

Except...

Rusty Koontz came walking up. He was tossing a handful of brass in his gloved hand and wearing a smirk. "Shells," he announced. "Nine millimeter. Found them at the third-story window, just where you said, Smithy."

Smithy shrugged modestly.

"Footprints in the dust, too," Rusty said, his gaze zeroing in on Sandra. "Small footprints. Like the kind a thirteen-year-old might have."

"I see. Make sure we get some good photos of the tread pattern for the file."

"No kidding."

"Now let me see if I understand this," she continued smoothly, moving authoritatively to the middle of the street and ignoring Mike's warning glance. "Two officers pulled up here." She pointed to the charred car. "One unidentified gunman stood there." She pointed to the empty third-story window.

"Child," Koontz interrupted coldly. "Poor, misunderstood child."

"Child, then. Let's assume it was Vee—"

"Who the hell else has been sending fan mail to the press?"

"Who we agree is an experienced shooter?"

"He *says* he's experienced. We haven't even been able

to prove the kid exists, let alone that he knows an automatic from a Tinkertoy.''

"Then we'll assume he's inexperienced. Now then, do you really believe, Detective Koontz, that someone can stand forty feet away from two standing targets, and miss them *completely?* Let alone the fact that he had a perfect downward angle, the two targets were totally unaware, and the storefront throws great light. And he fired six, seven shots?''

"Eleven," Koontz filled in tightly. "Eleven shells."

Sandra raised a brow. "Eleven shots at two good-sized targets with perfect positioning. You still think he missed purely by accident?''

Koontz glared at her sullenly. More officers had gathered and they were looking at her resentfully, too. It suddenly made Sandra impatient. They all knew what had happened here. Why was it so hard to admit?

Then she got it, she actually got it. They didn't want to hear that Vee had held back from killing two officers. They wanted the thirteen-year-old to be evil. These men in front of her, Alexandria's finest, wanted the excuse to *war.* They were frustrated with their jobs, angry with their community and tired of being disrespected. They wanted to break down every door and bust every kid who'd ever looked at them sideways. And they were perfectly willing to use a thirteen-year-old as an excuse to do so.

She suddenly felt nothing but contempt for all of them.

Mike spoke up. He said simply, "Warning shots."

Rusty skewered his partner with a look. "Yeah. Warning shots.''

"It seems to me," Sandra said slowly, so there'd be no mistake, "that Vee made a conscious decision *not* to shoot two officers.''

"Yeah, *he* made the decision," Koontz burst out heatedly. "But what about next time, or the time after that or the time after that? Better yet, take a look behind the yellow line, *Chief.* See any sympathy there? See any concern? Hell, they're *disappointed* the kid missed. They're thinking if only we'd stop paying attention, maybe they could finish the job. That's community relations these days. If we don't come down on this kid with everything we got, if we don't set a grade-A example of what happens to people who screw with us, our lives aren't gonna be worth the cheap tin used to mold our badges. *Get it yet?*"

Rusty stalked off to join the other officers, who stood clustered a few feet away. They opened up as a group to receive him, then closed in around him, anchoring him within their midst.

Sandra and Mike remained outside the group. Then she noticed a few officers inching away from Mike and refusing to meet his eye. A gap was opening up, she realized. They were consciously ostracizing her for being herself. But now they were also ostracizing Mike, because he had brought her here. He had spoken up on her behalf.

"I'm sorry," she murmured to Mike honestly.

"Not your problem, *ma chère.*"

"Well," she said briskly, "at least you didn't say 'Fine.'"

Sandra retreated to the smoking police cruiser. She watched the upholstery burn down to embers until one lane was finally cleared and the ambulance sped away.

One hour later, Mike drove Sandy back to her house. He'd been waiting for some token argument, but she'd said nothing. Instead she seemed to have shrunk in her seat since the shooting. Her skin was pale, her blue eyes bruised, and her red-brown hair wild around her shoulders. If Sandra could see her reflection right now, she'd scream bloody murder. Funny then, how Mike thought she looked pretty good.

Pulling up the driveway was awkward. What to do now? Say goodbye in the car? Shake her hand? Pretend he hadn't lived in this damn house a year himself, or that he'd once spent a Sunday afternoon kissing every inch of her creamy white skin? Hell, Mike hated awkward.

He got out of the car, opened her door for her and walked her to the door. Her hands were fumbling uncharacteristically with her purse. He took the Coach bag from her grip and dug out her keys himself.

"I'm fine," she said now.

"Sure."

"No, really, I'm *fine.*"

"*Ma chère,* we both know *fine* is my word, not yours. Why don't you have a seat on the couch."

He tossed her bag negligently onto her glass hall table and, without bothering to look back, headed for the marble wet bar. He might not be Sandy's husband anymore, but he remembered what she drank. A perfect V.O. Manhattan, served neat with a twist. Koontz had practically fallen over laughing the first time she'd tried to order it at the Code Blue, the local cops' bar. Sandy, of course, did not drink beer. For the Code Blue, however, she'd finally learned to stomach very bad whiskey.

Tonight, Mike mixed two Manhattans. What the hell.

He found Sandra sitting on her pale, L-shaped sofa. She'd dumped her blazer over the back of the sofa, kicked off her black leather heels and finally yanked out her hair clip. Now she sat with one leg curled beneath her and her head resting on her braced arm. Her chestnut hair was loose and curly, the way he liked it. Her white silk shirt was unbuttoned down to the top of her brocade vest, revealing tantalizing glimpses of satiny skin and a lace-edged bra. Her stockinged feet were tiny and somehow vulnerable. He used to rub those feet. He used to paint those toenails.

His throat closed up on him. His body went rock hard. He handed Sandra her drink and made it a point to sit several feet away. Apparently, some things didn't change, including Sandra Aikens's impact on his libido.

"Nice," she murmured after a moment, taking a first sip of the Manhattan and getting some badly needed color in her cheeks. "You remembered."

"Making a Manhattan is like riding a bike," he assured her, and was rewarded by a wan smile and even more color in her cheeks. He tried his own drink and welcomed the slow burn sliding down his throat.

"Mike, what was going on tonight? What was all that talk of ricochet?"

"Not too smooth, huh?"

"No, not smooth at all." She was frowning at him. Worse, she was looking genuinely hurt and he never could stand to see her hurt. "I don't get it. I honestly want to help Officers Fletcher and Johnson. I feel for what they went through tonight. I can't imagine anything worse. And yet…and yet I was treated as the enemy,. Things were going on they obviously had no intention of telling me about. How am I supposed to help them if they won't talk to me?"

"You are the outsider, *ma chère*. You come from the wrong side of the blue wall. Cops, by nature, aren't supposed to trust."

"So how do I get over it? You tell me that forcing my way into their world will only alienate me further. Tonight I tried being supportive and understanding, but that got me nowhere. So what do I do?"

"It takes time, *ma chère*. You'll learn as you go, and

one day you'll realize you're no longer studying cops, but actually thinking like one. You'll use too much lingo, talk in code. You'll find yourself looking down at outsiders, thinking they don't have a clue about how the world really works, and then you'll know you're a cop.''

"And I'll know about ricochet?"

"Lower leg injuries, Sandy. You'll know about lower leg injuries.''

She frowned harder, not getting it, and then suddenly— her eyes opened wide. "He shot himself! Good God, Fletcher shot himself! Trying to unholster his gun, right? Oh, my God, I need to do something about that.''

"No Sandy, you need to do nothing about that.''

"Mike, we can't have officers running around shooting themselves in firefights. Obviously we need more training, or better equipment. I've been reading articles on holsters that are easier to unsnap. Plus there's the whole issue of trigger weight. Maybe he had his gun set too light. I was reading that officers should have heavier triggers so they have to consciously and forcibly squeeze off the first shot—''

Mike set down his Manhattan. He looked his ex-wife in the eyes, and as close as he ever came to reprimanding her, he said levelly, "You say one word on the subject, Sandra, and no man on the force will ever take your order again. And I'll have to be one of them.''

She drew up short, looking genuinely startled. "Mike?"

He sighed. Lord, she was killing him. He wished she'd never taken this cockamamy job, never forced his worlds to collide. It was confusing the hell out of him. It was giving him a headache.

"Koontz said something today, and God knows I hate to give anything he says too much credit, but maybe he was right. Koontz said the difference between men and women is that men let each other be, while women gotta run around changing everything.''

"Nothing personal, Mike, but Koontz's opinions mean about as much to me as the village idiot's.''

"Listen, Sandy. Koontz's point is that some things you have to let go. Fletcher is one of them. You say something, you overhaul training, anything, and you're going to humiliate the man. And don't ask me to explain it, but in the Alexandria locker-room world, it's a bigger crime to embarrass a man than to try to prevent him from hurting himself. You were told ricochet. You want to earn points now, you repeat to every Tom, Dick and Harry you ever met that it was ricochet. That will buy you respect. Improving us, on the other hand, won't. Go figure.''

"Be part of the problem, not the solution?''

"Be part of the unit, and not the outsider looking in.''

Sandra was quiet. He knew such concepts went against her grain, but she appeared to be giving it genuine thought. Abruptly she nodded. "Thank you, Mike.''

"For telling you how evil we really are?''

"For telling me the truth.'' She shrugged, giving him an unexpected smile. "I know sometimes I'm too dogmatic, Mike. I come on too strong. I get lost in my righteousness, I guess. But I want to learn. I'm thirty-four-years old. I should know by now how to adapt. The world is a complex place. And being a cop is a complex job. It's good for me to think of those things.''

"Some of it's PR,'' Mike commented softly. "That's what Koontz was trying to say. Cops encounter lots of dangerous situations and dangerous people. We want mystique on our side. You admit that in a firefight, we shoot ourselves with our own guns. Hell, there's no voodoo there. You say we want to *understand, communicate, heal* people who threaten us, there's no voodoo there, either.

You can train us to act kinder and gentler—maybe that is what we need—but cops like Koontz simply don't want to *look* kinder and gentler. That's the difference.''

"Ricochet."

"Yeah. Ricochet."

"Mike," she said softly, no longer meeting his gaze. "I think you'd better go now. Maybe it's the Manhattan. Or maybe it's because we finally agree...."

"Too late, *ma chère*. I already want to stay."

He closed the space between them effortlessly. He dipped his hand beneath the curly veil of her hair. The first touch of his rough palm against her smooth cheek was electric. He could watch his impact in her big blue eyes now. The growing desire, the doubt and confusion warring in her gaze. He understood it. He felt the same. The overpowering need for the one woman who'd always stirred his blood. The sad, relentless knowledge that they'd been down this road once before, and it had simply hurt them both.

And yet, at times like this, it seemed like such a shame to not even try.

He dipped his head lower. He inhaled the delicate scent of her fine, upscale perfume. He watched her lips part.

"Mike?" she whispered again, part a protest, part a plea.

"Shh. Stop thinking of all the ways we were wrong for each other, Sandy, and let me show you all the ways we were right."

He kissed her. His blood was thundering in his ears, his body straining against his pants. He'd thought the kiss would be hungry and fierce, a four-year-old desire bursting into flame. But his lips were curiously soft on hers, coaxing. He nibbled the corner of her mouth, nothing more, nothing less, waiting for that welcoming sigh. And then it came. She turned toward him, her body arching into his, and he felt triumphant.

His hands were suddenly gripping her head, angling it back so he could deepen the kiss. And her mouth was open beneath his, her fingers digging into his shoulders, her breasts brushing his chest. He tasted whiskey and desire. He suckled her bottom lip, dueled with her tongue and delved deep into her mouth. He tasted home. He tasted everything he had ever wanted. He tasted the promise of so many future nights.

Then Sandra was pushing him away.

"No. Don't. No."

She bounded off the sofa before he could catch her arm. Her motions were jerky and agitated. What struck him most when she turned back around, however, was that her eyes glistened with tears.

"I've spent four years, Mike," she whispered hoarsely, "four *long* years, getting you out of my system. I don't want you back. I can't afford to have you back."

"Why not? You felt it, too—"

"*Of course I felt it!* For God's sake, sex was never our problem. You could look at me across the room and I'd burst into flame. Hell, I had to sell my *car* because I couldn't stand the memories. But what about afterward, Mike? What about outside of the bedroom? What about real life?"

He was taken aback by her words. Hurt. It made him stubborn and defensive. "Today was real life. We didn't do so badly."

"Oh, I see. One conversation and we're magically rehabilitated. Maybe if more people had gotten shot during our marriage we would've been all right."

"Hey, it's a start!"

"Down the long road to nowhere."

"Sandy, what do you want from me!"

"*I don't know!* I…just… You need to go home now, Mike. I want you to go home."

"Fine." He said the word more savagely than he intended. He got off the sofa forcefully. Blood was still pounding in his veins. His pants were too tight. And he was angry and confused. Hell, he didn't know what he wanted either, except then he looked at Sandy with her pale skin and curly hair and his desire took over his brain again. Seduce her and be done with it. All divorced couples relapsed at least once. Maybe it would get them out of each other's system. Maybe it would ease this ache in his chest.

He took a step forward. She cut him off at the pass.

"You walked away easily enough once before, Mike," she said lowly. "Don't tell me it's difficult now."

"I didn't walk away, *ma chère*. You did."

"You never tried to stop me."

"Yeah, like I was ever able to change your mind."

"Exactly! And here we go. All discussions lead to war. All wars lead to bed. All beds lead to a morning after, where we are right back where we started. I'm thirty-four years old, Mike. I can't afford another roller-coaster ride. I want a family, you know. I want children and college funds and retirement funds and growing old with someone at my side. I need a life mate, not a bedmate. I need someone other than you. I'm sorry, Mike, but it's true. Now go home. We can pretend this never happened, and then tomorrow at the office we'll finally have something together."

"Co-workers for life?" he snarled.

She said quietly, "It's more than we had before."

Mike turned away. He jammed his hands into his back pockets and exhaled shortly. She was right, and he hated that. Co-workers. It sounded so flat. Especially after that kiss, after having her in his arms once more. And that hadn't had anything to do with lust, though he didn't know how to tell her that. That had been about finally feeling right.

At the brink of leaving, he had to ask her one last question. It mattered to him, mattered to him more than it should.

"Why did you do it, Sandy? Why did you really become the chief of police?"

She opened her mouth. He could tell from the hostile look in her eyes that she was going to give him the pat answer. New challenge, expanding her horizons...

But something in her suddenly gave way. Her gaze softened, became more somber. Became haunting.

"Because I wanted to finally understand this precious world of yours, Mike. Because for one year I was married to a cop who would never tell me anything about his day other than it was fine. With Rusty you would talk for hours. With me, everything was a one-word platitude. So here I am. I'm part of your world now, and you finally have to talk to me about policing, don't you? You finally have to tell me about your day."

"Yeah," Mike said. "Yeah."

But his words were not soft or apologetic, they were harsh. They were hurt. Mike didn't think he should have to talk to his wife about the dirt he saw in his day. What was the point of making the world a better place if he brought the contamination into his home? His wife should trust him to be keeping the world safe.

But of course, fierce Sandra Aikens never trusted anyone, not even him.

Mike picked up his coat. He headed out the door.

This time, he did not look back.

Chapter 5

Letter to the Editor
April 19

Editor's Note: This is the second letter sent by "Vee" to the Citizen's Post. *Police have confirmed the shooting on Main Street at approximately 6 o'clock last night [see story, page A-1]. The police have also issued a statement encouraging Vee, or anyone who knows Vee, to please come forward [see box, page A-1]. For as long as this crisis continues, we feel it is our duty to print these letters to both encourage communication and inform the community. Once again, these letters express the view of the writer, not the staff of the* Citizen's Post.

Members of the Man:
Had you in my sight last night. Lined up the shot real nice. Be thinking about who to do first, when I

decided whut the hell. I did the car. Lit it up like the Fourth of July. Sat there 'n watched it burn. Ask any homeboy around. He'll tell ya, cars roast up nice.

Went down for a close up. Nobody noticed. Suits like you can go forever without seein' a kid like me. Unless I leave the east side. Then little old ladies cross the street to get away. Pretty young ladies lock their cars. I ain't ever hurt a girl. My mama raised me better'n that, I know whats right.

But you don't care in the west side. You look at my skin, you see a monster, you lock the doors. Ain't nothing I can do but peel off my own face. I tried that once, long time ago when I was little. Hurt like hell and didn't change a thing. It's better to stay in the east side. Homeys'll just shoot me here and I ain't got no fear of that. Maybe get me a clostamy bag. Or wheelchair. Or a casket. Ain't nothing I haven't seen before. Shootin' in the end, be more honest.

So tell me, Man. You think you can come into my streets now? You think you be safe?

I got my gun out, Man. Cleanin' it the way my brother taught me. I be thinkin' next time, I'm gonna hit more than a damn city car. Then maybe you'll start listenin' to me, Man. Then maybe, you finally learn to *pay attenshun!*

God take good care of my mama. God take good care of my sister. Devil sit on my shoulder, for he be better company for a brother like me.

Vee

Sandra finished reading the letter and crisply folded up the slim morning paper. She took a fortifying sip of strong black coffee, then absently rubbed the back of her neck where her shoulder muscles were already bunched up tight.

It was five-thirty in the morning. The *Citizen's Post* had called her about Vee's letter late last night. She'd called the mayor, who hadn't been surprised. He'd already spent time since the shooting being inundated by phone calls—from the African-American League, accusing the cops of provoking the attack by entering the east side. From the Chamber of Commerce, demanding to know if police officers were now going to abandon the struggling east-side businesses. From the East-Side First Congregational Church, quietly informing the mayor that if the police exercised any undue violence against a troubled thirteen-year-old boy, they'd bring the American Civil Liberties Union down upon his white middle-class male head.

Mayor Peterson was not amused.

Neither was Sandra. The situation was volatile, she agreed. Of course, they would resume regular patrols of the area. In fact, they would double up patrol cars, adding a lookout vehicle for the officers' protection. They would exercise caution and try to show restraint. But they would not abandon the east-side businesses or community members. They could not let a thirteen-year-old boy hold the police department hostage.

Mayor Peterson had said simply, it wasn't enough.

Getting up from the kitchen table, depositing her coffee cup in the sink, Sandra knew the mayor was right. She needed a more aggressive plan of action.

She needed to be doing more to manage her ex-husband, Mike.

His kiss last night. Slow, persuasive, melting. One hundred percent Mike Rawlins. Oh, God, she had missed those kisses. And the way he used to hold her, solid against his broad, hard chest, until she could feel herself fold into his frame, surrendering herself to the total possession of his embrace. He was the only man she'd ever met who could make her feel small and delicate. The only man who could take on her temper, twist it with a wink and grin and suddenly have her feeling feminine and attractive again. She missed sparring with her ex-husband. Frankly, she missed his body.

After last night's encounter, her dreams had turned on her, filling with erotic memories of the days that had been. Mike looking into her eyes with that intent Cajun gaze. Mike sliding into her body, hot and sweat slicked, whispering, "How's that, *ma chère?* You like that? What about this? And this..."

She'd woken up at five that morning to find her body soaked and her hands in a death grip on the sheets. Still dazed and confused, she'd turned to Mike's side of the bed, hungrily reaching for him. Then consciousness had returned like a bucket of ice water. The bed was empty. The house was empty. She was alone and the closest she got to fulfillment anymore was the yearning visions of her dreams.

She'd showered for a long time, trying to cleanse the images from her mind, trying to pretend she didn't have tears on her cheeks. Trying to tell herself it was only the stress of her new job that had her nerves so frayed.

In the end, however, she knew herself too well to be fooled. Right after the divorce, all of her nights had been like this. Dreaming of Mike, reaching for Mike, waking up alone. One week, crazed and sleep deprived, she'd driven all the way to his apartment. She'd sat in her car, rehearsing what she'd say.

I'm sorry about the house, Mike. Sorry I made you move into some beige and glass monstrosity that you never felt was home. We should've found a new house together, where we'd both feel comfortable.

I'm sorry about my parents, Mike. Sorry they made you feel second-rate or second-class. I should've told my mom to drop it—love me, love you.

I'm sorry about all the fights, Mike. Sorry I didn't know how to talk to you without it turning into war. Sorry I didn't know how to get you to understand what I needed, sorry I chattered so incessantly about work.

And I'm sorry you never felt you could talk to me about your day. I'm sorry you belonged more to the police force than to me. I'm sorry your family came first, then your partner, and in the end, you'd rather spend your evenings with anyone but me. I'm sorry that in the end, you didn't even want my body anymore, and I knew our marriage was over the first morning I woke up and found you asleep on the sofa. I'm sorry you grew to hate me that much and love me so little.

She'd put her car into gear and driven away then without looking back. And from then on, she'd focused on getting Mike Rawlins out of her dreams, not back into her life.

But here he was now. They were working together. She had to see him day after day, watching the way he strode confidently down the halls, memorizing the fluid movements of his hands, catching that careless wink. Someday she'd probably encounter him leaving the building with another woman. Or hear stories of some date. Watch him flirt, seduce, fall in love with someone else.

Her hands tightened on the edge of the ceramic sink. For a moment, that thought hurt so much Sandra didn't think she could bear it.

Then she forced her hands to loosen. She forced herself to take a deep breath. She reminded herself that these were the choices she had made. And she was strong; she could handle anything. Including her ex-husband. Including a troubled boy named Vee.

A minute later, Sandra was on the phone. Her first call woke the man up, but went well. Her second call was slightly more nerve-racking to make.

"Good morning, Rusty. Did I wake you? Good. Listen, Mike keeps telling me you're a good cop. I'm not sure I believe him, yet, Detective, but for his sake, I'm willing to give you a second chance. My office, ten o'clock. This time try to make it.

"You have a meeting with the high school principal at seven? Well, if you magically find Vee, all the better. If you don't, I'll assume you'll be at the meeting. Don't worry, Rusty, you won't even have to listen to me speak. You wanted someone who actually knows these kids and these streets. Well, I've found him for you. Don't be late."

Sandra hung up the phone. Then she went burrowing into her walk-in closet for her best power suit. It was going to be one of those days.

Dr. Howard Mayes was a bear of a man. Even a charcoal-colored three-piece suit did nothing to diminish the girth of his barrel chest or the thick size of his legs. Sandra suspected football somewhere in his background. She had escorted the grizzly-haired professor to one of the interrogation rooms while they waited for Mike and Rusty. Dr. Mayes read Vee's two letters, scrawling copious notes in the margins.

She left him long enough to meet with her lieutenants again. Patrol Officer Fletcher had gone home from the hospital last night and would be fit to return to duty by next week. Ricochet, Sandra reminded everyone firmly, and was pleasantly surprised to finally earn a few approving nods. They discussed doubling up patrol cars in the east side for safety. They discussed making vests mandatory for all officers until the crisis passed. They discussed the mayor's concerns if a shooting did erupt, and the need to handle the situation delicately.

Sandra wasn't sure, but she had the impression her lieutenants were satisfied with the decisions she'd made. Doing her best to protect her officers without backing down from a threat. Handling the politics with the mayor while trusting her police officers to get the job done. Maybe the animosity toward her ran a little shallower today. Maybe it was the suit.

At ten, Mike and Rusty joined her in the interrogation room with Dr. Mayes. The meeting with the high school principal must not have gone well for they both looked glum.

Rusty saw Dr. Mayes and his perpetual scowl deepened. Mike saw Sandra and performed a double take. Sandra definitely attributed that to her suit. This morning's hunter-green ensemble sported a formfitting jacket smartly tailored over a surprisingly short skirt. The saleswoman had assured Sandra that the authoritative lines of the jacket offset the unprofessional hem length of the skirt. Plus, she'd confided, Sandra had the legs for it. Judging from Mike's sudden inhalation of breath, he agreed.

Sandra started off the meeting feeling better than she had in days.

"Dr. Howard Mayes, may I please introduce the two detectives in charge of the case—Detective Rusty Koontz and Detective Mike Rawlins. Rusty and Mike, this is Dr. Mayes from Boston University's sociology department. In addition to being an expert on gang psychology, he grew up in South Boston with firsthand experience in the area."

"I lost my older brother to a drive-by," Dr. Mayes interjected deeply. "I lost my younger brother to cocaine. I

chose the church, figuring I might as well start out close
to God because everyone in my family ended up with him
anyway. Then education became my ticket out.''

Sandra nodded, doing her best to pretend that Koontz
wasn't rolling his eyes. ''I've asked Dr. Mayes to help give
us an understanding of how Vee thinks and how we might
best approach him once we identify him. I know the gut
reaction among many officers is to go in guns blazing, but
the mayor and I both feel it's imperative that this situation
not end violently. The boy is only thirteen, and he hasn't
actually harmed anyone yet. We need to keep that in
mind.''

''Tell that to Fletcher,'' Koontz muttered.

''Officer Fletcher is fine, Detective. Thanks for asking.''

Koontz glared at her. She returned his gaze until Mike
interjected casually, ''Come on, Rusty. As long as we're
here, we might as well listen to the good doctor. It's not
every day we get an expert visiting our small town all the
way from Boston. I think this means we're finally important. Or just unlucky as hell.''

Dr. Mayes chuckled. ''Not important,'' he declared in
his sonorous voice. ''Not unlucky. Just typical. We are
producing Vees all across this country, I'm afraid. Confused, angry African-American males, trying to come of
age in an environment of severe poverty, drugs and racism.
It's a confusing time in a boy's life. It's an angry time.
And in the inner cities, it can be deadly.

''Come on, Detectives. You must remember how it was
to be thirteen. Peach fuzz on the cheeks. Hair under the
arms. Starting to notice that girls smell differently, move
differently, have *chests*…''

Dr. Mayes paused strategically. Sandra noticed that
Koontz was looking self-conscious by the personal turn in
conversation but was nodding reluctantly. Mike, of course,

was nodding wholeheartedly. Alexandria's Don Juan was probably remembering exactly what girl he'd noticed first. How she moved, how she looked. That first kiss... Sandra edged back a few feet so she didn't give in to the urge to slug her ex-husband.

"Now, in any suburban or rural environment," Dr. Mayes continued easily, "there are outlets for this hormone-crazed time in a boy's life. Hard labor around the farm to blow off steam. Organized sports like Little League baseball or Pop Warner Football to marshal all that raging testosterone and give it focus. But in an inner-city environment, these resources are sorely lacking. No Little League games or amateur football. Pickup games of b-ball are the trend, but hoops are hard to come by. So that's our first problem—Vee's got all these hormones, all these raging emotions, and no productive outlet available.

"Which brings us to the second point. Vee is on the brink of manhood. He's looking around, searching for someone to emulate. Who does an inner-city black kid have as a role model? Statistics tell us most of their fathers are in jail, uncles, too. There are sports heroes, but they are distant models. Who does a child in the projects see day in and day out?" Dr. Mayes didn't wait for answer. He boomed, "Drug dealers, that's who. The young, successful urban entrepreneur is most likely a dope dealer, a high roller. And this young man is employing other youths, buying his mama a new car, and decking out his girlfriend in gold chains. He seems to be the only path to success. Except then there are the drug-related shootings and the gang violence that go hand in hand with the life-style. So now Vee's gotta think, being a successful black entrepreneur also means winding up dead. Good life, but a short life. What's a kid to do?"

"Shoot up cops," Koontz growled. "Freakin' fine role model there."

Dr. Mayes shook his head. He looked at Koontz almost pityingly. "Detective, you are not understanding this child yet. He doesn't hate cops. He hates young black males. And he's not trying to hurt cops. This boy is trying to hurt himself."

"Huh?"

For once in her life, Sandra agreed with Koontz. Even Mike was looking confused. Dr. Mayes took a deep breath.

"Let me try to make this clear. It has been a source of puzzlement for quite some time that the number-one killer of young black men is young black men. In sociology circles, we've been trying to make sense of this by interviewing urban African-Americans about what it means to be African-American. Frankly, that's a conflicting thing. These children grow up surrounded by their own race, but in an environment none of them like. So they try to leave. At some point in every inner-city child's life comes the first bus trip out. And if this journey is to a predominantly white neighborhood, what is the first thing this child encounters? Racism. Women locking their car doors or crossing to the other side of the street. Patrol cops stopping the child for no good reason. Store owners chasing him out of their establishments. It's shocking the first time. Then it's simply haunting. Everywhere this child goes, he gets the message he's unwanted. So he has to take the bus trip back to the projects, which he now recognizes as some kind of punishment for a crime he never committed. This is an inner-city black male's first lesson when he searches for his identity. He is a criminal. He doesn't understand why, but he's fundamentally unloved.

"At the same time, of course, a child like Vee is taking social studies classes telling him he lives in a country where all men are created equal. But this just makes things worse—what he's being told about the world and how he feels about the world don't meet. There's this huge disconnection, fueled by every white teacher who shies away from him and every well-intentioned social worker who looks down on him, that leaves him angry and confused.

"Young, urban African-American males report feeling trapped, feeling ashamed. There is a pressure building inside of them and they begin to resent that pressure. And what's causing it, what's putting them in this position? As far as they can tell, it's the fact that they are black. So they start to hate the fact they are black. And they start to turn on other black males—subconsciously, of course, fueled by gangland wars and survival instincts, but it's there."

"Yo, hold up." Koontz was looking confused again, but he was also engaged in the conversation, which gave Sandra hope. "If Vee hates being black so much, why doesn't he declare war on other gang members. Why us?"

"Because his feelings are too conflicted on the subject. Look at his letters, Detective. In the first letter, he writes about his sister being hit by a stray bullet in a drive-by. This obviously bothers him. In the second letter, he goes so far as to say that he was raised to know better than to hurt females, that it's wrong. Thus, he is not as much a homeboy as he would pretend in other places. There are things being done by his peers that he doesn't approve of. In the second letter, however, he reveals classic hurt and anger toward white society, as well. He tried to enter the white community and he was shunned. When he says here that he tried to remove his face, don't take him figuratively. Self-mutilation is a sign of keen self-loathing. Vee is receiving the message that he should hate his own skin, and he is reacting accordingly.

"Fundamentally, this child is at a crossroads. He is confused, disenfranchised by both blacks and whites. He doesn't like the violence of youth killing youth, hence his need to sound so casual and accepting of it. But nor can he accept white authority—these are the people who look down on him, who allowed his sister to be hurt, who may or may not have taken an active role in killing his father. Vee doesn't know where to turn or what to believe in, and yet he does want something to believe in. He is trying to provoke a reaction that will tell him which way to turn."

"What do you mean by that?" Sandra asked sharply.

Dr. Mayes shrugged. "He is walking a dangerous path, Chief Aikens. I believe there is some part of him that doesn't want to be pushed to violence, hence he fired warning shots last night. He writes with genuine affection of his mother and has stated twice that she's taught him what's right. That's a sign of some semblance of self-worth—a part of him sees himself as a good person capable of distinguishing between right and wrong.

"But day after day, Vee is also forced to live in a world where he feels he's invisible and unwanted. As time passes without something happening to alleviate his confusion and self-loathing, I fear he will edge closer and closer to violence. The anger and hopelessness is wearing him down, flattening him out. In several places, he writes there's nothing he can do to change things. That is the sign of someone abdicating responsibility for their own actions, a natural predecessor to doing something someone knows is wrong. He goes on to write that the devil be on his shoulder, definitely an indication of low self-esteem. Now look at the rest of the closing of his second letter—'God be with...' That is the tone of someone who doesn't expect to be around much longer. Someone who is letting go."

"He's a time bomb," Sandra filled in. "And if we don't

find him soon, help him make the right decision, he'll go off.''

"I think it's possible,'' Dr. Mayes agreed, "and I think if it happens, there will be no turning back. He is a self-destructive adolescent who talks about death, not prison.''

"Suicide by cop,'' Mike stated.

Dr. Mayes nodded soberly. "I believe that's how it might play out.''

For once, even Koontz appeared pale and troubled. "Sheeesh,'' the older detective sighed. "One confused thirteen-year-old and the whole city could go to hell.''

"On the bright side,'' Dr. Mayes commented, "it could go the other way. Maybe his mother says the right word one day or a schoolteacher praises his project and boom, that brings him back around. Teenagers are wonderfully fickle like that. Ask any parent.''

"But we can't count on that,'' Mike said dryly.

"Absolutely,'' Sandra agreed. "What do you recommend, Dr. Mayes? There must be some way of reaching this boy before things go too far.''

"Certainly. First off, Chief Aikens, you draft a reply to Vee's letter.''

"Oh, my.'' Sandra was taken aback. "What if I said the wrong thing? What if I made it worse?''

She gazed at all three men pleadingly. Koontz looked stricken, too, so maybe they had finally found common ground. Dr. Mayes appeared calm, however, and Mike seemed to be already considering the idea.

"I'd work with you,'' Dr. Mayes said. "We'd draft a simple letter, designed to let Vee know that his feelings are understandable and common. He needs to feel a connection with someone and receive validation of his self-worth. That alone could go a long way toward easing him through his confusion. At least it might keep him from taking any immediate action.

"Secondly, we work to identify him and bring him in so we can continue the conversations one-on-one. Vee needs professional help, but he's certainly not beyond reaching. Frankly, I find the letters very encouraging. And articulate."

"I don't know," Koontz said. "You start talking suicide by cop, I start thinking we should stay clear of his doorstep. What if he freaks, what if he overreacts? Hell, I've never tried talking to a thirteen-year-old gangbanger 'bout life. That's what prison's for."

"There isn't anyone more qualified than a cop to approach him."

"No, sir!"

"Detective, take away the badge and legal trappings and cops are nothing but a gang themselves. Think about it. Gang members are initiated through a hostile 'jumping in' program. How many rookies have you razed and tormented in your career?"

Koontz flushed. Dr. Mayes smiled knowingly and continued. "Gang members can have friends who are not gang members, but they will never be important. Likewise, cops are almost never close to people outside of the department. They have wives and families, sure, but they mostly hang out with other cops."

Sandra couldn't help herself; she gave Mike a look. He immediately glanced away.

"Then there are partners. A gang member will go to any extreme to avenge a fellow member's death. A police officer would surely do the same if the law didn't stop him, and we all know there are cases when a police officer finds a way to do that anyway."

Koontz fidgeted in his chair. Mike wore a self-conscious smile.

"So you see," Dr. Mayes concluded, "you already have a great deal in common with Vee. You simply need to approach him calmly, man to man. He cares about his mother, you care about yours. He's protective of his sister. Most likely you are protective of yours. He is an experienced member of the streets, just as you are experienced members of the law enforcement community. Engage him in a conversation, treat him respectfully, and hopefully he'll cooperate."

"Or pull out a gun and blow us away," Koontz said stiffly.

"It's possible."

"Don't worry," Mike told his partner. "I'll do the talking. You know no one can resist my Cajun charm."

"Yeah, like a thirteen-year-old straight shooter is a sucker for bedroom eyes."

"Works on you, doesn't it?"

"Rawlins, my partnering with you is nothing more than a pity date."

"Lasting eight years?"

"I got a big heart."

"Gentlemen," Sandra interjected. "Not to break up your pillow talk or anything, but I'd like to keep us focused. How close are you to finding Vee?"

Mike shrugged. "We struck out at the school. They can't think of anyone who writes like Vee or has a sister with a scarred face. Either she was hit with the bullet after graduating, or she dropped out of school."

"Do you have any fresh ideas?"

"We're going to try the hospitals next. Of all the information we've got, a bullet wound to the face still seems the most unique. Maybe an ER doc or trauma surgeon will remember something.''

"What about plastic surgeons or orthodontists who are covered by Medicade? If it was a facial wound, some reconstruction was probably done and they see fewer patients than an ER doctor. Their memories might be fresher," Sandra said.

Mike looked surprised and impressed. "Nice," he said thoughtfully. "We'll do that."

"Just trying to help out," Sandra said, feeling absurdly pleased by the praise. She was drifting closer to Mike when Dr. Mayes spoke up.

"Might I suggest something?"

"Please do."

"Why don't you go to the source? You are trying to find a thirteen-year-old gang member. You should talk to the kids on the street."

Koontz looked horrified. "Hey Doc, we're trying to find one of them. No way are they going to give a straight answer."

"You assume they are liars?"

"I assume their interests and ours conflict, and they'll resolve that conflict by lying, yeah."

"Maybe, maybe not. You won't know until you ask, Detective."

Mike clapped his partner on the back. "I'll do the asking. You just look mean."

"Freakin' job," Koontz said.

"Nothing we haven't done before."

"Yeah," Koontz muttered after a moment. "Yeah." But Sandra thought something else was still bothering him. She could tell by Mike's covert glances that he thought the same.

"Well," Sandra said after a moment, "I believe we're

done. Dr. Mayes, please come to my office. Rusty and Mike, good luck with the doctors.''

She ushered Dr. Mayes out of the room. Behind her, Mike whispered in her ear, ''Nice suit.''

Sandra walked faster.

Chapter 6

At seven that evening, Sandra was still hunched over her desk. A police radio was on in the corner of her office, volume turned down low. Not much activity tonight, but she could hear tension in her officers' voices as they called in reports. Everyone was watching and waiting. Fearing what might happen next. It was a hell of a way to perform an already difficult job.

"Late night."

Sandra started, jerking up anxiously, then immediately shook her head.

"Dammit, Mike, you scared the living daylights out of me."

"Really? I wasn't sure anything had the power to do that."

"Trust me, plenty of things do that. Abject poverty, nuclear holocaust, bubonic plague, a Democrat in the White House…"

"Huh. Just out of curiosity, which part of that list includes me?"

"Well, you're not a Democrat in the White House...."

She let the sentence trail off into a leading silence and he simply grinned. Damn, he looked good. Lounging in her doorway, shoulder snug against the doorjamb, ankles crossed, he sported a casual gray sports jacket over a collarless white shirt and well-worn khakis. The outfit should have looked sloppy and careless. On his powerful build, chest stretching the shirt tight, it simply looked impressive. One lock of black hair dangling over his forehead, five o'clock shadow staining his cheeks. The only way he'd look better would be naked in her bed.

Sandra set down her pen sharply. Mike took that as an invitation and strode into her office.

"Anything good on the radio?" he asked, jerking his head toward the scanner as he picked up her stapler and idly ran his thumb across the back.

"Quiet night." She forced her gaze away from his callused finger, then away from his hard-muscled chest, then away from his lean waist. The ink blotter. That seemed safe enough.

"Get the letter done?" Mike asked.

"Hardest thing I've ever written, even with Dr. Mayes's help," she said honestly. "It'll appear in tomorrow's paper."

"I'm sure it'll be good."

"I don't know anything about thirteen-year-old boys, Mike."

"Yeah, Sandy, but you always were a quick study."

He set down the stapler. The silence promptly grew tense. Sandra could smell his cologne—spicy, the way she liked it. She could feel the warmth radiating from his large body, and realized for the first time that she'd been cold.

The office seemed too small with him in it, the space too quiet, the police department too deserted. It was easy to believe they were the only two people in the building and that, she discovered, was a dangerous thought.

"How'd it go this afternoon?" she asked finally, valiantly trying to keep her tone professional.

"Long." Mike sighed and shoved his hands into his pockets. "Turnover at a city hospital is too high. We only found one doctor who'd been around longer than a year, and she didn't remember a gunshot wound to the face in that time frame. For some reason the hospital doesn't want to hand over all its patients' records, particularly without a date in mind. Tomorrow we'll go with your advice and try the plastic surgeons and orthodontists. Hopefully we'll get luckier there."

"It's amazing how easy it is for one child to slip through the system," Sandra murmured. "No wonder he feels he has no identity."

"I have to say, this case isn't going as easy as planned. But don't worry. Koontz and I always get our man." Mike slid his hip onto the edge of her desk and, changing gears, gazed at her frankly.

"You look tired," he stated flatly.

"Long day." She couldn't help herself; she started rubbing her neck. Her shoulder muscles were ungodly tight. She hadn't realized just how long she'd been hunched over her desk until now. And, she realized an instant later, that was why she was reacting to her ex-husband so strongly. She was stressed, feeling as though the weight of the world rested on her shoulders. Mike had always been wonderfully inventive about coming up with ways of easing that tension. For one brief year, he had been her shelter from the storm.

"What time did you arrive this morning, Sandra?" he

was asking now, his deep voice knowing. "Six, seven o'clock? You should go home, get some rest."

"There's too much to do," she said. "For a bit, I'm going to have to push myself hard. I don't mind, Mike. Besides, today was certainly better than yesterday."

"No new nameplates," he granted.

"Yep. And I think I might have even gotten a nod of approval from the lieutenants."

He appeared genuinely impressed. "Huh, maybe the boys are smarter than I gave them credit for. Well, you wanna know something else?"

"I don't know. Do I?"

"New pool," he told her. "We're no longer betting on when you're going to leave."

"Uh-oh. What are you betting on?"

"The length of your legs."

"*What?*"

"That's some skirt you're wearing, *ma chère*. And I mean that in the nicest way. Haven't you noticed the increase in traffic going by your office? It's been the talk of the department. Guys are doubling down bets on what you're going to wear tomorrow."

"I think I'm going to wear pants tomorrow!"

"And rob me of more money?" He leaned back, appearing injured.

"Rob you of money? How am I robbing you of money?"

"Because I got an unfair advantage in the pool. I know your legs better than anyone else. And I remember exactly every inch of your skin, from the supple line of your thigh to the taut curve of your calf to the delicate little indent of your ankle. I remember your tiny toes, your high arch, your ticklish heels. Hell, I still remember the night—"

"Hey…no…stop." Her mouth had suddenly gone too dry. "That's…that's not a professional conversation."

Mike winked. "I know."

"Mike!"

"Sandy!" he mocked back, then threw up his hands in surrender. "Okay, okay. You looked like you'd been having a long day. I figured you could use a little distraction. Surely Excel spreadsheets can't be everything a girl wants on a Tuesday night. Besides, that is one *helluva* suit, babe."

His tone was so approving Sandra lost her train of thought again. "It's a power suit," she murmured defensively.

He said, "Damn right."

"Oh, for heaven's sake. Mike Rawlins, get your mind out of the gutter!"

"But then I wouldn't be any fun."

"I don't need you to be fun."

"Sure you do." He held up his hands in surrender again as she started sputtering. "Come on, Sandy," he said reasonably. "It's late, you're tired, you obviously haven't eaten yet. What'd you say? You and me and a dinner platter."

"What? When?"

"Well, I was kind of thinking now."

"I don't know." Her gaze went straight to her desk and the budget she was still fine-tuning. She had a lot of work to do. She really did need to buckle down for a bit and she probably shouldn't be fraternizing too much with her ex-husband. But…he'd liked her suit. He'd complimented her on her job. She did still remember that night…

"Take-out Chinese," she muttered after a moment. "Split the tab fifty-fifty. No lingering over dessert."

"What if I get a really promising fortune?"

"Hope the waitress is cute."

"Ah, *ma chère,* I know you don't mean that."

"Those are the terms."

"Can I buy you a drink?"

"I'll accept one collegial Mai Tai."

"Sold." He slapped his hands on his thighs and stood. "I'll drive."

"I'll meet you there."

"You're not a very good date, *ma chère.*"

"That's because I'm not your date," she reminded him levelly. "I'm your boss."

"Methinks, the lady doth protest too much."

"Well, methinks the Cajun doth never think at all."

Mike grinned again, a slow, heated expression that did funny things to her chest. He slid off her desk. He strode toward the door. "Damn, I've missed you," he said.

And then he was gone.

Alexandria's one and only Chinese restaurant was a family-run operation sitting on the edge of downtown. The food was hot, cheap and good. The decor was an ode to red vinyl. After another brief discussion, Sandra decided they would take a table after all. Formica countertops and bustling business suddenly seemed a much safer environment than his place or hers.

Mike placed their order. General Tsao's chicken for him—the hotter, the better—chicken and broccoli for Sandra. He told her vegetables had no place in fast food. She pointed to his graying temples and told him he wasn't getting any younger—soon enough he'd have to realize that green food was his friend. He said only women ever thought that way. She said that's why so many wives outlived their husbands. He said husbands only died first because they were given the choice—more years of marriage or death.

By the time they sat down at a corner booth, they'd both worked up a sweat.

"So has your family stopped laughing yet?" she asked as two heaping platters of steaming food arrived.

"They're still having a good time with things. Last night my father called to ask if I was still six foot two. I said, of course. He said damn, he'd just lost a bet with my mother that you'd have already cut me down to size."

"It hasn't been for lack of trying," she assured him soberly.

"I'd say your tongue is as razor sharp as ever," he agreed.

"And coming from you, I take that as a compliment."

She helped herself to a piece of his chicken, sucked in her cheeks as a hot pepper exploded against her tongue, and grabbed her water. "God, how can you eat that stuff!"

"Ah honey, this is nothing. You should try my mom's blackened swordfish. Now that's hot. So how are your parents doing?"

Sandra shrugged. "Mom called last night to ask me if I'd come to my senses yet. Dad mentioned about eight times that he hadn't filled my job at the security company. I'm taking that as a sign they're not completely comfortable with my decision."

"An Aikens has never been a chief of police before," Mike observed. "You rebel."

"Pure black sheep, that's me."

His expression shifted, looking surprisingly serious. "Hey, Sandra," he said, dishing up more rice. "I think you're going to be fine. You're green, you're anal, you're working too hard, but those are all habits I'm sure we can break you of."

"Gee, Mike, thanks."

They chewed in companionable silence for a bit. Then Sandra set down her fork and, though she hated to break the mood, she had to ask. "Mike, what's going on with Koontz?"

"I don't know what you're talking about. Want another red pepper?"

"Come on. This morning in the meeting with Dr. Mayes, the thought of approaching Vee seemed to make Rusty extremely nervous. The minute Dr. Mayes suggested you guys actually interview teenagers, I thought Koontz might faint. Koontz is too experienced a cop to suddenly seem weak in the knees at the idea of approaching a few juvenile delinquents. What should I know?"

"Nothing. He's fine. Small talk just isn't Rusty's thing."

"He small-talks with you fine. And he makes wisecracks in front of a whole department a hobby. You know what I think it is? I think it's the idea of approaching African-Americans on their own turf. He's prejudiced. He's scared."

"Sandy, it's not my place to say—"

"You've picked up African-American suspects before, haven't you?"

"Of course—"

"Taken them to the station, interrogated them in small, stuffy rooms?"

"Sure—"

"So it can't be just questioning them. It's staying in the east side, isn't it? It's approaching these teens on their time on their turf. It's feeling like he's on enemy terrain. He's prejudiced and that makes him scared."

"Koontz isn't afraid of anything!"

"Sure he is, Mike. He just isn't going to say anything."

Sandra leaned forward. "I'm taking your advice to heart, Mike. Anything you say here will stay between you and me. But I need to know what's going on. This is important."

"And I *don't know* what's going on," Mike growled back. "He's doing his job, Sandy. We've been going all over this town trying to find this kid. Rusty's hardly daydreaming in the back of a squad car or drinking the day away. He's just...preoccupied, sometimes. I don't know."

"Not a hundred and ten percent?"

"A cop doesn't always have to be one hundred and ten percent."

"But Koontz generally is, isn't he, Mike? That's what it says on all his evaluations. He's obsessive about solving cases. That's what you like about him."

"Hey, so he's having an off week. It happens."

"He isn't going to do any interviewing with you, Mike. I'll put money on it right now. He'll have someplace else to go, or paperwork to catch up on, or something. You already know it in your heart—you'll go to interview the kids and he won't be around."

"And there's nothing wrong with that," Mike said firmly. "We've built a major case file at this point. The interview logs are running into twenty pages. If he wants to catch up on those while I do more legwork, then more power to him."

"Fine. I'll go with you."

"What?" Mike set down his fork. He wasn't amused.

"It's inappropriate for only one person to conduct an interview, Mike, you know that. Two pairs of eyes are always better than one. I'll go."

"No."

"With all due respect, it's not your decision—"

"Oh, don't you pull rank on this, Sandy. This is not

about rank. This is my case, you assigned me to it, now don't tell me how to run it.''

"You think that's what I'm doing? Stepping on your toes?''

"Damn right. You always want things your way, Sandy. Not just done, but done the way you want it, when you want it, how you want it. Obviously you feel you didn't get a chance to run my job when we were married, so you're going to take it over now.''

Her face froze up. She said tightly, "You egotistical bastard. How dare you think I took this job just to spite you. What the hell makes you think any part of my life or my decisions still revolve around you?''

"Because you said it yourself last night, Sandy! That I didn't talk about my job enough, that I didn't let you into my precious little police world. So now you've gone and inserted yourself into it. Well, congratulations to you. We can talk thirteen-year-old kids committing murder and babies found in trash cans all you want. You can come with me and roll in the filth to your heart's desire. Why should I try to protect you anymore? Why should I try to keep the garbage of my job from my wife or my home or my few after-work hours? You obviously never trusted me to be a good cop. You obviously don't think I'm capable of keeping the world safe. Hell, you had to go and become my boss. *Dammit!*''

He suddenly slammed his fist into the table. The motion startled them both and did little to alleviate his rage. The anger had sneaked up on him and dug its claws in deep. He didn't know where it had come from. He hadn't expected it to hit him so hard. But now his hands were trembling and his chest was too tight and he could feel the veins bulging along his neck.

Sandra was staring at him white-faced. As if she'd never

seen him before. And that made him feel worse than angry. That made him ashamed.

She said hoarsely, "I trust you, Mike."

He shook his head tiredly, rubbing the back of his neck now and wishing he could make this whole scene go away. "You're just saying words, Sandy. Take it from a Cajun, words don't mean a thing. Every night when I came home, you drilled me like a Marine Corps sergeant. How was my day? Any arrests? How'd they go down? How was the case shaping up for court? Did I feel prepared? What about Koontz? What about my lieutenant? What about my arrest record for the week? Hell, half the time I simply wanted to sit down with a cold beer and my wife. I didn't want to think about my day. No suspects or crime scenes or kids killing kids. I wanted to just be. In *my* home. With *my* wife. A little reward for a job on the front lines. You couldn't allow me that much, though, could you, Sandy?" He looked at her with genuine hurt. "Why was it so hard to trust me when I said things were fine?"

"Because 'fine' was all you ever said, Mike! Then Rusty would call, or your father or your brother and you'd talk for *hours*. I never doubted you as a cop. My God, I *loved* you for being a cop. I was proud of you. I just wanted... I just wanted to be the person you talked with for hours. I wanted to be your best friend, Mike, not simply the woman you took to bed."

"You were my *wife*. How could you doubt your importance in my life?"

"Because I did. Because that's what wives do. We worry, Mike. We doubt. We get married and the first time we discover we're still lonely, we get scared. Then I'd try to reach out to you. I'd seek reassurance. And you would simply say, 'Fine.'"

"But I—ah, hell." Mike pounded the table again, then

twirled his glass of cola. He didn't know what to say anymore. Half the time he looked at this woman, all he could think was good things. Then he'd look at their marriage and, God, what a mess. He didn't understand. He didn't know how to fix it.

"I didn't mean to make you feel like an outsider, Sandy," he attempted at last, his troubled gaze locked on his glass. "You'll discover it for yourself soon enough. After the really long days on this job, you come home empty. And you can't talk about it. You can't angst about it—hell, you can't even dream about it. You gotta just sit and recharge, let the good wash away the bad. That was all it was ever about."

"But Mike, if that was the case, why could you talk for so long to Koontz?"

"Because he's not part of my home, Sandy. He's not sanctuary. He's the freaking job. Don't you get it yet? All Koontz and I *do* talk about is police work."

"Oh." Sandra nodded shortly but still appeared subdued. Their collegial dinner had deteriorated, and he could tell she was as self-conscious as he was about the turn things had taken.

"Well, in the spirit of sharing," she offered haltingly, "I wasn't asking about your day because I didn't trust you. I've always thought you were a good cop. And I didn't become police chief to tell you what to do. Well, okay, so that was one appeal..." She shrugged, smiling wryly. "You have to admit, bossing around your ex..."

"Yeah, yeah. Revenge of the matrimonial impaired. I get it."

She sobered up again and said slowly, "This job...this job means a lot to me, Mike. I was raised to believe in giving your best and I was raised to believe in community. Except my family gives their best to their own company and donates money to the community. I wanted to do something more direct. I wanted...I wanted to be something more that Howard Aikens's daughter, spoiled little rich girl taking over her daddy's company. This position is the first job I've ever had that's been all mine and I like that. I want to be my own person now. To not just be successful, but to *feel* successful.''

''You've always been a bit different from your parents, Sandra. It's not too hard to understand you wanting to go your own way.''

''I don't know,'' she told him honestly. ''I'm thirty-four years old. Seems a little late for rebellion.''

''Ah, being chief of police isn't rebellion, *ma chère*. Marrying me, now *that* was rebellion.''

She granted him a smile. ''Not to add insult to injury, Mike, but all that episode earned me was a lot of 'I told you so's.'''

''And still you went out on your own. That takes guts.''

She laughed. ''Yeah, yeah. I suppose so.''

''Mike?'' she said quietly. ''One more thing. On the subject of the east side. I didn't bring up going into the east side with you because I doubted you. I want to go for *me*. So I can meet these kids and learn about their lives. Koontz is right. I'm a west-side girl from a west-side world. To succeed at this job, I have to fix that. I need to honestly learn how the other half lives.''

''It's too dangerous,'' Mike said immediately. ''Vee could open fire again at any time.''

''Then it's a good thing I'm going in with a very experienced detective.''

''I can't focus on interviewing a crowd of gang members and look after you.''

''Who says we'll be targets? We both wear street

clothes, and we don't drive a patrol car. We can look like
a young couple asking for directions.''

"A young, white affluent couple in the east side."

"Mike, please. You need a second person. I need the
experience."

"Maybe Koontz won't bail," he said stubbornly, though
he didn't really believe that would be the case. "This
whole conversation could be moot."

"If Koontz will go with you, I'll back off," Sandra
promised. "But if he doesn't..."

Mike looked at his ex-wife's pleading blue eyes. He
exhaled sharply. "If Koontz doesn't come," he granted at
last. "But then you gotta listen to what I say, Sandra. You
go in as a rookie, following my lead, obeying my orders,
and getting the hell out of sight at the first sign of trouble."

"I can do that."

He gave her a look.

"Well," she amended, "I can *try* to do that."

"That's more like it." He had to smile, though. Then
he wondered what she'd do if he leaned over right now
and kissed her. He said, "Come on, *ma chère,* I'll walk
you to your car."

Outside, the night air was cool and crisp. Stars studded
the sky and a pale waxy moon rose up to the west. They'd
been in the restaurant for over an hour and now it was late.
Traffic had slowed down. Few cars populated the parking
lot. The area had grown quiet.

"Still no news," Sandra murmured, and Mike knew she
was thinking about Vee.

"Maybe he's studying books for a change, instead of
loading up his gun."

"Maybe." She sounded unconvinced. He escorted her

over to her Lexus and held open the door. She didn't get in right away, though.

"It's hard to believe sometimes," she said, looking out over the peaceful area, "that just fifteen miles from here there exists a virtual war zone. Some young girl is preparing right now to go work some corner of the street. Some mother is probably fighting cockroaches to get dinner on the table for her family. Some boys like Vee are gathering on someone's porch, contemplating who to fight, what to do. Here we are. There they are. Is it any wonder there are so many rifts in this community?"

"White liberal guilt," Mike said quietly.

She shook her head. "It doesn't make it any less true."

"Maybe, but you can't drive yourself crazy over it."

"Somebody ought to."

"Sandra Aikens," he murmured. "You never give up. But then, that's what I always liked about you."

He lowered his head. At the last minute, he saw her eyes widen in surprise, but she didn't pull away. Shock or acquiescence? He didn't know and didn't care. He took command of her lips and drew out the kiss leisurely.

This was the taste of Sandy Aikens's mouth. This full bottom lip here, this tender corner there. This ridge of sharp white teeth, this sweet duel with her tongue. Her body shifted, turned into him wordlessly and he deepened the embrace.

She fit nicely against him. Her rib cage felt small and fragile beneath his hands, but her heart pounded powerfully. Her legs nestled against his passively, but her hands dug into his shoulders. He could feel her growing tension and desire. The shifting in her hips against his groin, the swelling of her breasts against his chest. The way her head now angled back on its own and she opened her mouth wider for him, gave herself over to his kiss.

He plunged his hands into her thick hair, anchoring her head in place, and though he'd told himself this was going to be a controlled experiment, he devoured her lips wildly. He suckled on her lower lip, tormented her mouth with his tongue. He grazed his teeth along the delicate line of her throat and pursed his lips around her earlobe.

She rewarded him with a low mewling sound that sent his blood soaring.

He straightened. He set her back from him a bit so she wouldn't know exactly how strongly she'd affected him. And then he dropped one last kiss on the tip of her nose.

"What…what was that all about?" she asked breathlessly.

"Collegial kiss. One co-worker to another. Good night, Chief Aikens. And sweet dreams."

He sauntered away. And he knew how well his experiment had worked by the low oath that escaped his ex-wife's lips and by the ferocity with which she slammed her car door. A moment later, her Lexus whipped by him in the parking lot and headed out onto the street without looking back.

Mike remained standing by his pickup truck for several moments more. He needed the cold night wind to rein in his throbbing body. He needed a quiet moment to organize his thoughts.

She had responded to the kiss immediately. Even after last night's "we must be friends" speech, she had never held back. Surely that had to mean something. And he could have sworn that, for one instant, when she'd seen him standing in the doorway of her office tonight, she'd been happy to see him. At yesterday's shooting, she'd also been grateful to have him there.

Sometimes, he knew for certain that his ex-wife was a lonely woman. Smart, controlled, capable, but also isolated on the inside. Not the type to be overly outgoing, slow to make friends. The opposite of himself in many ways.

Except they were both loyal to a fault. To their families, to their friends. And in Mike's case even to his defunct wedding vows. He'd never tell Sandy, but he'd had very few dates since the divorce. He joked about it, he laughed about it, but he never actually did it. Date another woman. It just never seemed right.

He'd once had Sandra Aikens as his wife. And as he'd come to learn years ago, as he grew certain of tonight, her taste still fresh upon his lips, after having had Sandra Aikens, no other woman would do.

Chapter 7

"So what do you think happened to Vee last night?" Mike asked his partner the next morning. "Think he had a change of heart?"

"Dunno. Maybe he and his gangbanger pals decided to pick on someone their own size." Koontz turned a corner, read the address out loud and grunted. "Damn, where can this office be?"

"Three blocks back," Mike said dryly.

Koontz made a face. Since picking Mike up at eight that morning to interview a plastic surgeon, he'd grumbled about the traffic, grumbled about the roads and grumbled about the frost still daring to coat the streets. Then he'd lit up a cigarette, even though he and Mike had a deal about him smoking in the car. Something was on the man's mind. Mike figured if he was patient, sooner or later Koontz might even tell him.

"Think it was Sandra's letter in this morning's newspaper?'' Mike dared to ponder as Koontz stubbed out his cigarette in the car's ashtray, then drove around the block.

''Yeah, right. If writing letters was all it took to stop crime, Ann Landers would be a Supreme Court justice. My guess is the closest Vee comes to answering our fearless leader is burning the paper in the trash.''

''I liked the letter,'' Mike said mildly. ''Didn't preach, didn't whine. Just talked to Vee matter-of-factly. Seems a good approach for a thirteen-year-old boy.''

''No offense, but Sandra Aikens could knit a handgun right now and you'd be so smitten you'd carry it around in place of your side arm.''

''Hey, I like my Beretta.''

''Yeah?'' Koontz slid over a deceptively sleepy look. ''Did you take it out for Chinese food last night?''

''Actually, I did.''

Koontz exhaled sharply, his fingers thrumming the steering wheel. ''Dangerous game, man. It's a small department and you know the walls got ears. One dinner and the whole place is already buzzing. Where can this lead, Rawlins? Let's say you do get back together. On the one hand, the whole freakin' thing falls apart, except now you gotta work with her. Or on the other hand, the whole freakin' thing works out, except now your fellow officers are gunning for your hide. 'Rawlins is sleeping with the boss. Rawlins gets the good cases 'cause he's literally greasing the wheels.' Either way, you're burned.''

''I'm a Cajun. I don't mind heat.''

''Dammit,'' Koontz said. ''Where is this stupid office!''

''One block behind now. You were so busy lecturing me, you drove right by.''

Koontz scowled, pounded the brakes and brought the old sedan to a screeching halt. The narrow avenue was technically one-way. After eight years, however, Mike knew better than to point that out as his partner shifted into reverse. He simply hung on as Koontz slammed the gas pedal to the floor. They rocketed backward at approximately forty miles per hour. Another car, coming up an intersecting street on the left, saw them and had the audacity to honk its horn. Koontz gave the driver the bird.

Then he neatly swung the car into an empty curbside parking space. "Ha," he said. "Now *that's* driving."

Mike raised a brow but climbed out of the car without saying anything. It was going to be a long day with Koontz.

Inside, the news didn't get any better. Yesterday, they'd called Medicade and gotten a list of plastic surgeons authorized to perform reconstructive surgery. The list was small, and the number of permissible operations limited. Medicade would only kick in for "necessary reconstruction," meaning the disfigurement had to interfere with the patient's health, not be merely cosmetic. Mike and Rusty weren't sure if a gunshot wound to the face was considered cosmetic or not.

They started their search with Dr. Morgan. He also donated time at a free clinic downtown, making him the most likely candidate to have met Vee's sister.

Dr. Morgan was waiting for them in his office, reviewing notes for an upcoming surgery and clearly in a hurry.

"What's the time frame again?" he asked, slapping two X-ray slides onto a lighted board and frowning at the glowing shapes. Cheekbones, Mike realized. The man was studying someone's cheekbones.

"We don't have a time frame," Mike said.

"Female, you said?" Dr. Morgan prompted, cracking his X-ray slides as he yanked them down and threw up a fresh set.

"Yes."

"Age?"

"We don't know."

"Extent of damage?"

"We're not sure. The letter describes the wound as leaving her with a scar in one cheek, so maybe the bullet didn't pass all the way through."

Dr. Morgan snapped off his light-board and faced Mike long enough to give him a skeptical glance. "I thought on the phone you said she was the victim of a drive-by."

"That's what we think."

"Correct me if I'm wrong, Officer, but not many drive-by shootings are done with small-caliber weapons. And a large-caliber gun is going to do significantly more damage than scar one cheek. The least you could hope for was it passing through her open mouth, making a clean line cheek to cheek. But frankly, that would make it a case for the record books. Far more likely, the bullet ricocheted off her teeth, maybe her jawbone, shattering bones and teeth and shredding the tongue before lodging someplace in the soft palate or throat. I've seen bullets lodged behind someone's septum. I've seen bullets nestled right up against the aorta. Either way, you're talking extensive reconstruction work."

"This would be covered by Medicade?"

"Certainly. A damaged tongue can swell and block airways—it would need to be repaired or possibly even replaced. Likewise, a shattered jaw would have to be fixed for the patient to be able to eat again, and that might require a bone graft. Finally, a damaged palate or soft tissue of the gums might also need to be rebuilt before it could hold bridgework. Depending on the extent of the injuries, we could be talking many follow-up surgeries, not just one."

Mike frowned. "But you haven't handled a case like that?"

"I've handled four cases like that. All males, however, and you're looking for a female."

Koontz was perplexed enough to turn away from a poster of model noses decorating the wall. "We're talking the east side, a family without much money. Who else could they go to?"

"No one else. And not just because I'm the best plastic surgeon in the city, gentlemen, but because my price is right. A case like that, I would've done for free."

"But she was wounded," Mike murmured. "We got the letter."

"Unless the letter is a hoax," Koontz grunted.

"The shots fired on Johnson and Fletcher didn't feel like a hoax to me—"

"Gentlemen, the letter. May I?" Dr. Morgan held out his hand. Belatedly Mike dug out a folded copy of the letter from his breast pocket and handed it over. The doctor needed only a minute.

"Ah, here's your problem. She was inside the house when the bullet caught her. That complicates matters. A large-caliber bullet could certainly pass through Sheetrock or a window while retaining enough force to be deadly, but we don't know if that was the bullet's true trajectory."

Mike and Koontz got it. They muttered the one word together as a single curse. "Ricochet."

"Precisely. If the bullet came from a long distance away, or ricocheted off other objects first, there's a good chance it dispersed the majority of its force before impacting the subject's cheek. Now we're talking the possibility of a minor injury. The bullet penetrates the cheek, then lodges beneath the tongue. Any ER doc could irrigate the wound and stitch her back up."

"But we're talking a major hole in someone's cheek," Koontz tried.

Dr. Morgan shook his head. "It's no longer medically relevant, gentlemen. Cheeks are little more than skin and muscle. A doctor would stitch it back up and it would heal. Certainly, there would be damage. The patient would lose muscle tone in that side of her face, she would be unable to smile with that half of her mouth. But in terms of vital functions like chewing, swallowing…" He shrugged again. "For her sake, I'm sorry to say that follow-up surgery would no longer be considered a medical necessity."

Mike sighed heavily. He couldn't believe what he was hearing, and yet he could. "So there's a good chance she never had any reconstruction done. She went to the ER, received one helluva stitching job, and that was that."

"It's definitely possible. You need more information, gentlemen. There's just not enough here. Now if you'll excuse me…" Dr. Morgan handed them the letter, gathered up his file, and led them to the door.

Two minutes later, they were sitting back in their car, Koontz at the wheel. Eight-thirty in the morning. The sun was shining. The day was cold and bright. And their best lead had just been shot to hell.

"Time for plan B," Mike said.

"We don't have a plan B."

"Sure we do. Dr. Mayes's suggestion. Let's talk to the gangbangers."

Koontz rubbed his hands around the steering wheel. "I think we should review the information we already have," he said, "before we get too far ahead."

"We don't have information, Koontz. We have paper."

"You never know. Sometimes you get little nuggets here and there, and you just don't recognize them as leads at the time. You have to sift through again to see them."

"Yeah, sure. It happens." Mike waited a moment. He saw from the tight set of Koontz's jaw that Sandy had been right. Koontz didn't want to do the interviews in the east side and this was how it was going to go down.

"Why don't we split up?" Koontz muttered shortly. "I can mull over the paperwork. You hit the streets."

"I can do the interviews," Mike said.

"Cool." Koontz turned on the car and shifted it into gear. He pulled them out onto the road and headed for the department. Mike didn't say anything more, though for the first time in eight years with Rusty, he was disappointed. His partner had copped out on him, especially after Mike had sworn to Sandra that he wouldn't.

And then Mike started thinking. How many interviews of African-Americans had Rusty been present for? Mike could picture his partner in interrogation rooms. He could picture him leading cuffed suspects into the holding cell. But the preliminary interviews, working the streets...

Mike was no longer comfortable with where his thoughts were taking him.

Presently Koontz said, "Did I ever tell you about my uncle?"

"An uncle? No, I don't remember that."

"Oh. Well, I had an uncle. He took me in after my parents died. A permanent bachelor kind of guy. Lived in a one-bedroom house with laundry piled from floor to ceiling. Couldn't cook to save his life. Good guy, though. Never complained about suddenly being saddled with his baby sister's kid. Took me to a lot of Bruins games, got me through high school. Did his job."

Mike nodded.

"So anyway," Koontz said, "one night, ten years ago, Frank makes a late-night pretzel run to the local minimart. Bruins are on TV, it's intermission, you know how that is. He's got something like seven bucks on him. It's not enough."

Koontz turned toward Mike. He said matter-of-factly. "Some eighteen-year-old punk blows him away with a close-range shotgun blast to the chest. Kid's high as a kite on PCP, and furious my uncle doesn't have more money. So he lights him up like the Fourth of July in the middle of the minimart. Then he does the cashier. Then he throws down his empty shotgun and digs into the Hostess display. When the cops arrive three minutes later, here's this skinny black kid, sitting between two dead bodies, licking cream filling off his fingers. Kid got outta jail two years ago. They gave him a light sentence 'cause they said he was too drugged to know what he was doing. Kid was a victim. Kid had a hard life. We white guys can't possibly know what it's like to grow up black. Kid's probably shooting up on a street corner right now. My uncle…well, my uncle is still dead."

"That's rough," Mike said. "You ever look the kid up?"

"No man, I know better."

"That's good, Rusty. It's good to know your limits."

"I thought about it, though."

"You didn't do it. That's what matters."

Koontz nodded. They drove in silence the rest of the way to the station. As they pulled in, Mike turned to his partner one last time. "You do the paperwork. I'll hit the streets."

"That's the plan."

"Koontz. Sorry about your uncle."

And Koontz said, "I knew you'd understand."

When Mike approached Sandra about accompanying him downtown to do the interviews, she was elated. After last night's kiss, she'd gone home and promised herself she'd forget all about him. Instead, she'd dreamed of him

over and over again. That had ticked her off and started a
fresh wave of resolutions. Which had lasted until she fell
asleep again and her ex-husband invaded her dreams.

Frankly, Mike Rawlins was still in her blood. And some
part of her—no, a big part of her—was starting to wonder
if there might not be some way of making things work out.
Funny how one conversation over Chinese food could
elicit so much hope. He hadn't meant to shut her out, she'd
found herself thinking at five o'clock. It was merely the
side effect of the job. She was a cop now, too; she could
understand that. They had fewer differences now, she told
herself at five-thirty; more things in common. And still
such a spark...

By seven, she'd decided she was thinking too much under the influence of hormones. At nine, he walked into her
office, tall, dark and handsome, and she was positive hormones knew best. Then he told her he wanted her to join
him interviewing kids on the east side and her fate was
sealed. He had listened to her last night. He respected her
enough to include her in his job.

The two of them working together to protect the city. It
sounded wonderfully romantic and strong.

Then Sandra was promptly terrified. She didn't know
anything about how to talk to kids, let alone inner-city
kids. Let alone angry, disillusioned, inner-city kids. She'd
struggled enough writing the letter and, having heard nothing back from Vee, she didn't know if she'd even done
that right.

At noon, Sandy called Dr. Mayes. He laughed sympathetically at her fears and gave her some advice for approaching teenagers. Dress the way she normally dressed,
talk the way she normally talked. She was who she was,
and kids had an inherent distrust of fakery. Yes, they

would be hostile toward her in the beginning. That's what patience was about. Oh, and good luck.

When Mike arrived at her office at two in the afternoon, Sandra was nervous but as ready as she was going to get. She'd selected a simple dove-gray pantsuit with an open jacket and a man's white dress shirt unbuttoned to below her collarbone. She'd read somewhere that exposing your throat made you appear more approachable. She wasn't sure if this applied only to vampires, but at least Mike's gaze lit up.

"Very nice," he said.

"You don't think it's overdone?"

"I honestly have no idea. Hey, wait a minute. Isn't that one of my old shirts?"

"You'd left it at the dry cleaners. I decided to put it to good use."

Mike blinked his eyes several times. "My shirt covering your breasts. Honey, that's just plain erotic."

"Ah, but will it help you win the pool?"

"To hell with the pool. My interests have gone way beyond money."

"Too bad," she murmured as she sauntered out the door. "I would've let you buy me another Mai Tai."

Mike's face held a reluctant grin as he caught up to her in the corridor. He was still grinning when he held open the car door for her. She could tell he had turned some corner in his mind, too. There was a spark between them, the tension and sizzle she remembered from their dating days. It was combined with a fresh, hesitant vulnerability. They weren't completely certain of what they were doing, but they were going to do it anyway. At least until it blew up in their faces.

As they headed downtown, however, they both turned to business.

"The sister lead may be a dead end," Mike said flatly as he negotiated heavy traffic. "We spoke to a plastic surgeon who says her wound may not have been serious enough to warrant surgery. Any results from the letter?"

She shook her head. "No reply has magically appeared on the *Post*'s doorstep. It is early, though. The last two letters were left late at night."

"Maybe tonight then."

"Hopefully. Other than that, all I have to show for my efforts is a new nameplate."

He looked at her quizzically and she filled in, "'Dear Abby.' Hey, at least now they're showing a sense of humor."

Mike, however, didn't smile. For the first time, she noted the crow's-feet creasing the corners of his eyes and the tight carriage of his shoulders. He was worried, she realized, and a moment later, that simple observation rattled her. She wasn't sure she'd ever seen easy Mike Rawlins worried before.

"The case is in bad shape," he said after a moment.

"I know."

"Koontz is reviewing our notes to see if there's anything we've missed, but at this point I'd say we're on day three of an investigation into a very dangerous boy and we've got *nothing*."

She nodded.

"Soon we may need another shooting just to have a break in the case, and that's not a great feeling for a detective. When you're waiting for the perp to strike again because you need the additional information."

"Is there anything more I can do? More resources you need, other outside experts?"

He hesitated. She got the definite impression there was

something weighing seriously on his mind now, something that troubled him, but he wasn't sure about sharing.

"Maybe some additional manpower," he said after a moment. "A few more bodies searching the streets would be nice."

"I'll see what I can do."

He nodded but didn't look relieved. "This could be dangerous, Sandy. If I say get down, don't argue with me, get down. If I yell at you to hide in the car, no heroics, *ma chère*. Hide in the car."

"I promise to duck, hide, and retreat as necessary. This is your show, Mike, I'll do as you say."

"That's my girl."

A moment later, they passed into the east side.

Old textile mills came into view, brick facades crumbling and walls sagging on their foundations. When they had arrived two nights ago it had been dark so Sandra hadn't noticed much. Now she observed the steady change sweeping over the landscape as they descended into low-income housing. Corner grocery stores gave way to pawnshops, delis to bail bond offices. She saw more and more signs advertising lottery tickets and check-cashing services, hope and resources for people who didn't have much of either.

The buildings grew grayer, streaked with old graffiti paint and not even important enough to be tagged again by newer street artists. More windows were boarded up. More streetlights blown out. More kids roaming the street, though most of them should have been in school.

Sandra could feel the environment press against her. By the time Mike pulled up to an old park with a cracked asphalt basketball court and two broken swings, her expression was sober.

It was easy to write a letter telling a thirteen-year-old

child he had choices, she thought. It was harder to stand in a decrepit park on a worn city block and believe. My God, those were discarded hypodermic needles littering that gutter. And that was definitely a used condom hanging from that tree. How did you grow up surrounded by this and still have hope for your future? How could you preserve peace of mind?

A small cluster of teenagers were eyeing them warily from a park bench. Sandra took a deep breath, then followed Mike out of the car. Professional detachment. That's what she needed.

It was a chilly spring afternoon. The four kids sported heavy coats, two of the young men wearing what appeared to be black down vests with black knit hats. At a glance, Sandra would have guessed that their ages ranged from fourteen to eighteen, plus one toddler who was sitting on a young girl's lap. The mother appeared to be sixteen and her baby was just at the age where he could stand precariously on her knees. Both the young girl and her child wore matching gold necklaces. Maybe a gift from the dad.

"Afternoon," Mike said to an audience of sullen stares. "I'm Detective Mike Rawlins. This is Sandra Aikens, Chief of Police."

An older boy got to his feet. The self-appointed leader of the group, he climbed down from the table until he stood in front of Mike. He wore a pair of baggy jeans that threatened to slip from his skinny frame. High-top tennis shoes seemed to catch his pants more than protect his feet. His white T-shirt held a red Nike swoosh beneath his down vest. He wasn't particularly large, an adolescent at that stage where his bones were growing faster than his weight could keep up. What he lacked in size, however, he made up for in attitude.

"So what's that gotta do with us?"

"Not much," Mike said calmly. "We were just in the neighborhood and thought we'd swing by for a chat."

"Cops don't chat."

"Really? Must have missed that at the academy. So what's your name?"

The boy glared at Mike harder but, faced with the larger man's impassive expression, finally said, "Mac-Two. They call me Mac-Two. Can you figure that?"

Sandra gazed from Mike to the young man back to Mike again. They seemed to be engaged in some kind of contest, she decided. The boy was sizing up Mike, waiting for an answer, and Mike was taking his time, staying in control. She wasn't sure how the winner would be declared or what might be at stake. Then Mike spoke again.

"Mac one-one," he said. "As in MAC-11, as in the automatic pistol."

Mac-Two's brows shot up. He rocked back on his heels and gave Mike a fresh appraisal.

"Not bad," he finally grunted. The boy climbed back on the picnic table and apparently Sandra and Mike made the grade, for he introduced them to the group. The two boys were named G'Day and Lil Man. They were friends of Mac-Two and didn't say much. Sandra thought Lil Man appeared flustered when she shook his hand, turning away quickly before Mac-Two saw him blush. The young girl turned out to be Mac-Two's sister, Keisha. Her son was almost a year old and named Bobby.

Bobby's father was working this afternoon, Keisha explained softly. He held down two jobs, a real trooper for her and the baby. Someday, they wanted to own their own house. Maybe somewhere out in the country where they could have their own backyard with a dog and a swing set. Some place where they wouldn't have to worry about Bobby getting hit by a stray bullet. That would be nice.

Mac-Two scoffed at this. He told his sister coldly that she'd already messed that up. If she'd really wanted to leave the east side, she shouldn't have gotten herself pregnant. Everyone knew once you were sixteen years old and had a baby that you were stuck. Hadn't she looked around the neighborhood lately?

"Karl is different," Keisha said stubbornly. "He's a stand-up man. He'll take good care of Bobby and me."

"Stand-up man? The boy don't even have a GED. What kinda life he gonna provide without an education? He's a stock boy now and he's gonna be a stock boy ten years from now. If he makes it that long. If he don't one day decide to hell with the hard work and give in to his brother."

"He ain't talking to his brother," Keisha replied heatedly. "He ain't going down that road. He *promised* me."

Mac-Two scoffed again. He looked at Mike and Sandra with a hard, unrelenting face. "Karl Jones's brother be an O.G.B. Good rep, good piece of business. He drive around in a Mercedes. Got a wife and two kids of his own. They all got matching diamond necklaces, not these stupid gold chains here." He waved a dismissive hand at his sister's and nephew's jewelry and Keisha flinched. "Karl wanna be a provider like his brother, but at least he got the brains to stay out of the gang. Of course how he gonna provide, then? Around here, you got two choices. Dealin' and rich, or straight and poor. That's life. If Karl Jones don't wanna face that, then so much for being a stand-up guy."

"He works hard," Keisha said again, but compared to her brother's matter-of-fact speech, her voice was weak. "He's gonna take care of Bobby and me, you'll see."

"What about you?" Sandra asked Mac-Two. "Where do you want to be five years from now?"

Mac-Two merely shrugged. "Alive, that's my goal. It be big enough."

"Come on, you must want more than that."

"Lady, look around. Why the hell you down here anyway? Pity field trip? White liberal guilt? Damn, this place ain't got anything to do with you."

"I'm the new chief of police," Sandra said reasonably. "This place has everything to do with me."

"You gonna clean this up?" He waved his hand around the abandoned playground.

"I think we'd better."

"Uh-huh. And the morning after that and the morning after that? Listen here, lady cop—go back to your political meetings and fussy white friends. Give them speeches 'bout what you wanna do. They'll be happy for you, they'll pat you on the back. We, we know better."

"Like Vee?" Mike interjected. "Like Vee knows better?"

Mac-Two's gaze narrowed shrewdly. He gave them both a fresh appraisal. "Yeah," he drawled. "Like my good brother Vee knows better."

Sandra inhaled sharply. She glanced at Mike and could tell he felt it, too. Mac-Two knew something.

"I would like to meet Vee," Sandra said quietly.

"Uh-huh."

"As the new chief of police," she continued, "I'm very concerned about what happened to his father. It's not right for officers to be shooting people in the back. I would want to look into that…if I had more information."

"If you had more information."

"I'd like to meet him, too," Mike said. "I have two sisters and I'd hate it if anything happened to them. In fact, I spoke to a doctor this morning who thought he could help Vee's sister, free of charge. If he had more information."

"If you had more information." Mac-Two rolled his eyes. Suddenly he slapped G'Day and Lil Man on the back. The two younger kids lurched forward, caught off guard. "Take a hike," he commanded harshly, and the two kids, charged by the unexpected savagery in his voice, obediently took off running.

That left Mac-Two, his sister, and Bobby, who was happily blowing bubbles. On instinct, Sandra picked the baby up and cradled him against her chest. He smelled of baby powder and warm skin. He felt unbelievably soft against her bare throat. His stubby fingers grabbed at her jacket lapels, then twisted her shirt collar. He had drool on his hands, dirt, too. Keisha looked embarrassed as he left a long muddy streak across Sandra's shoulder, but Sandra didn't mind.

He was a precious child. Holding him in the middle of a gray, cracked park, Sandra could understand why Keisha held so feverishly to her dream of a house and white picket fence. Holding him in the middle of a needle-strewn park, Sandra could understand why Vee felt so angry. And sad, too, she realized for the first time. The thirteen-year-old wasn't just mad. He was also heartbroken.

Mac-Two had turned to Mike. "How much money?" he asked.

"Twenty," Mike negotiated.

"Hell, man, the kid's shootin' at cops. Don't insult me."

"Forty."

"One hundred. You walkin' in the east side with a pretty lady, you obviously got nothin'."

"We give you a hundred dollars," Sandra spoke up,

"and you're going to tell us who Vee is? Just like that? I thought... What about loyalty?"

"He ain't no brother of mine."

"Do others feel that way?"

"Sandra," Mike growled warningly.

She shook her head, pulling away from him and still holding the baby. "No, I want to understand this. This boy is writing letters to the paper. He is saying he's tired of kids killing kids. He's tired of violence against people's sisters. You have a sister. You live here, too. Doesn't any of that mean something to you?"

Mac-Two's nostrils flared. "Don't you walk in here and tell me what I'm supposed to feel."

"I'm not telling you, I'm asking you."

"No way. You're tellin' me I gotta be loyal to some letter in the paper. Look, lady. I gotta be loyal to my hood. I gotta be loyal to my family, I gotta be loyal to my homeys. Now don't tell me I gotta be loyal to some letter. I don't got *room* for that. I don't got *time* for that. You got a hundred bucks or what?"

Mike gave Sandra a stern look. She backed off, though there was something about the whole exchange that unsettled her, left her wearier than before.

Mike handed over five twenty-dollar bills. Mac-Two gripped them fiercely.

"Where can we find Vee?" Mike asked.

"Hand over Bobby to Keisha."

Sandra obeyed, though she promptly felt empty without the child.

"Where can we find Vee?" Mike repeated.

Mac-Two grinned. It was the only warning they got.

"Right behind you," he said, and then like a shot, he and Keisha were gone.

Chapter 8

"**D**own!" Mike yelled.

Immediately Sandra flattened, feeling gravel and glass dig into her palms as Mike whipped out his firearm and dropped into a crouch beside her.

"Where?" she cried. "I don't see…"

And then she caught it. A flicker of movement across the street. Someone was in the flat brick building across from the park.

"Dammit, we're sitting ducks out here," Mike growled. "On the count of three, run behind the car. One. Two. *Three.*"

Sandra sprang to her feet and ran. Mike was right beside her, curling his arm around her waist and covering her with his body as they raced for the protection of the car. They jumped behind the passenger-side door, ducking low and breathing hard. Still no sound from across the street. Somehow, that frightened Sandra more.

Mike had his 9 mm gripped with both hands in front of

his face. Sweat beaded his brow, but he still sounded remarkably composed as he said, "Do you have a gun?"

"In my purse on the floor of the car."

"Get it out."

He moved to the end of the car, peering earnestly across the street while she cracked open the door and dragged out her purse. Seconds later she had a small .22-caliber pistol in her grip, though her hands weren't nearly as steady as Mike's.

"I think he's gone," Mike said. "Damn."

"Damn?"

"Face it, *ma chère,* this may be as close as we come to catching him. Okay, you sit here. Don't move a muscle. I'll be back in a sec."

"What are you—"

Mike didn't wait for her question. He bolted across the street with his head tucked between his shoulders. Sandra was left peering out from behind the bumper, nervously waiting to see what happened next. The building across the street appeared to be an old garage of some kind. The front facade was brick with evenly spaced square windows. Unfortunately, the glass was so caked with dirt and grime it was impossible to see in.

Was Vee still inside? Had he already run off or was he serious now? Two cops had come into the east side and were asking about him. Maybe that had made him mad. Maybe it was enough to jolt him into action.

Dr. Mayes had said Vee was mostly angry with himself. Suddenly Sandra wasn't so sure.

A loud popping sound emitted from across the street, followed by a startling crash and a fierce curse. Next thing Sandra knew, a small body came tearing out of the building and made a beeline for the fence down the street.

Vee, she realized. That was Vee.

Acting on instinct, she took off in pursuit.

Vee had a good head start on her, so they were hardly neck and neck. From this distance, she couldn't even tell if he was carrying a gun, but assumed he must be. Mostly she was struck by his size. Small, wiry. More boy than man. And fast. He tore down the sidewalk like hell on wheels, his arms pumping furiously at his sides.

"Stop, police," Sandra yelled belatedly.

He kept on running, not even glancing over his shoulder.

Dammit, she was never going to be able to catch him. The kid moved too fast and she'd been an idiot to wear heels. She honestly needed Mike and had no idea how far behind her he might be. She'd heard more cursing from the building as she'd run by it; he was probably tangled up in there.

Then she was seized by another realization. Vee was a small boy, obviously intent on getting away. Sooner or later he must plan on ducking through something, cutting through somewhere.

She spotted it. An opening in the fence up ahead. The boy could dive on through and come out on another block or cut through a backyard. If he made it, she was sunk.

Sandra came to a halt in the middle of the street. She identified a car capable of offering protective cover if she needed it, and she made her stand. She raised her gun above her head, and knowing what she did of Vee's father, she fired.

The boy immediately halted. He was three feet from the hole in the fence. She could see him lean toward it longingly, weighing his chances.

"Don't make me shoot," she called out.

Very slowly, Vee turned around. Now she could see the 9 mm dangling from his fingertips. It looked frighteningly large in his hand.

"Drop the gun, hands over your head."

He didn't move.

"Drop your gun," she said more forcibly. "Hands over your head!"

He didn't move.

"Drop your weapon!"

The boy shook his head. Sandra had one last impression. Huge brown eyes framed by thick lashes. An expression nearly as frightened as her own. Then his face settled, became too stoic. Vee jerked his arms around, gun coming up.

"No!" Mike yelled from behind her, still running to the scene.

"No," Sandra gasped.

The boy threw his gun at her with all his might. Then he dove through the hole in the fence as Sandra's knees gave way in shock and she collapsed in Mike's arms.

"Are you okay, are you okay?"

They were back in Mike's unmarked police car. Minutes had passed since the confrontation, but it seemed like hours. Sandra was cradled on Mike's lap. She knew it was unprofessional and yet she had no intention of going anywhere.

"I'm okay," she said in a shaky voice, still clinging to his shoulders and searching his face earnestly for signs of damage. "You?"

"Banged my stupid head on a collapsing beam. What the hell were you doing running after him like that?"

"I had to do something. You said so yourself—this might have been our only chance to find him."

"He could've shot you!"

"He didn't."

Mike gripped her harder. "Don't you ever stop in the

open like that again, Sandy. For heaven's sake, when you confront an armed suspect, you find cover. You hear me? *You find cover.''*

"I'm sorry, I'm sorry, I'm sorry." Then she couldn't speak. He was crushing her too tightly against his chest. He was tipping her head up. He was devouring her lips with his, feverish and punishing. And she welcomed the onslaught. She sympathized with his need to claim her as she was consumed by the need to claim him.

Nothing had happened to Mike. Dear God, why had she never realized before what it would do to her if something had happened to Mike?

He finally dragged his head up. They both gasped for air. Then she was the one who found his lips in another bruising kiss. He was warm and hard and solid. He was strong and real and fierce. She wished they weren't in a police car anymore. She wished they were at home in her bed, where she could strip his clothes off and he could drive into her body before the adrenaline wore off and they both had time to think. Time to come to their senses. Time to realize they were no longer lovers, no longer spouses, and nothing ever got resolved in bed.

Mike finally drew back. In a gesture that made Sandra's eyes burn more, he tucked her head beneath his chin and rocked her against his chest.

"You scared the living daylights outta me," he whispered hoarsely.

"I think we scared Vee even worse."

"What if he'd opened fire, Sandra? What if he'd shot at you? *Mon Dieu!''*

"I don't know. I didn't think of that."

"You're developing a soft spot for the boy," Mike said seriously. "You're bonding and it could get you killed."

Sandra didn't say anything. She thought of Vee's eyes

again, his round, frightened stare, then his overly stoic gaze. She thought of this park with its needle-ridden pavement and broken children's toys. She thought of Mac-Two and Keisha and baby Bobby, who would now grow up in these bullet-torn streets.

"Hold me," she murmured to Mike. And he did.

Twenty minutes later, they were back in the station house, buffeted by questions as news of the encounter spread. Vee's gun was bagged and tagged, then sent down to forensics for testing. They would dust the weapon for prints, then try to match the gun with shells retrieved from Monday night's shooting. Mike had already told Sandra that the 9 mm would most likely prove untraceable; the serial number had been erased from the barrel with acid. Forensics had a number of tricks up their sleeves, however, and might be able to come up with something.

In the meantime, Sandra worked with a sketch artist to create a composite of Vee's face, while Mike blew up a map of the east side and pinpointed the various sites where the boy had been spotted. This was a common technique for trying to locate the home or hideout of a suspect. Hopefully, as more information became available, they could narrow in on Vee's location.

Police officers came and went in droves. Had they really seen the thirteen-year-old? What kind of firepower had he been carrying? What had he said? What had he done? Had Sandra really given pursuit? What? She let him get away...

Mike's head wound received a great deal of attention, as well. He received a bandage, a cold compress, and then a good deal of ribbing. Two enterprising detectives drew up a manila case file for a Mr. Dead Wood, suspected in the April 20 assault of a homicide detective. Known associates: Mr. and Mrs. Brick. Known hideouts: Deserted buildings. Fingerprints: Ten carefully inked-up wood slivers. Considered heavy and abrasive. Do not approach with eyes closed or head held high.

They hung the case file on the police bulletin board for Mike's immediate attention, offering a two-beer award for the first person to capture Mr. Wood. Mike got to say, "Yeah, yeah, yeah." He laughed, he claimed good-naturedly they ought to see the other guy, and he hoped no one noticed that his hands were still shaking.

He simply couldn't shake the image of Sandy staring down a thirteen-year-old hood. He shouldn't have brought her into the east side. He shouldn't have left her alone. When Vee's arms had come back around like that...

Mike had aged ten years. And while Sandra still seemed convinced that Vee didn't mean any harm, Mike wasn't so certain. He thought he'd read something else on the boy's face. Growing desperation. The need to take a stand.

A little after four, Sandra finished with the sketch artist. The composite wasn't much. Both she and Mike had spent too much time staring at the back of the boy's head to notice any distinguishing characteristics. In the end, they had described a fairly typical thirteen-year-old. Rounded cheeks, flat nose, thickly lashed eyes, broad forehead and short black hair beneath a backward baseball cap.

"Congratulations," Lieutenant Hopkins observed. "You just narrowed our search to one thousand juvenile delinquents."

Sandra sent the drawing over to the *Citizen's Post* anyway, where it would run on the front page of the morning paper. They still had not received any replies to her letter. Then again, Vee had had a busy afternoon.

"Why do you think he was at the park?" she asked Mike when things finally quieted down. The night patrols headed out, officers still wearing vests and traveling in pairs.

"I don't know. Maybe he lives by there." Mike was standing in front of the blown-up map. He pointed to a series of blocks running by the park. "Any of these neighborhoods would fit the demographics."

"We just stumbled onto his home turf."

"Possibly. We were looking for him."

"So why didn't he take more aggressive action? It would seem that he spotted us long before we were aware of him. He could've opened fire at any time."

Mike shrugged. "We were also standing in the middle of four kids and, for a while, you were holding a baby. That doesn't make for a clean shot."

Sandra hesitated. "So if I hadn't picked up Bobby..."

"I don't know, Sandra. I honestly don't know."

She nodded, and Mike could tell that her mood was still subdued. Unconsciously, he moved closer to her, his arm sliding around to offer comfort. At the last minute, however, he remembered where they were. His arm dropped to his side. He moved pointedly back. He saw that she followed his withdrawal and seemed to nod slightly.

In a police department, the walls had ears, and she knew it, too.

"Well," she said briskly. "I need to catch up on some paperwork."

"I need to find Koontz."

"Hopefully, he learned something going through the case file."

"Maybe." Mike kept his tone neutral. "Gonna work late?"

"Yes."

"Mmm, maybe we should debrief later? I may have some developments that need your attention."

"I don't know. It's been a very busy day for the case. Maybe we should take a break." She hesitated, looking slightly vulnerable. "Maybe we should make sure we haven't lost our objectivity."

"Instinct is a powerful investigative tool, Chief Aikens."

"It doesn't hold up in court."

"That doesn't mean it's wrong. Sometimes, it's thinking too much that gets you into trouble."

"True," she acknowledged softly, "thinking too much can be a problem."

"I think this afternoon we were on to something. I think we should follow that lead."

"It was a...nice lead."

"Eight o'clock?"

"All...all right."

His voice dropped. "Your place?"

Her breath picked up slightly. "Yes."

He made the mistake of looking at her then. Her blue eyes were wide and luminescent, her lips pearly pink and half-parted. Damn, he wished they weren't surrounded by homicide detectives and patrol officers. He wanted to kiss her. Kiss her hard. Feel her body shivering against his the way it had just a few hours before. Except this time he would deepen the kiss, bury his hands in her wild, curly hair. This time he would take the moment all the way through until her body was hot and writhing beneath his and finally... Finally...

"Eight o'clock," he said hoarsely.

"Mike. Don't be late."

Mike never did find Koontz. In the end, Rusty found him.

Mike was in the police locker room. He'd showered

after the long day. He'd changed into a pair of fresh khakis with a dark green shirt, slapping on the aftershave and starting to look forward to his evening. Then he looked up and Koontz was standing there, a strange expression on his face.

"Partner," Koontz drawled.

"Rusty," Mike acknowledged. He glanced at the locker room. Four other guys were around. They were all staring at him and Rusty intently. Something was up.

"Heard about your encounter in the east side," Koontz said after a moment. He moved over to an empty bench, propped up his foot. He was wearing fancy brown leather shoes with today's navy-blue silk suit. Mike found himself studying the tooling pattern formed on the leather.

"We came close to catching the kid," Mike said.

"You and Sandy."

Mike looked his partner in the eye. "Me and Sandy," he agreed.

Koontz slammed his foot back down on the floor. He suddenly whirled on the other officers. "Get out!" he yelled. "Can't you see we're trying to have a conversation here? Scram, dammit! Scram!"

The other men jumped belatedly to their feet and scrambled. Seconds later, Mike and Rusty were alone in the locker room and Mike knew it was going to get ugly.

"So that's the way this goes down," Rusty stated. "I leave you alone for one afternoon 'cause I got other work to do, and *bam!* you replace me."

"Sandra asked to accompany me for her own information," Mike said.

"Oh, come off it! You've been waiting for this all along. You and Sandy, back together again."

"I was conducting interviews. I needed a second and you weren't available."

"So you took the least experienced person you could find? Give me a break. You ended up in a confrontation and she let the kid get away! She's not a cop. She doesn't know jack about this job and she's screwing this case pretending otherwise."

"Screwing this case?" Mike's own voice picked up incredulously. "Because she tries? Because she's asking questions and getting involved? Hell, Koontz, you were the one who challenged her. You were the one who said she didn't know anything about these streets—"

"And she doesn't!"

"So she found an expert! She went out on a limb trying to start a dialogue with this boy. Then she put herself on the line today trying to catch this kid—"

"And let him get away! She's a bureaucrat, Rawlins. A spoiled little rich kid trying to play cop so she can impress her ex-husband. She's got no place in this department and the fact you can't see that just means you're once more under her spell."

"Hey, Sandra is turning into one helluva good cop and she has every right to be in this department. And you want to know why, Koontz? Because she cares. Maybe she isn't experienced, maybe she's naive, but at least she's taking an interest in this community. When was the last time you really cared about that, huh, Koontz? When was the last time any of us around here really *believed* in this job?"

"My God, you've gone over to the dark side."

"No, Koontz. I'm just coming to my senses and realizing it's not supposed to be us against them. Do you really want to end up shooting at thirteen-year-olds? I don't."

Koontz said flatly, "You told her, didn't you? *Tell me the truth!* You told her everything!"

Mike stepped up to his partner. "I told her nothing."

"I don't believe you—"

"Then that's your problem! You are my *partner,* Koontz. I don't like your attitude. You want to hear it all? I think you do have issues. I spent this morning thinking about it long and hard and you know, you never are around for interviewing black suspects. And then there are the jokes and quips you're always making. Truth is, you're afraid of African-Americans, aren't you, Koontz? They make you uncomfortable. They make you nervous. Truth is, you *are* a racist. And it interferes with your ability to do the job."

Koontz's nostrils flared. "I am a damn fine cop. Look at my arrest record."

"Where were you this afternoon?"

"Perusing old leads—"

"Scud work."

"It's gotta be done—"

"It's scud work!"

"Dammit, don't you tell me how to do my job! I know how to do my job!"

Mike yelled back, *"No, you don't!* And that's why you're here now and that's why you're angry. Not because I took Sandy to the east side. Not because you think I told her anything—you know me better than that. You're angry, because deep in your heart, you are a decent cop and you *know* Vee shouldn't have gotten away today. It wasn't Sandy's job to stop him. It was yours. And you blew it."

Koontz recoiled. It was the first time Mike had ever seen him hurt.

Rusty walked back a few steps, putting plenty of distance between him and Mike.

"You don't know what you're talking about," Koontz muttered after a moment.

Mike didn't say anything.

"This is her talking through you. She poisons you, man.

She gets under your skin and turns you against your friends.''

Mike remained silent.

"Dammit, I've been on the force fifteen years! I am a *good* cop and I know how to get the job done. You're the one who's jeopardizing the case. *You're* the one whose using poor judgment. I never thought I'd see the day, but you're turning against your own kind, Rawlins. You're siding with the bureaucrats. You're hanging your partner out to dry. Man, we're under attack from all sides these days. And just when you oughta know it's time to be lookin' out for one another, time to be watching each other's backs, you go and pull this.''

"If that's how you feel, maybe we shouldn't be partners anymore.''

"Yeah. Maybe.''

"At the end of this case, you can request a new assignment.''

"I'll do that.''

"Fine.''

"Fine!'' Koontz scowled again, then shook out his arms the way he always did when he was uncomfortable. He adjusted his silk suit jacket, playing with the single button, then squared his shoulders as if he was all together now. Nothing could faze him.

The familiar routine suddenly tightened Mike's chest, made him look away. They had been partners for eight years. That was a lot of miles, a lot of cases. A lot of beers at the Code Blue.

The silence went on, long now. The locker room became too cold, too empty.

"I gotta go,'' Mike said at last. He picked up his bag. He brushed by where Koontz was standing. His partner didn't say a word.

Outside the locker room, the four banished men were still waiting. It was obvious from the looks on their faces that they'd overheard the entire exchange. As Mike walked by, one by one, they turned away.

Mike made it a point not to look back.

Nightfall. The kid who called himself Vee sat alone in his room, pretending to be listening to some discs but not really paying attention. He had the paper on the floor. He'd bought it first thing this morning. Letters to the editor appeared on page two. He'd read one of those letters, two, three, ten times.

Dear Vee: My name is Sandra Aikens. I am the newly appointed chief of police of Alexandria County and I am writing to you on behalf of our citizens. I am writing to tell you that you are not alone. I am writing to tell you that we all care. I am writing to tell you that your letters touched me personally, and I would like to do whatever I can to help you. This need not end in violence.

Vee hadn't expected a reply. He didn't know what he thought about this. A couple of kids at school had laughed over the letter. *Looky here, Vee's got a pen pal. The new chief of police has gone sweet on him. Ah, ain't that cute?*

Vee hadn't said a word. Just listened. Everyone around school was talking about this kid named Vee as if they knew him. Vee be an O.G.B., they liked to say. Serious rep. A man of stature. Of course he hang in my hood.

Nobody knew a thing. Vee was a made-up. Didn't have no more substance than Zorro or Robin Hood or some freak like that. Vee'd invented the name to go with the letter. He'd also invented the rep. The kid who called him-

self Vee wasn't really no straight shooter. He wasn't in a
gang; he didn't hang in no hood. In the words of the street,
he was nobody. A thirteen-year-old nobody. Sometimes,
that fact hurt the worst.

'Course that might all be changed now. Mac-Two had
seen him go into the building this afternoon. He'd spotted
Vee's gun and seemed to know what was going down.
Would he talk? Tell others? Did it matter?

Vee didn't know anymore.

Today he'd had his finger on the trigger. He'd seen their
car in the park when he be walking home from school.
He'd gone straight into the building, watching the curly-
haired woman across the street. The sun had hit her hair
and set it on fire. Pretty chief of police. He hadn't known
that. It made him feel funny.

Then she be picking up the baby. Kid streaking dirt all
over the woman's fancy suit while she smiled and coochy-
cooed. It had bothered Vee. The mother should take her
kid back. Show some respect. A pretty, classy lady like
that didn't need to be covered in no east-side dirt.

But the chief lady had been happy playing with the
baby. She'd held it close.

Finally, long-time later it seemed, she handed it back.
Vee watched Mac-Two glance at him in the building. Vee
watched the other kids bolt. All alone now. Clean line of
sight. All he had to do was pull the trigger. Take out the
lady cop and big detective. Just do it.

He be staring at the mud streaks on the pretty jacket.
His finger slide off the trigger like it got a mind of its own.
He be a loser after all, not an O.G.B. like his brother. He
be nobody.

*Dear Vee...I am writing to tell you that your letters
touched me personally, and I would like to do whatever I
can to help you. This need not end in violence.*

Ah lady, it all end in violence, he thought. You too rich, too white to know a thing. You stopped in the middle of the street, when any experienced dude knows to jump for cover.

Vee kicked away the paper. He reached under his bed, where a big old cardboard box held dozens and dozens of firearms. He got a 9 mm, he got a .38 special, he got shotguns. No matter how many guns he threw at cops, he always came home to more. This was his brother's legacy, the arsenal that was supposed to keep Big S Sammy safe.

At the funeral, Vee had tucked two 9 mms in his brother's coffin. Just in case heaven didn't turn out no better than the east side, and Big S Sammy still had some more killing to do.

Vee went to the kitchen. Fixed himself some mac and cheese. Cupboards didn't hold much else. In a day or two, they'd be empty.

Vee went into the living room. His sister rocked in front of the TV, her face turned away so she'd be pretty. When he walked into the room, she turned toward him, and the big shiny scar looked like a hot penny seared into her cheek.

"What you staring at?" she screeched.

"Nothin," Vee mumbled, and ducked his head. He shuffled back into his bedroom, where he could once more be a straight shooter named Vee, and not just some little kid annoying the snot out of his big sister.

He sat on the bed with dinner. He stared at his pile of guns. Then he read the letter to the editor, two, three, ten more times.

This need not end in violence.

Lady, lady, you don't know a thing.

Chapter 9

Waiting for Mike to arrive, Sandra was nervous. At six, she took a long bubble bath, scented by a healthy dollop of her favorite perfume. She told herself she was older and wiser, she knew what she was doing now. She and Mike had had their differences. Of course, a few good conversations didn't magically change everything, but it was a start. Plus, you couldn't deny their chemistry. Heavens, you couldn't forget their chemistry.

She followed her bubble bath with a heavy dose of rich lotion, smoothing it onto her legs, her arms, her face. She rubbed her skin until it glowed and then she thought of Mike's rough palms moving over her skin as well. The way he used to caress her body, so slow, so patient. Whispering sweet words in French…

Her insides went hot and liquid. She thought less of the fights they used to have—the endless succession of fights—and more about how well they made up. On the floor, the sofa, the kitchen counter, the bed.

At seven o'clock, she was sorting through her scant selection of lingerie. She used to have more, but as any good divorcée, she'd tossed an armful of delicates the day after signing the papers. Her marriage had failed. Surely that meant her underwear had not gotten the job done.

She had a weakness for soft, lacy items, however, that extended long after Mike's departure. She liked the feel of fine fabric against her skin. She liked wearing stern power suits with mannish shoulders, knowing that underneath she was pure lace. It gave her a secret to carry around with her all day. *You think you know who I am just by looking? Honey, you don't know a thing....*

Mike knew what was beneath her suits, of course. And if memory served, his favorite color was peach.

She owned one teddy in that shade. Very thin fabric, not a lot of material. She slipped that on. She dabbed perfume everywhere she could think of, then dabbed it a few new places just to be sure. She saw that her hands were shaking now. Mike would be here in just a half an hour. And then...

What was she doing? So there was chemistry. There had always been chemistry. From day one they had torn off each other's clothes. But what about after that? Remember all the nights of him coming home and barely saying a word? Or the long Saturday afternoons at his parents' house, his mom looking at Sandra as if she wished she'd burst into flame. His brothers and sisters, laughing and joking and leaving Sandra alone on the fringes.

Better, the Sunday afternoons at her parents' house, when her mother would look at Mike as if she wished he'd drop dead. Then those endless dinner parties with everyone chattering about money, money, money while Mike fell asleep over the entrée from pure boredom.

What about the times when Sandra was anxious about

her job, trying to talk about her day, and Mike just looked at her and said, "Relax, *ma chère,*" as if that should make all her worries go away? What about the times she would find him staring off into space, looking troubled, and yet when she asked him about it later, he simply said, "I'm fine, *ma chère.* Just fine."

What about all those moments? The doubt, the hurt, the mistrust? The millions of tiny ways they failed each other every day without ever knowing they were doing so? Funny, she'd been so sure marriages ended over big, cataclysmic issues. She had never suspected they could also erode like a rock, constantly battered by small, swirling waves.

Then, Sandra realized she didn't care. She was thirty-four years old. She was standing in the middle of her bedroom in nothing but a peach teddy, and she wanted her ex-husband. She wanted his arms around her again. She wanted to listen to his Cajun drawl, watch the way his dark eyes crinkled at the corners when he grinned. She missed the way he held her, the way he could always coax her into a smile. She missed the warmth and spontaneity he brought to her life, the times she would look at him and see the father of her children, plain as day. She had tried other men, richer, better dressed, more successful choices—her parents' kind of people. They all left her feeling empty.

No, the only man who had ever held her attention—for better or worse—was Mike.

Seven forty-five. Sandra blew her kinky hair into soft ringlets framing her face. A light dusting of blush here, mascara there. Pink lip gloss for her mouth, drop pearls for her ears. Perfect. She promptly threw on jeans and Mike's dress shirt to cover everything up. Just in case.

The doorbell rang. Sandra checked her hair one last

time, played nervously with two curls, then headed down the hall.

She had no sooner opened the door than Mike swept into the room. His eyes were dark and burning. She'd seen that look before. He shrugged out of his sports coat.

"Like your shirt," he said. Then he pulled her into his arms.

The first kiss was hot. Blazing. She could feel his intensity, his need. He angled her head expertly, and brought her against him hard. She shivered. He was in a mood. The logical part of her mind recognized that. The rest of her was too flattered to care.

He pushed her into the living room. No need for small talk now. They backed up against the sofa, wrestling with the buttons on each other's shirts. Mike's fingers were faster. The minute he discovered the teddy, he sucked in his breath.

"You like it?" she asked hesitantly.

"*Mon Dieu,*" he breathed. "Peach."

"I remembered…"

"Ah, *ma chère…*"

This kiss was softer. Slow. For a moment, Sandra swore she saw tears in her ex-husband's eyes. Then his lips were upon her throat, nibbling a line up to her ear. He drew in her earlobe, and settled her more intimately against his body.

She finally managed to get his shirt unbuttoned. She pushed it off his shoulders at the same time he dropped her white shirt to the floor. She pulled him back into her arms immediately, gasping at the first electric touch of exposed skin to exposed skin. She always loved that moment when she had him naked against her. She always marveled at how hot his skin could feel. She liked pressing her breasts against the hard plane of his chest. She liked to run her hands over his collarbone, down the rippling curves of his arms. He was strong and powerfully built. No matter how many times she saw him naked, it always turned her on.

"Stop it." He finally caught her hands with his own. His breath was coming out rough, his words a mere growl. He took her hand and placed it against the front of his pants so there could be no mistake.

Yes, he was hard. He felt positively delicious.

"Take off your clothes, Sandra," he whispered thickly. "I want to see you wearing nothing but that teddy. Then I want to kiss every inch of your skin."

She yanked off her pants hastily, impatiently kicking them aside. He stripped off his own, as well, standing before her in nothing but a lopsided grin and a pair of cotton boxers decorated with Winnie-the-Pooh. The sight made her giggle. Then it made her want him more.

"I like your underwear better," he said.

"Okay. Take it off."

He took his sweet time, his hands devilishly slow and controlled as they danced across her shoulders. How could she have forgotten the delicate whisper of his fingertips against her skin? The rasping feel of strong fingers sliding down her neck, hovering just above the swell of her breasts. And then his lips, kissing her teasingly, coaxing her head up, her body into his, while his fingers still lingered, brushing her skin but not moving one inch lower when she desperately wanted them to.

Then, just when she thought she might scream from frustration, his fingers flickered over her silk-covered breasts. His thumbs massaged her nipples. His palms cupped her breasts. Her own hands finally slipped the thin straps of the teddy off her shoulders. The top fell down, exposing herself completely to his hands.

He ducked his head and took one nub into his mouth.

She whimpered. She buried her hands in his dark, thick hair. She held his head against her and thought if he ended it now she'd die. No, she would kill him first. Then she'd die.

"Please," she murmured. "Please."

He moved to her other breast, laving it with equal care. Then he drew the nub between his lips and suckled hard. She released her pent-up breath as nearly a scream and found the waistband of his boxers. She jerked them down savagely. She pressed herself against his hard length, rubbing her silk-clad belly against him.

He responded by tossing her over the back of the sofa and following her down into the pillows. Now they had her teddy off. Now they were naked body pressed to naked body, sweat-slick skin against sweat-slick skin.

His hands seemed to be all over her. Then they found her hot, wet folds, slipping into her body, moving with exquisite care. She grabbed his arms so tightly her fingers welted his skin. It had been too long for her. She could feel the pressure building up to unbelievable levels and she thought when the climax finally came, it would tear her apart. She didn't want to be shattered alone.

"Now," she murmured. "Now!"

He settled between her legs. She had one last glimpse of his face. His eyes were so dark they were bottomless. Sweat beaded his brow. Tension set his jaw. He looked handsome and a heartbeat later, as he plunged into her body, she thought he looked sad, torn in two.

He ducked his head against her shoulder. He whispered her name in a tone of guttural need. And suddenly she was rocking him against her at the same time he was moving inside her. She offered him comfort while he took their bodies up, up, up. She held him tight while the tension built then burst, and then she was murmuring his name over and over while he exploded inside her and their bodies writhed together on the sofa.

In the aftermath, he fell against her heavily. She stroked his back and wondered how he could make her body feel so good while holding so many secrets in his eyes.

A short time later, he rose and wordlessly led her to the bedroom. He spooned her against him and seemed content to stroke her hair. But those touches soon led to his hands on her arms again, then her breasts. Then he was kissing her feverishly. Once again they made love with an urgency she didn't understand.

And Sandra discovered that in spite of her best intentions, she could not bring herself to ask Mike what was really going on. She was too afraid he'd say, "Nothing." She was too afraid he'd say, "I'm fine, *ma chère,* fine."

So she curled up against him silently in the dark. And she was not surprised to wake up hours later and find her ex-husband gone from her bed.

The clock read 2:04 a.m. Sandra got up and retrieved her silk robe, pausing for a moment to listen. There were no sounds coming from the rest of the house. Most likely, that meant Mike was in the living room. Six months after they were married, Sandra would find him sitting there a lot in the middle of the night. Always alone in the dark. Never giving up his thoughts.

I thought we were going to talk this time, Mike. I thought we were going to work on being more than lovers. That we were going to be friends.

Sandra took a deep breath, told herself this was the mature thing to do and walked out into the hall.

She did find him in the living room. He was sitting on

her pale sofa, nursing a glass of something and studying an icy sliver of moonbeam as it slid across the floor.

"Hey," she said at last.

"Hey."

"Couldn't sleep?" She took a hesitant step into the room.

"Just restless. Didn't mean to disturb you."

"You didn't disturb me." She walked a few steps closer. He'd pulled on his boxers but nothing else, and moonlight rippled across his bare chest. Sandra decided to take a seat on the small chair across from him. Distance seemed safer.

"You should get some sleep, *ma chère*," he said after a moment. "Until we catch Vee, it's gonna be a rough week."

"I'm not tired."

"Don't you have a press conference tomorrow? That community policing stuff? Don't want shadows showing up under your eyes."

"I'll wear more makeup."

He looked away, then took another sip of his drink.

"Whiskey?" she guessed after a moment.

"Yep."

"You don't generally drink much."

"Just in the mood, I guess."

"Mike, what's going on?"

"I'm fi—"

"Don't say it, Mike. Please, just don't say that."

He ducked his head. She could see his frustration, illuminated by the moon and set harshly on the planes of his face. Something was definitely bothering him, and once more, he seemed intent on keeping it to himself. And it hurt her deeply.

"It would be better," he said hoarsely, "if you'd go back to bed."

"I can't do that."

"Why, Sandra? Can't I have moods, too? Can't I be the tense one sometimes, the angry SOB? You could be the one who lets it all slide and trusts me to be fine by morning."

"I want you to be fine by morning, Mike. But I also want to know what's going on inside your head. Why is it so hard to tell me what you're feeling?"

Her voice had risen. She hadn't wanted that. Now he slammed his highball down on the glass coffee table with more force than necessary. She hadn't wanted that, either.

"I feel a need to be alone. That's all I'm asking, Sandy. All right?"

"No, it's not all right. It's our old pattern. Unbelievable intimacy inside the bedroom, total withdrawal outside of it. Dammit, I *care* about you, Mike. I want to know all of you. The good and the bad, the fun and the fierce, the happy and the moody and everything in between—"

"*And I can't give you that right now.* I just...ah, damn!" He swiped his hand through his hair, rose jerkily off the sofa and paced a few steps. "Sandy, I'm a guy. Sometimes guys need to be left alone. It's nothing personal."

"But it *feels* personal."

"But it's not! I just can't talk to you about everything. Sometimes...I gotta work it out for myself first."

"How? By coming over and seducing me? By stripping off my clothes and jumping into bed with me just so you can leave me six hours later?"

"One thing has nothing to do with the other."

"Like hell it doesn't! We hadn't been together for four years. *Four years!* And then there was this afternoon, and then you arrive tonight, and all I can think is how good it feels. I missed you. I've been lonely. I've been thinking about our marriage and why we couldn't make it work. I wanted to make it work.'' Her voice broke; her eyes were tearing up. She brushed back the moisture impatiently. "So here you are, Mike. And into bed we go. And not *six hours later,* here we are again. You shutting me out, and me feeling lonely. Damn you for that. I thought we were going to be better this time. I thought we were going to try harder. Damn you!''

"Hey, I'm not doing anything I didn't learn from you.''

"What's that supposed to mean?''

She'd risen as well. Now he turned and met her gaze squarely from across the room.

"Come on, Sandy. You're standing here lecturing me about sharing. That's a laugh. Which one of us prides herself more on independence anyway? Sure, you'll tell me about your day. You'll come home and rant and rave about the politics of your daddy's company or the co-worker who messed up your project. But what about when you have a *real* problem, Sandy? What about when someone writes *Bitch* on a nameplate outside your new office? That's for you to handle, right? What about when you're scared of attending a cop shooting? Another problem just for you. Fear is your burden. Proving yourself is your burden. Facing down all the big bad chauvinist pigs in the world is also your problem. 'Cause heaven forbid anyone ever help Sandra Aikens. Not even her *husband* is allowed to do that.''

"I…I try to include you.…''

"You rejected my name, my family and my house. How the hell were you including me?''

"I don't know! I'm the only Aikens left. It seemed a shame to lose the name completely. I thought you understood that. Our children still would've been Rawlinses. I promised you that.''

''Maybe. It's harder to believe that though, when I put it together with everything else. You got married, and what really changed for you, Sandy? You have the same name, you live in the same house, you insist on Saturday cocktails with your parents. I get married, I gotta move into some art deco monstrosity, toss out all my furniture—''

''Hey, duct tape wrapped around a foam cushion doesn't count as furniture!''

''But it was mine! And then there was nothing of mine left. You rejected invitations to my family's house, you didn't fit in with my friends, and you had me living in some house where I was terrified to walk through the door most nights in case I tracked working-class dirt on the marble tiles. But you know what hurts most of all, Sandy? The fact that you still insist I did nothing to save our marriage. My God, I rearranged my whole life for our marriage. It just wasn't good enough for you.''

For once, Sandra was stunned into silence. She had never thought of things that way, never tried to look at their new life from Mike's perspective. Funny, at the time she had honestly not possessed any ill intent toward her new husband, and yet she had done plenty of damage anyway.

''I...I guess I wasn't thinking,'' she said at last. ''My house was larger than yours, so I thought it made sense to keep it. My furniture was nicer. My neighborhood has better schools. I don't know. I wasn't trying to hurt you.''

Mike kept staring at her. She finally bowed her head.

''I do value my independence,'' she admitted. ''I liked keeping my stuff and my world. That way I didn't have to throw myself at your mercy, or suddenly feel dependent upon you. I guess...I just didn't want to be one of those

women whose lives revolved completely around their husbands. I wanted to still feel like myself, capable of taking
care of myself and solving my own problems.''

''Well, there you go, Sandy. You want your independence and I want mine. So hell, maybe the bedroom is the
only place we can meet in the middle. The rest would
involve too much compromise.''

He took off for the bedroom. She followed him belatedly, feeling even more confused than before. ''Where are
you going?''

''Home.''

''Mike?''

''I want to be alone. How many times do I have to say
it? Dammit, don't look at me like that. I just need space!''

''Don't leave like this. We have to be able to work this
out.''

He threw on his shirt and pants. ''There's nothing to
work out.''

''Mike!''

''Sandy!'' He had his shoes on now, his jacket under
his arm. He stopped in the foyer just long enough to meet
her eye and she was taken aback by the depth of anger in
his face. ''You told me you would trust me, Sandy. You
told me you would understand when I didn't want to talk.
Well, I don't want to talk. When I'm ready, I will. But I
won't be bullied into it beforehand just to meet your needs.
I've got needs, too, you know. How about thinking of
those for a change? How about thinking of something
other than yourself?''

He stormed out the door. Sandra remained standing in
the darkened foyer.

''I'm...I'm sorry, Mike,'' she whispered. But by the
time she got the words out, his car had already backed out
of her driveway and there was no one around to hear.

Another reconciliation, another fight. Funny, how the arguments were never what she wanted and, yet, all she seemed to have in the end. Apparently they weren't older and wiser after all. Apparently they were still oil and water, forever unable to mix.

After a moment, she closed her front door and locked the dead bolt. Sandra returned to her living room and curled up on the sofa where only hours before they had made love. She didn't cry. Instead she closed her eyes and long before the sun lightened the sky, she did her best to inhale the lingering traces of Mike's scent. She held the pillows close, since she was now more certain than ever that she would never have him.

At eight o'clock, Sandra's phone rang. From the kitchen table, she eyed the plastic hand piece warily. It was late; she should be at work. Instead she was lingering over her cup of coffee, still in her silk bathrobe. She just couldn't get herself moving this morning. She didn't like to think about having to face Mike at work.

On the third ring, she reluctantly picked up the phone. It was good old Lieutenant Hopkins.

"You planning on coming to work today?" he asked immediately.

"I'm on my way," she lied coolly.

"Good, 'cause the *Citizen's Post* ran that drawing of Vee this morning, and we got a problem."

"Someone identified him?"

"More like nine hundred people have identified him. The switchboard is jammed, the call officers are booked, and the leads are still streaming in. Congratulations, Chief. You've officially crashed the Alexandria police department. Now what do you plan on doing about that?"

Sandra jumped into the shower, threw on a suit and headed for work.

By ten, Sandra had assembled Mike, Koontz and Lieutenant Hopkins in her office for a situation update. She'd already spent thirty minutes on the phone with the mayor. She'd spent another fifteen minutes talking to the *Citizen's Post*. Her press conference, officially to talk about community policing, had been moved up to one o'clock. She would now be talking about the Vee "crisis" as well. If the mayor had his way, she'd be announcing that Vee was safely in custody. That, of course, remained to be seen.

For now, she adopted her most somber expression and eyed the three men across from her. All three of them had shunned the offered chairs. Koontz was leaning against the left wall, wearing a double-breasted gray suit and looking as if he'd rather be any other place on earth. Lieutenant Hopkins stood in the middle, still smirking slightly at the mess Sandra had made. Mike was all the way in the back, closest to the door. His face was carefully shuttered, his dark eyes remote. She thought he looked tired, but wasn't sure if that was wishful thinking on her part.

She didn't look at him long anyway. She was too afraid her eyes would give her emotions away.

"All right," she said briskly, "I've spoken to the mayor and we've outlined a plan of attack."

"Better late than never," Koontz muttered.

Sandra ignored him. "Given the high volume of calls we are currently experiencing, the mayor has authorized the establishment of a temporary command center. We will form an official "Vee" task force, overseen by Lieutenant Hopkins here. Mike, Rusty, you will remain the lead agents on the case, but the mayor has also approved an additional manpower request, so you'll now be assisted by the Gang and Vice detectives as well. Basically, I've appointed eight troopers in charge of the phone lines. They'll take all calls and fill out a log sheet with the information. It's up to you to evaluate the leads and assign detectives to follow up on the ones you think are most important.''

This was standard protocol for a large-scale manhunt. That a thirteen-year-old could qualify for so much procedure still staggered Sandra, but she had not expected many comments on the organization itself. Of course she was wrong. Koontz promptly pushed away from the wall and stalked toward her.

''Come on, when are you going to get serious?''

''Excuse me?''

''Haven't you been listenin' to Lieutenant Hopkins here? These calls are a waste of time. Every shop owner who's ever been robbed and every citizen who's ever been mugged is now tying up our phone lines. Let's face it, politically correct platitudes aside, to most white folks, all black kids do look alike. So we're not gonna get anywhere there.

''Worse, now we also got gangs taking credit for Vee like he's some kind of hero. That damn picture has given him substance. Now it's 'our homey, Vee' this, 'our brother, Vee' that. You know it's only a matter of time before either the kid blows up from the pressure, or someone else does it for him. We're talking copycat shootings, organized attacks on cops, maybe some good old-fashioned looting and vandalism.''

''I'm aware of those dangers, Koontz. Patrols are under orders to travel only in pairs, and everyone is suited up in vests. We're doing everything we can to protect ourselves, but you know as well as I do that we can't retreat.''

''No kidding. But as long as the patrol officers are risking their butts out there, let's take the offensive! We bring

the composite drawing to the junior high. The principal
and teachers can probably pinpoint two dozen kids who
roughly match the sketch. Perfect. Now we got a list of
names. Furthermore, we know this kid is packing. He had
a gun when he encountered you two, right? Most likely,
he's armed twenty-four seven. So let's have the principal
open up the lockers—"

"That's getting into dicey ground—"

"Who cares! We need to find this kid. We pop the lockers, we search for weapons. Chances are, that narrows our
list from several dozen to one. We bring them here, we
set them up in interrogation rooms, and I'm telling you, in
less than two hours, we can hand you Vee. Bing, bang,
boom, and for a fraction of the cost of a twenty-four-hour
command center. How do you like that?"

"Koontz, we go into a school and pull out a dozen African-American children after an invasive locker search.
Then we drag them to the police station without benefit of
their parents or legal council? It looks aggressive, it looks
insensitive, and at least half of our population is going to
scream bloody murder because it's illegal."

"Oh, my God!" Koontz rolled his eyes. "Do you ever
listen to yourself speak? What kind of cop do you think
you are?"

"I'm not a cop, Rusty. I'm the chief of police, and it is
my job to think beyond this department. In fact, I'm paid
to manage the mayor's, and the city council's, and the
public's perception of us. You may not like PR, but you
don't have to. You're a detective. I'm the chief, however,
and I don't have that luxury. This is a politically sensitive
case at a time when this department is on very shaky
ground with the African-American community. We act inappropriately, and the public outcry will bury us alive."

"Yeah? Then don't act at all. Wait till this kid blows

away some hardworking officer—better yet, a twenty-something, freckle-faced poster boy with a new wife and baby on the way, and then you see who the public buries alive.''

Sandra exhaled sharply. She glanced at Mike again. He remained leaning against the doorjamb, still not saying a word. She shook her head, this time his silence hurting a little more.

''Fine,'' she said after a moment. ''Let's do this—Lieutenant Hopkins, you man the command center. Rusty, Mike, you take the picture to the junior high. Draw up your list of possible boys. See if you can tie any of the names more closely to Vee. Do they have a sister who was shot? Did they have an older brother? Maybe someone heard them mouthing off about shooting cops. Anything concrete. In the meantime, I'll talk to the D.A. about legal grounds for a locker search. But I honestly don't want to go there if we don't have to. Bringing a dozen kids to the station is too much and going to get us backlash. Let's hope, through standard procedure, we can limit ourselves to three or four boys with good cause. That'll look better all the way around. Make sense?''

Koontz shrugged, probably the closest to agreeing with her he'd ever come. Lieutenant Hopkins nodded. Mike smiled sardonically and said, with meaning, ''Fine.''

Sandra figured she deserved that.

''One thing,'' Koontz spoke up again. ''I don't think it's necessary for both Mike and me to go downtown.''

Sandra frowned, not understanding this. Mike was shifting uncomfortably in the doorway now. For the first time, she picked up on the tension between the two men. ''What do you propose?'' she asked Rusty carefully.

''I can handle it.''

''You can handle it?''

"Yeah. Why waste two detectives flashing around a portrait? I'll go to the junior high." He glanced at Mike and said almost belligerently, "I don't have a problem with that."

Sandra didn't like this. She shook her head. "Rusty, talking to the principal, teachers, and all the students is a lot of work. Two detectives are perfectly appropriate."

"I don't mind."

"It's not safe. You two go together or not at all. Anything else?"

Koontz thinned his lips stubbornly. There was definitely something going on between the partners; Sandra could see that now. Was that what was eating away at Mike? He and Koontz went way back. Sandra had never personally liked Rusty, but she understood that he was Mike's partner.

"Great," she said briskly. "Meeting adjourned."

She picked up a pen to signal she was done with them. Just as Mike opened the door, however, she said in her most casual voice, "Detective Rawlins. One moment, please."

He stalled, Rusty snickered. A moment later, Sandra and Mike were alone in the room. She waited until he closed the door again. Then she set down her pen.

"I'm sorry," she said quietly. "For last night."

He regarded her balefully.

"I…I know I agreed to trust you more, to respect your feelings when you don't feel like talking. I'm sorry I pushed so hard. I just…" She realized she was about to launch into a speech about her own needs again, and quickly caught herself. "If, when, you'd like to talk about what's bothering you, I would like to listen. Just so you know."

His stance finally relented a fraction. "I'll keep that in mind."

"I hated the way things ended last night."

"I know."

She smiled ruefully. "Guess we never forgot how to touch each other, or how to fight."

His gaze fell. He looked truly tired now. "No, I guess we didn't forget how to fight."

"Funny, it's never the way I want things to go."

"It's not what I want, either. Sandy..." He sighed. She could see lines around his eyes now, bruises beneath his eyes. Whatever had happened between him and Rusty, it had been a doozy. Mike looked like he'd been put through an emotional wringer.

"I know I shouldn't have stormed out like that," he said abruptly.

"That...hurt."

"I didn't mean half of what I said...."

"Sure you did, Mike." She held up her hand to silence his next protest. "It's okay. Most of what you said was right."

"I still shouldn't attack you like that. I don't mean to. You just keep pressing and then..."

"You blow."

"I blow," he agreed.

"Mike," she said hesitantly, "has it ever occurred to you that if you spoke sooner, maybe it wouldn't build to the point of blowing? You know me, I spout off at the drop of a hat. I'm not saying that's right, either, but you are the other end of the spectrum. Easygoing Rawlins. You shrug everything off, except I don't think it really rolls off as easy as you pretend. Instead it gets stored inside of you. Where it grows, layer upon layer, until...boom," she concluded softly.

"Boom," Mike echoed dryly. He rubbed the back of his neck. "There might be something to that."

"I still shouldn't have pushed you," she added hastily.

"You had your reasons."

"I really did like our evening. Up until that point."

Slowly he nodded. "I liked our evening, too. Even when I'm not ready to talk... I needed to see you last night, Sandy," he said. "I needed to be with you. And then to see that teddy you wore. Peach. Just for me. I loved that."

Her insides warmed. Some of the tension finally left her. "Maybe we could try again tonight?"

"You'd be willing to do that?"

"Yeah, I'd be willing to do that."

"*Ma chère,*" he murmured. "Sometimes you take my breath away."

"I learned it all from you."

The door was still shut. Her office had no windows. He moved in close. Just when she thought he was going to simply brush her cheek, he kissed her instead. It was slow and sweet, what they both needed.

She settled deeper into his embrace and for a long time they simply stood together and let the moment feel right.

Then without another word, they separated and returned to work.

Vee still waited somewhere in the city streets, and though they had not discussed it, they were both nervous.

Chapter 10

Mike and Rusty journeyed to the east side in silence. Koontz was driving, his hands gripping the steering wheel abnormally tight. In the tiny space of the automobile, yesterday's argument loomed as a large gulf between them. Mike didn't know how to bridge that gap, or if he was supposed to even try.

They turned into the parking lot of the junior high. Though it was eleven in the morning, over a dozen kids loitered outside the building, several of them smoking. They regarded the police sedan with flat stares as Koontz pulled into a front parking space. Mike watched a fresh sheen of sweat dot his partner's upper lip.

"Damn kids," Koontz muttered.

They opened their doors and headed out.

Nobody approached them. The students didn't appear any older than fifteen, and they seemed content to hold their ground. But Mike was feeling his partner's nerves now as well. There was something about the way the kids watched them, frank and shameless, as if they knew something Mike and Koontz didn't. As if they'd already sized up the two older, larger detectives and found them wanting.

By the time they reached the front school doors—once glass, but now boarded up to hide the bullet holes—Koontz was shaking out his silk suit jacket over and over again. Mike didn't blame him.

Alexandria's junior high was twenty years old and looked forty. Like many buildings built on city budgets, it featured cheap linoleum floors and low drop ceilings. Over the years, bored students had tossed enough pencils up into the corkboard panels to have permanently imbedded yellow pieces of wood. The walls also featured student-supplied decorations in the form of bright graffiti and fist-sized holes. To complete the inner-city theme, two metal detectors guarded the front doors and a security officer stood beside them—not that either kept the school weapon-free.

Random searches of student bags and lockers continued to turn up enough firearms to convince the school board that they had a problem without ever actually making a dent against it.

Mike and Rusty met first with the principal. Marty Rodriguez was a small man, sharply dressed and firm with his handshake. He smiled easily and seemed genuinely enthusiastic about his school, if not realistic about the lives and opportunities his students faced. He also didn't care for the composite drawing.

"Yes, I saw the sketch in the *Citizen's Post*. But I'll be honest—that picture fits half the boys here."

"Focus on one aspect," Koontz said. "Not everyone has the same features."

"The cheeks are round. This is junior high. Most of the

boys are still carrying some baby fat. The eyes are dark and evenly spaced. Again, nothing unique. Seeing the hair might help—some kids are sporting their initials shaved into their scalps these days—but you show him with a baseball cap turned backward. That doesn't limit my options.''

''What about height?'' Mike spoke up. ''He's a smaller kid, maybe four-ten, four-eleven. About a hundred pounds.''

Principal Rodriguez considered it for a moment. ''That helps. What about dress?''

''Baggy jeans, oversize blue sweatshirt with a hood and front hand pouch.''

''Gang colors?''

''Didn't see any, but we were chasing him at the time, so it wasn't a detailed viewing.''

''Still, the bandannas are fairly obvious. If you didn't see it, then he probably wasn't wearing colors. So now we're talking about a thirteen-year-old, a bit on the small side, not in a gang. That limits my choices.''

''Enough to generate a list?'' Koontz pressed.

The principal hesitated. ''I'm not sure how comfortable I am with that.''

''Hey, the kid has opened fire on cops. He's pledged to kill one sooner or later. This is serious business.''

''So is giving out a list of student names, Detective. We work hard to make the students feel safe here. If word gets out that we're letting police officers roam our halls, it's going to look like we're siding with the enemy. I'm being realistic.''

Mike leaned forward, putting on his most charming smile. ''Then we promise to be on our best behavior. You give us names, access to a few teachers for questioning, and we'll be all done. Otherwise, we may have to interview all the students. We may have to hang out here for quite some time. Wouldn't you say, Koontz?''

"Days," Koontz agreed. "Maybe weeks."

Principal Rodriguez scowled. He knew he was being pressured, but like any good school principal, he also understood that some fights weren't worth the effort. "I can only provide a general list," he warned. "Vee may not even be one of our students."

"We'll keep that in mind."

"How many teachers do you want to talk to?"

"How about Mrs. Kennedy, the English teacher?"

"Fine. I'll arrange it in the teacher's lounge. That would be best."

"We can hardly wait."

Mike thought Mrs. Kennedy looked wary when Principal Rodriguez ushered her into the faded teacher's lounge. She was wearing a pastel flowered skirt with a matching blue sweater-blouse, tiny silver earrings dangling beneath her upswept hair. Very pretty, very classy. Mike imagined half of the boys in her English class had a towering crush on her. Looked like Principal Rodriguez might have a small one himself.

Since Koontz was back to being uncomfortable, Mike took the lead. Yes, Mrs. Kennedy had read Vee's second letter in the paper, as well as Chief Aikens's reply. She'd also examined the picture run this morning. Really, it could be any thirteen-year-old boy. Why did they keep coming back to her?

Mike thought he detected hesitation in her voice now. He glanced at Koontz and saw that his partner had noticed it, too. Mrs. Kennedy was holding back.

Mike brought out the principal's preliminary list of

thirty seventh- and eighth-grade boys. "Last time, we left a copy of Vee's letter with you, correct?"

Mrs. Kennedy nodded slowly.

"I imagine you've had to read some more homework assignments since then. Kids turning in essays, reports..."

She nodded again.

"Anything jump out at you this time? Maybe a sentence here or there that suddenly reminded you of the letter? Look at this list of names again. Think about the letter. Help us out here."

She absently fingered the list of names, and Mike could tell she didn't really need to see them.

"Mrs. Kennedy?" he probed quietly.

She said, "I noticed something."

Mike sat up straighter. Koontz promptly whipped out his notepad. Mrs. Kennedy was speaking in a rush.

"It's funny. To read the letter, I was thinking of someone hard-core. A real tough boy, probably one of my students who doesn't even do his homework assignments. I know what a straight shooter is. I understand I have a few in my class. Sometimes I think I can pick them out just by looking. That boy there has killed someone, this boy here. It's uncomfortable, to be looking out at a class of thirty-five students, wondering how many of them are already murderers. It's just not right."

"You're scared? You think you need protection? We can take care of that."

"But that's just it." Her gaze finally rose to meet Mike's. "When I looked at this picture this morning, I didn't see a hard-core gang member. My first thought was a different child completely. He sits in the back of my third-period English class, never says a word. Just shuffles in at the start of the period, then shuffles back out at the end. I've never seen him hang out with any other students.

My impression is that he keeps to himself and, for whatever reason, the other students let him be.''

"Maybe 'cause his brother was somebody important,'' Koontz murmured.

She shrugged. "I don't know, Detective. But I can tell you I honestly never pictured him as the violent type. He's small, quiet, unobtrusive. More the kind of student doomed to fall through the cracks of the education system.

"I went back this morning to see if I had any samples of his writing. He's turned in quite a few assignments, I discovered. He's actually quite bright. I'm surprised I didn't notice it more before. There's a certain poetry to his writing, a need to be heard. I...'' Her voice broke off awkwardly. She looked genuinely regretful. "I'm sorry. I have a feeling I was supposed to have heard. But one hundred and twenty students. So many papers to grade... I didn't get his message, his need to be noticed, and so he took it to a larger audience.''

"The kid who wrote the papers also wrote the letters? You're sure.''

"Pretty sure. I am really so sorry.''

Koontz and Mike leaned forward. "Give us his name.''

The kid who called himself Vee was trudging back to school. Lunch break. Students weren't supposed to leave the school grounds, but most of them did. Cafeteria food sucked at Alexandria Junior High. Kids all went to the local minimart and loaded up on Nutter Butters and Cup-a-Noodle soup instead. Best lunch you could get for a buck fifty-five.

Vee didn't get to eat today, though. He didn't have money, spent his last dollar two days ago and now his stomach hurt. One bowl of mac and cheese a day just didn't sit right. He'd have to get a job, he thought. His sister definitely wasn't gonna work and they couldn't live on what the government paid her. Landlord took most of the welfare check for rent. Heat and electricity gobbled up the rest. God knows the last time the cupboards had food.

Vee would get a job. Not much out there for thirteen-year-olds, though. Unless he wanted to be a lookout. That's how Big S Sammy had started. Low in the gang ranks, moving on up from there. Yeah, he'd gotten the ultimate promotion in the end, right on up to the big house in the sky.

Lord, Vee's stomach *hurt*. He cut across the school parking lot and some big kid came out of nowhere and grabbed him around the shoulders.

"Shuddup, little bro." The big kid quickly dragged him behind some big old car. Four other big kids were there, geared up and looking mean. Vee gazed from one pair of flat, black eyes to the next. He thought he knew what would happen next.

They'd pound him. Pound him hard. Crack ribs, swell his eyes shut. Beat him till he stopped whimpering. Then it be done. He'd belong to their hood. He'd be a gangbanger and his broken-down mama would cry.

Damn. For a moment, Vee was so hungry he didn't care. If he be a gangbanger, he could go to some homey's house. He could eat his food.

"You be Vee?"

The kid who called himself Vee nodded, trying to look tough. He'd thought this might happen. Picture in the paper wasn't that good, but maybe good enough for other brothers, particularly ones who knew Mac-Two.

"You gotta split."

"What?"

The older boy cuffed him across the mouth. "Don't

what me, little bro. Pay attention here. There be two cops in the school looking for you. Time to split.''

Vee just looked at the older boy dumbly. He couldn't split. Who would take care of his sister?

"Man," the older boy said, "for someone who wrote such *down* letters, you don't got a brain in your head. Here, take this. If you run home now, you probably got a chance at beating the cops. Grab what you need, find a hotel. Things get real dicey, you can hole up with us. We got a scrapbook on your brother, you know. We take care of our own.''

Vee looked down at the roll of hundreds that had been thrust into his hand. Money. He could give some to his sister. He could buy food. Then he thought, *Black Guerrilla Family money.* You take care of your own? Tell that to Big S Sammy.

No more time for thinking. The big kid cuffed him again, harder this time. Everyone looked nervously at the school.

"Split," the four big kids hissed. "Split."

Vee started running, roll of money clutched in his fist. He didn't know what else to do.

At twelve-thirty, Sandra got the call from Mike. He and Rusty finally had a name. They'd left two patrol officers at the school in case Vee showed up; now they were on the way to the boy's house. After a long week, they thought they'd broken the case and they were feeling good.

Sandra made Mike promise to be careful. Then she headed for her press conference.

Everything went well. The reporters jumped over the news that the police had a break in the Vee case and expected to resolve the situation shortly. Of course, Alexandria's law enforcement still needed to improve their relationship with the community, Sandra transitioned smoothly, hence the new focus on community policing.

Amid a flurry of note scribbling, she described the general principles behind community policing—that many so-called ''soft'' crimes such as graffiti, vandalism and prostitution, paved the way for ''hard'' crimes such as drug dealing, mugging, and murder. Since the police did not have the resources to pursue all crimes, especially minor violations, community members could assist local efforts by attacking these offenses. For example, community leaders could organize whitewash parties every Saturday morning when locals would paint over graffiti tags done during the week. Studies showed that after enough time, taggers generally moved on and so did some measure of gang activity.

Community leaders could also organize local patrols of the city blocks, even videotaping suspicious activity for use by the police later. In one city, local business owners took out a restraining order against the prostitutes on their block. The women had to move their activities or were arrested for violating the restraining order the minute they showed up for work. Police discovered that once the prostitution ceased, so did many of the drug-related activities.

They had to start by focusing on small zones of security, Sandra concluded thirty minutes later, community members and law enforcement working hand in hand. These pockets could then attract investment dollars and community goodwill to help them expand over time, until someday perhaps the whole east side could be a safe zone where children could play in clean parks, walk down well-lit streets, and sit on their front porches without fearing for their lives. Surely it was worth a try.

A few reporters nodded vigorously. A few others looked bored. Sandra could live with that. They all promised to print the police department's request for volunteer community liaisons. Hopefully, that would get the ball rolling.

Sandra also promised to keep the reporters posted about the situation with Vee. The *Post* still felt it had first dibs on the story. She let them feel that way.

Five minutes later, she had retired to her office and was hovering anxiously over the police scanner, waiting for news of Vee's arrest. None came, but at a little after six, Mike and Koontz burst into her office.

"We got him," Koontz announced, eyes shining bright. "Kid's name is Toby Watkins. Little Toby Watkins."

"Did you arrest him? Is he here?"

Mike shook his head. He looked as jazzed as Rusty. "No, not yet, but we know he's Vee. When we knocked on the door, a young woman answered. Big round scar on her right cheek. It's him, all right."

"Check this out," Koontz announced, flipping through his spiral notebook. "Toby Watkins, age thirteen, youngest of three children born to Yulanda Watkins. No record of criminal activity—that's why we couldn't find him in NCIC. According to his sister, he also doesn't belong to any gang. His mother made him swear he'd never adopt colors after his older brother was shot during some gang war. Big S Sammy was the older brother's name. He died three years ago. Toby now lives with his sister, Opal, and his mom, but the mom was recently taken away."

"Taken away? Taken away where?"

"She had a breakdown," Koontz said casually, and shrugged. "Some kind of nerve thing. She's at the county hospital doped up on Valium and Prozac. I doubt she knows her own name."

Sandra turned to Mike for guidance. He was definitely more compassionate in his approach. "She was taken away three months ago and Vee was left in his sister's care. Opal

Watkins is twenty-two and capable of serving as a legal guardian. Unfortunately, from what we could tell, she's not working at all—''

"Dedicated herself to soaps," Koontz snickered.

"The situation isn't ideal," Mike said. "No food in the kitchen and a pile of garbage on the floor. From the letters, it sounded as if Vee was close to his mother. Once she was taken away…" He made a helpless gesture with his hands. "Vee probably started to unravel a little, too."

Sandra nodded. "We need to find him," she said seriously. "This situation is still precarious."

"Oh, we got him," Koontz assured her. "According to attendance records, he's pretty good about going to school and according to his sister, he doesn't have any friends or other relatives. Now we got unmarked patrol cars at each location. I'd say any minute now, that radio is going to be beeping with good news."

"I think we should still approach with caution," Sandra said. "Even if he doesn't have a history of violence, he's been under a lot of pressure. Now he has his face featured in every newspaper. He must be feeling frightened and overwhelmed."

"We'll approach with caution," Mike agreed. "We did find a small arsenal under his bed. Oh, and the manual typewriter."

"Great work," Sandra said seriously. "The mayor will be delighted, and I know we'll all feel better once we've gotten this boy into custody."

Mike grinned. After a moment, Koontz grinned, too. Sandra was mildly taken aback. She wasn't sure she'd ever seen Koontz smile before. For the first time she could see the pride he took in his work.

The detective clapped his hands together and rubbed

them briskly. "Come on, Rawlins, let's go down to the Code Blue and wait for the news. My treat."

Mike hesitated, his gaze slipping to Sandra so imperceptibly she hoped Koontz hadn't noticed. But Rusty immediately stilled. Something harsh and cynical slipped over his face.

"Oh, yeah, how could I have forgotten? Excuse me."

"Hey, man, the Code Blue sounds great."

"Oh, no, no, no. I overstepped my bounds again. Forgot about you two lovebirds here. Can't be having that."

"Rusty—"

Koontz wasn't hearing it. His eyes were already dark with anger, his motions jerky. Whatever rift had been temporarily sealed by closing the case came tearing back open as Koontz headed for the door.

"Rusty, wait." Sandra spoke up instinctively.

"What?"

"I…it's just…we're professionals here Rusty. Mike, you, me. We don't need to get into this stuff. You and Mike are great partners. You want to go have a beer at Code Blue, more power to you."

"You mean I got your permission?" Rusty drawled sarcastically. Mike immediately opened his mouth, looking angry now. Sandra held up a silencing hand, determined to try again.

"I mean it's none of my business."

"Damn right."

"Damn right."

The fact she'd agreed with him made Rusty scowl harder. "Don't go doing me any favors, Sandy. You want Rawlins here, he's all yours. I've been meaning to ask about a new partner anyway. So how about it?"

Sandra's eyes widened in shock. Even knowing the partners were going through a difficult time, she had not seen this coming. "Mike?" she asked after a moment.

He wouldn't meet her gaze. He was engaged in an in-depth study of the badly scarred floor. That told Sandra enough. Mike was embarrassed. He was hurt. He was angry. He wasn't going to say a word. Let this be Koontz's decision, just like for him, the end of their marriage had been hers.

It made Sandra's decision easy, after all.

"No," she said.

Both men stared at her in surprise.

"What do you mean, no?" Koontz demanded.

"I mean no. You're my best detective team. I won't split you."

"Hey, Aikens—"

"Now, Sandy—"

She cut them both off. "I don't want to hear it. Whatever problems you have, work them out. You are the two best damn detectives on the force. You just broke the toughest case we've had, and I won't split you. Good night."

She picked up her pen. Both men remained flummoxed. When it became blatantly apparent she wasn't going to change her mind, Koontz stormed for the door. He slammed it behind him, which Sandra took as his way of getting in the last word. Mike had to open the door back up to pass through it.

At the last minute, Mike turned. The lines were back around his eyes. He looked strained, but he also looked grateful. He said simply, "Thank you." And then he was gone.

Alone at last in her office, Sandra set down her pen and regarded her closed door. She didn't know if she had just done the right thing. Koontz hated her. Maybe it would have been best to remove him from Mike's life. It probably would have made things easier for her.

Except that Mike would have been hurt, and she couldn't bear to do that to him.

Maybe she was older and wiser after all. Maybe she could grasp the spirit of compromise.

Of course, she thought ruefully, she was still spending the night alone.

"Wait up." Mike caught up with Koontz just inside the parking garage. Rusty was walking fast and looking ready to spit nails.

"Buzz off, Rawlins."

"Like hell."

"Don't you got a hot date tonight?"

"Not if you stand me up."

Koontz came to a screeching halt. "Oh, no," he said, "don't you treat me like that. I'm not your pity date, Rawlins, the third wheel to fill in if Sandy's got other plans. I'm your partner. You're either in or out."

"I said yes, Koontz. You're the one who got mad."

"You hesitated!"

"I'm human."

Koontz scowled, still not looking mollified. Mike finally lost his temper.

"What do you want from me? You've been on my case since the minute Sandra walked through those doors. So you don't like me getting involved with her. So you don't like her. You don't have to. It's *my* life."

"Oh, so now you're getting all uppity. Your personal life is your personal life and I suppose mine is mine, too."

"Of course."

"Then what the hell were you doing calling me a racist!"

"Talking to you about your job!"

"Well, there you go. Sandy's part of the job now, too."

Koontz started walking again. Mike swore and caught his partner's arm. He said forcibly, "Don't do this."

"Do what?"

"Destroy us. Eight years, Koontz. Eight years. We've been a good team."

Rusty finally looked undecided. His feelings remained hurt, however. He shifted from foot to foot. "I'm not a racist," he growled.

Mike didn't say anything.

Rusty bowed his head. "Dammit, I don't know what I am. I hate this PC world! Hate it!"

"I'm no expert at this stuff, either," Mike said quietly. "After what you went through with your uncle—I don't know. Maybe you need to talk to someone about that. Get a better perspective on things."

"You mean like a shrink?" Koontz sounded as if he was strangling.

"Yeah! Maybe. Hell, I don't know."

"You," Koontz said, "have been spending too much time around women."

Mike shrugged, Koontz scowled harder. "I hate Sandy."

"No kidding, Rusty. And for the record, she hates you, too."

Rusty blinked, obviously taken aback by this blunt disclosure. Then his lips twitched. For some reason, the news that the animosity was mutual amused him. That Sandy disliked someone was probably the first thing about Sandy that Koontz could understand.

"She's got a mouth on her, Rawlins," Rusty said after a moment.

"It reminds me of someone else I know."

"Yeah, but she always wants the last word. How do you put it up with that?"

"Pretty much the same way I put up with you."

"Sandy and I really do go at it," Rusty acknowledged. "Maybe it is kind of fun, goading each other on." Rusty looked at Mike abruptly. "Kind of sucks to be you, though, doesn't it."

"Yeah," Mike said softly. "It kind of sucks to be me."

Rusty finally looked chagrined. He gazed off into the distance. He shook his head. "Why didn't she just let us split up?" he said finally. "It's gotta make her life easier. You go your way, I go mine. She can have you all to herself. I mean, what's she trying to prove?"

"Maybe she's not trying to prove anything. Maybe she means exactly what she said—we make a good team. She respects that."

"God, these neophyte chiefs of police. You'd think we had nothing better to do than break them in."

"You'd think."

Koontz said more hesitantly, "I always figured she did nothing but bad-mouth me behind my back."

"Rusty, I don't need her to think for me any more than I need you to think for me. Got it?"

"You still called me a racist."

"You backed out on me. We had a job to do, and you weren't there."

Koontz studied the ground. Slowly he nodded. "Maybe—maybe I should think about that. Ah, hell. I hate this stuff. Buy you a beer?"

"Two beers. Imports."

"Then you're going to go to her place, aren't you?"

"If I'm lucky."

"I'm so much more fun, Rawlins."

"Yeah, but she's got better legs."

Koontz finally looked at him. "Tell me honestly. Do you love her?"

"Yeah, Rusty. I think I do."

Chapter 11

Mike left the Code Blue a little after ten, later than he would have liked. He and Rusty had consumed six beers in the end, plus two orders of macho nachos. Then they'd booed the Red Sox who managed to lose it in the ninth inning. Then they'd slapped each other on the back—hard.

Male-bonding rituals. They worked.

By the time Mike slipped out the front door, he was feeling better about things. Quite a few cops hung out at the Code Blue and by morning, word would spread that Rawlins and Koontz had not only solved the cop-shooter case, but they had also patched things up. Life at work would improve for both Mike and Sandy.

In Sandra's case, Koontz would probably lighten up a little. And, if a sarcastic, hard-to-impress cop's cop like Koontz started to go easier on her, others would, too.

All in all, not a bad night's work.

Now Mike wanted to show his appreciation to his divinely intelligent ex-wife. In his beer-hazed state, he decided to go all out. Buy her a dozen roses. Yeah, and more peach lingerie.

Of course, florists weren't open at ten o'clock. It was the damnedest thing. He ended up in a cab going to a gas station minimart that sold single pink rosebuds for a buck. The cabdriver assured Mike that a rose was a rose, who cared where it came from, so Mike bought six. In the back of the cab, he managed to fashion them into a single bouquet. The driver was very impressed.

Arriving at Sandra's home in the upper west side, Mike saw that lights were blazing. Sandra was awake; he was in luck. He threw a wad of money at the cabdriver—who continued to be more and more impressed by Mike—and jogged up to the front door.

Sandra answered after his first knock. She was wearing that icy-blue silk robe he loved so much. Her eyes widened appreciatively at the sight of half a dozen slightly mangled roses.

"For me?"

"Yep." The word came out funny. Mike pursed his lips. He ought to be able to sound clearer than that. Now his ex-wife was smiling at him.

"Had a few beers, did we?"

"Mmm, maybe."

"Uh-huh." She let him in. He followed her down the hall to the kitchen, where she retrieved a vase for the flowers. Damn she looked good in that robe. He wondered if she was wearing anything beneath it.

"I take it things are better between you and Rusty?"

"Mmm, yep. You're very pretty, you know."

"Yes, I bet I am." Sandra arranged the roses in a vase.

"I wanted to buy you 'nother peach teddy. You know the stores around here close at seven? How's a person supposed to get anything done?"

"It's very difficult."

He moved closer. She was still smiling and her eyes held a warm, welcoming glow. It made his heart beat harder in his chest.

"Can I take off your clothes?" he asked politely.

"Possibly."

"Can I take off my clothes?"

"That's not a bad idea."

"We'll both be naked then."

"Whatever will we do?"

He drew out one of the roses from the vase. "I have a few ideas."

Mike led Sandra back to her bedroom. He untied her silk robe and discovered she wore absolutely nothing beneath it. Then he took off his own clothes, already hard and hungry.

But it was the nice thing about being an easygoing Cajun. He knew how to wait. And it was the nice thing about making love to Sandy. He knew exactly where to touch, with his hands, his lips, and the petals of a rose.

The first time he brought her to climax, he lay beside her and savored the sight of her closed eyes and flushed skin. Her naked legs were intertwined with his, her long limbs golden by candlelight. He loved the way she turned herself over to him, her body supple and pliant. He loved the taste of her, the feel of her. The way she gripped his head and held him closer. It made him hungry all over again.

So he started back at the top, kissing her neck, nuzzling her ear. Working down to her high, firm breasts, where her nipples were turgid and rosy from his attention. Her hips began to writhe, leading him on with her rhythm. Man, she was sexy.

He settled between her thighs, brushing his cheek

against her belly, inhaling the warm, musky fragrance of her body. Then he had the rosebud trailing down her thighs, taking his cues from the sharp inhalations of her breath. A little here, a little there. Sliding the silky petals a little closer.

Suddenly Mike found himself flat on his back, his hands pinned over his head and his ex-wife rising up like an avenging goddess.

"My turn," she whispered, and took the rose from his fingertips.

Mike discovered Sandra had learned a thing or two from him. Soon his hips were the ones writhing and arching, aching for her touch. Until finally she was there, settling above him, sliding down. Moving slow and sure, while his hands gripped her hips and urged her to move faster. Much, much faster.

And then...her whimper, her small scream, the signal he'd been waiting for. He rolled his ex-wife onto her back. He drove into her hard. He let the pressure build. He roared as it burst, and then he was drifting down, down, down into Sandra's waiting arms, content and satiated and thinking that this time he'd make things work. Somehow, this time he'd get it right.

An hour later, Mike rolled over to discover Sandra wide-awake beside him. She was propped up against the pillows, absently stroking his back and looking at nothing in particular. He yawned, rubbed the sleep out of his eyes and peered at her groggily.

"Can't sleep?"

She shrugged. "I keep waiting for the phone to ring. It's made me anxious."

"Vee?"

She nodded as he sat up. The clock read a little after eleven-thirty. It was getting late for a case he and Koontz had promised would break in time for the five-o'clock news.

"No more information?" he asked.

Sandra shook her head. "I talked to Lieutenant Hopkins shortly before leaving. The command center is still inundated with calls. It seems like a waste of manpower at this point, except we can't very well say we have a positive ID on the picture and are merely waiting for the suspect to appear. That would scare Toby Watkins away from his house permanently."

"But the fact that he hasn't gone home yet…"

Sandra looked miserable. "Yes, the fact he hasn't gone home yet. You and Koontz said he had no other family and friends. That he was basically a shy kid. Mike, what if something has happened to him? He's only thirteen."

Mike took her into his arms. He settled her comfortably against his bare chest, slowly brushing back her hair from her temples. "I don't know," he said at last. "Maybe he's hiding out in some warehouse for a while. Maybe he saw Koontz and me at the school and got spooked. He's close to his family, though. Sooner or later he's bound to show up."

"He's under so much pressure. His picture is in the paper, he's probably heard we have a lead. He must be feeling like his whole world is falling apart. And who can he turn to? Who does he have to trust?"

"Sandra, you can't keep doing this."

"Doing what?"

Mike tipped up her head gently. "Acting as if this kid is solely your responsibility. No, don't argue with me. You care, Sandy, and that's a good thing. I've been thinking lately that that's a great thing. Maybe we're all getting too hard these days. But at the same time, if you accept everything as your responsibility, you're gonna burn out. Be-

ing a cop is sobering, *ma chère*. We all suffer heartbreak.
And you gotta learn to let go. Bottom line is that you're
not Vee, you didn't make his decisions, and you've done
the best you could.''

She sighed unhappily. ''I don't feel like I've done the
best I could.''

''That's because you're a perfectionist.''

She finally nodded, rubbing her cheek against the
smoothness of his shoulder. Then she wrapped her arm
around his waist and settled more deeply against him. He
replied by wrapping one of her silky chestnut curls around
his palm. The red, shimmering highlights always fasci-
nated him.

''So you and Koontz are fine again?'' she murmured.

''I think so.''

''Are you ever going to tell me what it was about?''

''No.''

She angled her head up. ''Why not?''

''Because it's between Koontz and me, and partners are
like a married couple. What goes on between them, should
stay between them.''

''You don't talk about us to Koontz?''

''Never.''

''Really?'' She sounded genuinely surprised. He smiled
crookedly.

''We're guys, Sandra. Just because we've been together
eight years doesn't mean we talk about anything personal.''

She rolled her eyes. ''Now that I should've seen coming.''

She settled against him again. He was quiet for a moment, then he said, ''I've been thinking about us, you
know.''

He felt her tense slightly. ''Yes?''

"It seems to me that we've always attributed our problems to our differences—different backgrounds, different families, different personalities. But I've been wondering lately if many of our fights aren't because we're so different, but because we're so much alike."

Sandra sat up. She appeared genuinely intrigued by this line of thinking. "How do you figure?"

"I was thinking about what we both said last night. Me accusing you of never needing me. You saying that you pride yourself on your independence and need your own space. Maybe I'm like that, too. Thing is, even if Rusty wasn't my partner, I don't know that I would tell you about him. It's…*my* relationship. Something outside of you and me. Maybe that's why I wasn't very good at talking to you about the job, either. That's also my thing. I need that."

"But what will happen now, Mike? I'm part of the police department, too. Is that going to be a problem? Are you going to resent me for it?"

He considered it, honestly not sure of the answer. Then he shook his head. "No, I can handle you as the chief. I respect your opinion. You show good insight. Plus, I trust you not to get bogged down in politics and nepotism the way other chiefs did. Now, if you were my partner…I wouldn't like that. That would be too much."

"So I can be your boss, as long as I leave you and Rusty alone?"

"That's pretty much how it works, Sandra. Two detectives go off and build the case. The lieutenant or chief simply receives updates, adds her own two cents and monitors progress. Frankly, there are too many crimes going on in Alexandria for a single police chief to get involved in the details of every single one."

"But what if you and Rusty have problems again? Then your relationship becomes my business."

"Yeah, and we'll both hedge like mad, just as we would if anyone else stepped in. Rusty and I don't suffer intrusions well. No partners do. Ask the last police chief or the chief before him. It's nothing personal."

"So some walls do exist, both personally and professionally, for both of us. We have to learn to respect those walls."

"Yeah, *ma chère.* I think so."

She gazed at him frankly. "But Mike, what if those walls are too much? If we always need our space, what's left for our marriage?"

"Well, that's the other thought I had. I always pegged you as the fierce one, Sandy. Hell, that's what I love about you. The way your chin comes up, the way you're always ready to spit fire. It's really sexy."

She actually blushed. "Really?"

"Oh, yeah, honey. Oh, yeah. But then you made the point today that I'm not so easygoing myself. I think I let things roll off my back. I was certainly raised to do that, but maybe it's not that simple. I know the job gets to me. Koontz is the one who's great at going home at night. Case is closed, and he sleeps just fine. Sometimes...sometimes I can't let it go like that. I think about Vee, too, *ma chère.* I think about his letters, the conditions we found at his house. I wonder what it would be like, growing up watching your family disintegrate like that. And what are we really going to do for him in the end? Send him to juvie, get him some overworked social worker? His English teacher said he was very bright. She regretted not noticing it sooner. Then I wonder where Vee will be ten years from now. Unfortunately, I think I know the answer. Then I wonder what's the point of this job."

"Aha—you have an overdeveloped sense of responsibility, too!"

"Yeah," he said quietly. "I guess I do."

"You also have to remember about the choices Vee made."

"Absolutely."

"We are a lot alike."

"I believe I've proved my case."

"We could talk about these things, couldn't we? I won't pry about the details of your job or Koontz. You were right—too often I turned our evening conversations into some kind of twisted police audit. But in turn, maybe we could talk about how the job makes us *feel*. The tough parts, the long days, the frustration. Mike, I would really, really like that."

He said softly, "I think I would like that, too."

"Mike," Sandra blurted out, "I love you!"

"Know what, Sandra? I love you, too." He ruffled her hair. She smiled at him, huge and radiant and his heart squeezed in his chest again. But then her expression faltered.

She said roughly, curiously, "Why am I suddenly so afraid?"

"Because last time we said all this, we broke each other's hearts."

"Mike? Tell me we'll do better this time."

"I want to."

"Tell me we're older and wiser."

"I have more gray hair."

"Then tell me you love me again."

"More than the sun and the moon and the stars."

"Damn, marriage is hard."

She settled back into his arms. He held her closer. Neither one said a word.

In the abandoned warehouse building, Vee shifted for the fifth time in twenty minutes. It was getting cold. Wind had a bite and he hadn't thought to grab a jacket. Least his stomach didn't hurt anymore. He'd splurged a whole six bucks on a hamburger, fries and a chocolate shake. Seemed like extravagant living to him, and he'd been real excited. Halfway through the potatoes, however, he'd lost interest. Living large wasn't half so much fun when you were alone.

He'd wandered, trying to figure out what to do. According to the BGF homeys, he couldn't go back home or to school. He knew a lot of abandoned buildings, sure, his neighborhood had way too many of them, but how long could a brother live in condemned squalor on the east side? Didn't seem to make much sense. He had to keep buying food, going out in public. Sooner or later, he'd need to shower. What then?

He'd grabbed three more guns from beneath the bed, a shotgun and two hand guns, but they just weighed him down. Seemed he'd started out writing some words and now he was on a fast track to nowhere. First cop that saw him would bust his black hide. What would Big S Sammy think of that?

Vee shifted around on the old wood floor. He shivered as his back came up against cold brick. He wished he was back home with his mama and sister again. Then he wiped the moisture from his face.

Outside there be too much action. Some homeys be hanging out on the corner, drinking beer, looking for something to do. Not too long ago, a not so bright brother tried to cross the street. The other kids moved in fast. Kid had really squealed for a while. Vee wanted to tell him to shuddup, it be over faster if you shuddup, but he knew better than to show his face. BGF protection don't mean nothing when homeys be in a bustin' kind of mood.

Least now the beating be down to the quiet parts. Kid just *umphed* from time to time. The other brothers would lose interest soon. That's the way it went.

Then Vee heard sirens. Two *whirp-whirps*. Cops be arrivin' at the scene.

Vee knew better, but he leaned over and stared down at the street.

Cops popped open their doors. Yelled, "Hold it, police."

Brothers looked up. They appeared so goofy startled, Vee nearly laughed. The homeboys had drunk themselves stupid. Now the cops would call the detox van and that would be that. 'Cept for the kid moaning on the ground. Sucked to be him.

Brothers backed off slowly, arms obediently in the air. Cops relaxed, shoulders coming down. Vee could hear their exchanged words. "Must be eight of them there. Damn, the paperwork. I wanted to go home early tonight. Dumb, black—"

Suddenly some dude broke out of the building, maybe a doper, startled out of cover. Man started running hard. The police appeared confused, but then gave chase. This roused the brothers back out of their stupor. They started hollerin', "No, no, leave him alone."

Then the brothers started running, too. The bangers chased the cops, the cops chased the doper, and the world be going nuts. Window broke. More shouting.

Abruptly one cop turned. He had his gun half-out of his holster. Vee could see his face. Cop be scared, pee-his-pants scared. Had eight big brothers bearing down on him and they all seemed a little crazed. Man pointed his gun at the homeboys. Man assumed the stance. In the distance, the other cop yelled something. Maybe no, maybe hell, yes.

Vee couldn't hear anymore. He just saw.

Cop pulling the trigger. Spark of gunpowder against the night sky. First kid tumbling down.

Brothers scattering, cops yelling. Screaming, screaming, screaming. Scared cop still taking aim.

And Toby saw his father, running. Toby saw his brother, laughing. Toby took out his shotgun. He thought of everything he'd written. *I be a straight killer since I wuz ten. Now I be thirteen and I ain't got no need to grow no older. Call me Vee.*

Toby pulled the trigger.

The blast be so damn loud, it burst his ears.

The scared cop fell to the ground. The scared cop fell hard.

And the whole wide world went insane.

The phone rang at two in the morning. Sandra picked it up after the first ring, some part of her brain reacting instantly. Vee, she was thinking. Finally the call that they'd picked up Toby Watkins. Mike was already stirring by her side.

Lieutenant Hopkins, however, was not talking about apprehending a thirteen-year-old boy. He was talking about a shooting in the lower east side. Two juveniles down. Officer down. Civilians gathering angrily. Cops grabbing full riot gear.

The city was about to go to war. What would the chief of police like to do?

Sandra told him to secure the scene, get the CSU on site, *now,* and not leak a word to the press. They were operating code red. Officers on full alert, scene locked down tight, and all information sealed. That was an order.

Then Sandra was flying out of bed, Mike right behind her. She told him about the situation as they grabbed their clothes. Then there was no time for talking. They were racing downtown.

Even after listening to Lieutenant Hopkins's dire tone of voice, Sandra was not prepared for what they found on the lower east side. Civilians had not merely gathered, they had *converged* upon the scene. Ambulances could not get through. Police cars were bogged down. She and Mike had to park six blocks back from the shooting, and they could already see groups of boys siphoning off from the mob and running down side alleys. In a matter of hours, maybe just minutes, the first window would be broken, and the angry mood officially sparked. Soon, vandalism, looting, arson and car rolling.

Lieutenant Hopkins was right. They had a riot on their hands.

Sandra got on her cell phone to the mayor, while Mike pushed their way through the crowd.

In the center of the ring, the situation grew worse. Now Sandra could see a large black woman, convulsing against two somber-eyed teens as she cried for her baby—the bloodied black youth being hastily strapped to a gurney. Now Sandra could see Alexandria's finest, patroling the perimeter in bullet-proof vests, clear face shields and combat boots. Many were aggressively slapping batons against their palms, meeting the hostile crowd with angry stares.

"They got vests," the crowd hissed. "Look at all them white boys hiding behind their shields. And what do we got to protect ourselves? What do we got to protect our children?"

On the cell phone, Sandra spoke faster to the mayor. Then Lieutenant Hopkins came running up.

"Three down," he reported crisply. "One cop, two teens. Officer Brody took a shotgun blast to the front, lower body. His vest protected his gut, but he still has extensive damage to his upper legs. EMTs are working to stabilize him now."

"And the civilians?"

"First is sixteen years old, took a good beating. Couple of cracked ribs, lacerations. Officer Wallace said he and Brody had come upon a group of teens attacking the victim. That's what got things going. In the ensuing confrontation, a second kid, seventeen years old, known gang member, sustained a single bullet wound to the right shoulder. He's lost a lot of blood, but the EMTs think he'll be okay once they get him to the hospital."

"So why aren't these people at the hospital?"

Lieutenant Hopkins gave her a look. "That's your first problem, Chief. Those fine folks out there have closed off all the streets. Second ambulance can't get through—"

"Get it a police escort."

"Tried. They rolled the police car."

"Oh, God." Rolling police cruisers. They were in trouble. "Who's in the worst condition?"

"The officer."

"Damn. We load him up first and this crowd will blow."

"We load him up last, the officer may die."

"Helicopter," Sandra said. She flipped back out the cell phone and dialed Alexandria County Hospital. She kept her tone clipped. "Can your helicopter do a rooftop landing? That's what I thought. Here are our coordinates. Pick your landing pad. Fine. You have five minutes."

She turned back to Lieutenant Hopkins. "Sixteen-year-old is stable, right? Okay. Load the seventeen-year-old up in the ambulance. Let the crowd see we're trying to help him. Get Officer Brody strapped to a backboard, but wait for the helicopter to arrive. When it lands, let the ambulance go. Then while people are focused on the ambulance, get Officer Brody to the top of that building right there. Don't give Brody an armed escort, that's just asking for trouble. We want to keep things smooth, swift and controlled. Got it?''

Lieutenant Hopkins got it. He went racing off to the EMTs. Mike said simply, ''Not bad, *ma chère.*''

Sandra nodded, not feeling better at all, as they moved deeper into the scene. Mike spotted Koontz and went toward him. Sandra found the mother, who was still weeping against her children. The woman had obviously been called out of her bed. She was wearing a ratty nightgown and her whole body was trembling. Sandra grabbed two blankets from the EMTs and carefully draped them over the woman's shoulders. Fresh murmurs arose from the crowd.

''They killed my baby,'' the mother wailed. ''Your officers killed my child!''

''We're doing everything in our power to help your son, Mrs....''

''Forge,'' the woman sniffled. ''Annie Forge.''

''Mrs. Forge, they're going to take your son to the hospital at any minute so they can fix his shoulder. The EMTs are optimistic, but we definitely want to get him the best medical treatment possible. Now, let's make arrangements to get you to the hospital as well. I know you want to be with your son. And are these your other children? What are your names?''

Sandra introduced herself to Delilah and Daniel. They told her they didn't have a car, and while their uncle could come give them a ride, they didn't know if he could get through the streets. Sandra went back over to the EMTs. They could fit one person into the back of the ambulance; that was it.

She returned to Mrs. Forge. Why didn't Annie ride in the ambulance with her son? Sandra would call Mrs. Forge's brother and get him to come pick up the children as soon as possible.

After a moment, Mrs. Forge nodded. Thinking about the logistics had calmed her some. She trembled less as Sandra dialed the uncle and made arrangements for him to pick up his niece and nephew.

"We're going to take good care of you," Sandra repeated to the shell-shocked woman. "We're going to help you through this."

The front of the crowd was shifting again, a fresh grumble turning into a collective roar. Sandra turned to see Officer Brody being lifted onto a backboard. Even from this distance, she could see that the officer was seriously hurt. And it frightened her that the crowd didn't seem to care.

Keeping her features composed, she patted Mrs. Forge's hand one last time, then headed over to Officer Brody.

The young man was strapped in, a blanket placed for privacy. The EMTs had already sliced away his pants, exposing a horrible array of pellet holes peppering his upper legs. The trauma looked bloody and intense, and yet Sandra knew the officer was lucky. At a close enough range, loaded with the right kind of shell, a shotgun blast could rip straight through a Kevlar vest.

Other officers knew it, too. They wore grim expressions and looked out at the crowd with growing animosity.

"We're trying to help one of their own and they won't let the ambulance through. What does that tell you?"

Sandra searched immediately for the source of the voice, but all the men turned away, protecting their own. Then the police radios buzzed to life. Windows shattering over on thirteenth. Report of a car on fire, and a theft in progress. Requesting immediate assistance.

Sandra closed her eyes. It was starting now. She had gotten the mayor's permission to request full state backup. No one knew it yet, not even her own men, but soon helicopters would take to the sky with huge searchlights. Armored vans would pull up and disgorge SWAT officers in full riot gear. Tear gas would be fired if necessary. Rubber bullets if worse came to worst.

And some people would fight back. Angry, drunk, who knows why. Little skirmishes would take place all over the city, and Alexandria's police department would win. The civilians were right—the cops were better equipped. But who would really feel the victor in the morning? Who would really come out ahead?

On the ground, Officer Brody's breathing grew more labored. The EMTs moved in and Sandra somberly withdrew.

Mike and Rusty were waiting for her.

"Sidebar," Mike muttered, and swiftly drew her behind the ambulance.

"You hear about the shooting?" Koontz asked, his eyes darting from side to side. They were closer to the yellow tape here, the murmurs of the crowd harder to ignore. *Cops, can't trust 'em, look at what they do, shooting at kids. Bet if he was white, he wouldn't be spread out on the pavement. No, no, they only use bullets on us black folks...* Koontz hunched further in on himself. His face was covered in sweat.

"What about the shooting?"

Koontz glanced at Mike. Mike broke the news. "We talked to the partner, Officer Wallace. They were on routine patrol when they came across a group of kids beating up another teen. When they pulled up, however, some guy broke out of a building and started running. They gave chase. Next thing they knew, the kids were running after them, shouting and yelling. Things got a little tangled. Then Officer Brody opened fire.''

Sandra peered at her two detectives, not getting this. ''They were under attack, so Officer Brody discharged his weapon?''

Koontz shifted again, definitely unhappy. ''Wallace didn't see a weapon.''

''Oh, no.'' Now she was getting it.

''He was behind Brody,'' Mike said, ''so maybe Brody saw something Wallace didn't. But we've paced out the scene, inch by inch. We can't find a shotgun anywhere and the sixteen-year-old beating victim swears none of the kids drew down. They were drunk, they were unruly—''

''And they were unarmed,'' Sandra finished for him. ''Wonderful.''

''Cop got spooked,'' Koontz said. ''Late at night, this thing going on with Vee. Everyone's got the heebie-jeebies. It was only a matter of time.''

''Speaking of which—'' Mike said dryly.

Sandra closed her eyes. After the last announcement, she'd seen this one coming. ''The shotgun blast. If the kids were unarmed, then who shot Officer Brody? Enter Toby Watkins.''

''Shot came from that abandoned building,'' Mike said quietly, pointing up to a hollow-eyed window. ''Downward trajectory. That's why it caught Officer Brody in the legs. Too bad. A couple inches higher, the vest would've absorbed the spray and he'd be home free.''

''I don't think Toby Watkins is a shy kid anymore,'' Koontz muttered. ''I think he just came of age.''

''When the news teams get a hold of this—'' Sandra sighed.

''Too late.''

Koontz looked up. When Sandra followed his gaze, she

saw that the buzzing coming from the sky wasn't the rescue chopper. It was the Channel 4 news team. Denied the streets, the reporters had gone airborne, too.

"We're in trouble. Look, talk to Lieutenant Hopkins. Someone get Wallace down to the station, *fast* and round up as many of the kids involved as you can find. We need statements from everyone and we need them *out of the way* of the press. If one of these kids starts talking, we'll get rumors circulating fast, and then we'll have a justifiably angry mob on our hands."

Koontz looked at Mike. He muttered something low under his breath. It sounded like, "drop gun."

Sandra's eyes grew wide. She knew about drop guns. They were extra hand guns, generally recovered from a crime scene and never entered into the evidence log that cops would carry as backup pieces. Subject turns out to be reaching for his wallet instead of a weapon when you opened a fire, well *drop-gun* the scene. Look, the perp was carrying, after all.

Sandra shook her head, her voice coming out fierce. "Koontz, mess with my crime scene and I'll take your badge."

"Makes for better press," he countered levelly. "Kid has a rap sheet."

"For heaven's sake, it was a shotgun blast. How are you going to explain a seventeen-year-old kid in jeans and a T-shirt magically producing a shotgun, let alone a shotgun that only one witness—Officer Brody—managed to see? The whole thing will reek of cover-up, and then we'll have not one, but two crises on our hands. Officer Brody made a mistake. It happens. Now we take responsibility for that and we move on. It's the only way to feel better."

"Who feels better? The kid? The mother? Hey, Officer Brody has a weeping mama, too."

"Officer Brody is a cop. Risk and injury is part of the job."

"Absolutely. And stopping to help a black kid getting punked up by a bunch of brothers was also part of his job. Anyone out there talking about that? Anyone out there talking about how this whole thing started? Officer Brody tried to help a sixteen-year-old kid who had no business being on the street at two in the morning anyway. Now, look at what happened to him."

Koontz stormed off.

"You're going to have to control him," Sandra said at last to Mike. "You don't want me interfering? Then you *do* something about him."

Mike nodded.

The hospital's helicopter finally arrived. On cue, the ambulance sirens roared to life. The crowd rumbled, but at the sight of Mrs. Forge's son passing through the doors, even they grew silent. An officer removed the yellow barrier. The ambulance pulled forth.

The crowd parted and just for a moment, it seemed everything would be all right.

Then somebody shouted, "If he dies, I say we kill 'em all. Kill the pigs, kill the pigs, kill the pigs!"

Mike's arms went around Sandy instinctively. They stood together as the shouting gained momentum, then the first state police helicopter flashed its powerful searchlight and blazed across the sky.

Chapter 12

By six that morning, the streets of Alexandria had finally been brought under control. Small street gangs were rounded up and juveniles processed. Fires were extinguished and some property recovered. Store owners began boarding up shattered windows and filling out insurance forms. The mayor instigated a city-wide curfew to extend through the week.

Officer Brody's condition was upgraded to stable. The seventeen-year-old shooting victim, Charles Smith, aka Ice Tray, was also listed in good condition. The sixteen-year-old was treated and released.

Life returned to normal, just in time for the morning commute—except for the burnt-out cars still smoking on the streets, the sidewalks littered with shards of glass and the scared mothers who kept their children home from school that day and the next.

At six-thirty, Sandra finally returned to her house, covered in soot and badly in need of a shower. She did not think she had ever felt so tired, yet in twenty minutes, she would be returning to the station. Vee had yet to be located. Word was out that a white Alexandria cop had opened fire on a group of unarmed African-American youths. City leaders were crying for an update. What was Alexandria's police department doing? How could they let a thirteen-year-old run the city? And what would they do now to keep the east side safe?

In the end, Sandra cheated and showered for a whole fifteen minutes. She needed the hot, stinging spray on her face.

She'd no sooner stepped out of the shower than her phone rang. It was her mother.

"Oh, my God, Sandra. Are you all right? We've been watching the news. Horrible, just horrible. Please tell me you weren't downtown for all that."

"Good morning to you, too," Sandra said.

"Is it true there were riots? We saw pictures of cops with shields and plastic masks chasing groups of hoodlums through the streets. It looked like a Third World country or something. My God, we made the national news with this!"

"The situation is now under control."

"Sandra, I have to be honest about this. You are scaring the living daylights out of your father and me. Tell us you've changed your mind. Come back to your father's company. Really, enough is enough."

"I'm not going back to Daddy's company. But thanks for the offer."

Her mother, however, remained undeterred. "Sandra, be realistic. You're a young, intelligent woman. You could have any job you want. Certainly you could do better than, than...*this*."

"Than managing crises that affect the whole city? I think not."

"Would you like to get into politics?" her mother spoke up brightly. "That would be nice."

"I would like to do exactly what I'm doing, Mom. But really, thanks for calling."

There was silence on the other end of the phone. Sandra sighed and began toweling off. She didn't know why she bothered with these conversations. Her mother wasn't going to understand. She was still struggling with the concept of women in the workforce, let alone in the police force.

Her mother said abruptly, "It's because of *him*, isn't it?"

"I make my own decisions."

"Oh, no. You would never have gotten interested in policing if it hadn't been for Michael Rawlins. He's the one who got you into this. And now what are you doing? Risking your life, giving your father and me heart attacks just so you can be closer to some blue-collar—"

"Stop it. Stop it right there."

"Sandra! I am your mother. I will not—"

"You are my mother, and I love you. But finish that statement, and I will no longer be your daughter. I mean that."

She managed to stun her mother into silence. When Melissa Aikens spoke up again, her tone was genuinely hurt and defensive. "I don't understand."

"I know, Mom. I know." Sandra closed her eyes. She was curt, she was weary. She shouldn't be having this conversation right now. Yet, on she went. "Mom, I love him."

And her mother, God bless her, said, "Oh, no!"

"Oh, yes. Listen to me. I know you don't understand me or my life. You've never liked Mike, and you certainly don't want me in law enforcement. But those are the things I want, Mom. And I'm a good chief of police. Not that you can tell by looking at the news clips this morning, but on the other hand, I've gone days now without having *Bitch* written on my nameplate."

"What?"

"And you know who's helped me with all of this, Mom? Mike. He's been at my side, helping me learn the ropes, helping me understand the department. I really think this time, we might be able to make things work. At least I'd like to try."

Her mother made a strangling sound. Then she put her hand over the mouthpiece and yelled, "Howard, come talk some sense into your daughter."

Sandra shook her head. Seconds later, her father was on the phone. "How are you, dear?"

"Tired. Late for work. Not in the mood for this."

"We saw the news," her father said somberly. "It looked like a terrible scene."

"It was a rough night, but everything is fine now."

"Your mom worries, you know. I do, too."

Sandra didn't say anything. After a moment, her father sighed heavily. "You're not coming back to Security, Inc., are you, young lady?"

"No, I'm not. And since Mom's going to tell you this next, I'm reconciling with Mike."

Sandra could hear her mother in the background again. "Is she coming back to work, Howard? Is she making sense now?" Her father hushed her.

"Are you sure about this?"

"Yes."

"It's only been a few days, sweetheart."

"I'm not so sure that's true. It feels to me that we're finally having the conversations we should've had four years ago. Instead, we walked away. I think we were too hurt and inexperienced to know what else to do. But we've had four years to turn things over in our minds. Four years to realize that while we did have problems, we're even more unhappy without each other. I think we really were meant to be together. Now we just have to figure out how to make things work.''

"You've given this some thought."

"Dad," she said tiredly, "it's me. When have I ever been impulsive?"

Her father finally chuckled. "Why don't you bring Mike over to dinner, Sandra. We'll get reacquainted and talk about your new job."

"Barbecue. Family only. The first time someone talks down to Mike, we're outta there."

"My, my, Sandra, you have taken to your new job."

"Absolutely."

"Barbecue it is. Family only. Your mother and I will be on our best behavior." Her mother made a shocked noise. Her father said, "Shh!"

"Thank you, Dad."

"No problem. Now you get to work, young lady. And, sweetheart, good luck."

Now it was Sandra's turn to make a strangling sound. She hung up the phone and prepared for her day.

At eight o'clock, Sandra convened a debriefing for all of her officers, regarding last night's incident and the situation with Vee. As on her first day, the men looked sullen and defensive. Her lieutenants were clustered together in the front. Mike was lounging against the wall in the back. He smiled at her; otherwise, the mood was pretty much the same, and the only person missing was Koontz. Sandra hadn't seen him since he'd walked off last night. Maybe he didn't do mornings.

Sandra took a deep breath and addressed a group of tired middle-aged men who were sick of hearing that everything they did was wrong.

"Good morning," she said. That didn't even earn her a nod. She gave up on small talk and simply launched into her spiel. She summarized the events leading up to Officer Brody shooting seventeen-year-old Charles Smith late last night. She described what they believed happened next: Spotting the incident, Toby Watkins had fired upon Officer Brody from a warehouse window, then fled the scene himself. CSU had finally found the shotgun, in a Dumpster behind the abandoned building. Preliminary fingerprint analysis revealed a match between prints recovered from the shotgun and prints found on the 9 mm Vee had thrown at Sandra two days before.

"So what's this all mean?" one officer spoke up from the back. "According to the paper, it sounds like Brody's the bad guy for firing when under attack, while this kid Watkins is the hero for shooting a cop. What's the deal with that?"

Several officers grumbled their agreement. They stared at Sandra accusingly.

"That story is *not* coming from this office," she said firmly. "While Officer Brody is now on probation as the disciplinary board investigates the shooting, we still consider him a member of Alexandria's police force in good standing until the board concludes otherwise. Officer Brody has an excellent record and we stand behind that. Even if it does turn out that he opened fire inappropriately, there are a lot of other factors that must be weighed and analyzed. The mayor and myself appreciate that fact."

People finally nodded. So the brass wasn't going to make Brody the sacrificial lamb. Yet.

"Now then," Sandra said. "The good news is that Officer Brody and the two teens are recovering from their injuries. The bad news is that Toby Watkins is still out there. We have reason to believe he's heavily armed. He's also frightened, confused and volatile. We must apprehend this boy. *Peacefully.*"

That earned her another collective mutter of disgust. Sandra leaned forward, her own voice angry and intent.

"Hey, we have a major community crisis on our hands. Half of the gang members we arrested last night talked about Vee as if he's a local hero. It appears that gangs may also be helping Vee hide from the police. As his stature continues to grow in the eyes of the community, Vee will have even more resources at his disposal. And he may feel more pressure to fire on local law enforcement as a means of proving his newfound reputation. Obviously, we have to consider Vee dangerous and proceed with care. But we also have to consider how he is viewed by the public at large, particularly within the African-American community."

"Wonderful," someone muttered in the front row.

A second officer spoke up in the middle. "So what are we supposed to do? Roll over and play dead? This kid's a killer and against a shotgun, vests don't mean a thing."

Sandra smiled tightly. This was the risky part of her speech. She was depending heavily on something Mike had told her the first day. She should trust her men more. She should give them some credit now and hope it came back to her later.

She said, "I don't know what to do."

Total silence. A few raised brows. Finally, an admittance of weakness from their sharply dressed chief of police. Sandra had figured they would like that.

"I'll be honest," she said. "I'm too new to this to have ready answers. On the other hand, in this room we have over two hundred years of combined policing experience. We have some of the finest officers in the state and a police force I firmly believe in. This is our crisis. This is our community. Let's put our heads together and resolve this matter. Let's prove once and for all what being an Alexandria cop really means."

More silence. Alone on the podium, Sandra feared her ploy had failed. Then a voice in the back of the room said, "We could find Vee. Hell, we go undercover all the time to find drug dealers. What's one thirteen-year-old kid?"

Sandra homed in on the Vice detective. "Please explain."

The forty-something cop stood, arms crossed over his barrel chest. "We go door to door as cops and nobody is gonna tell us a thing. You want the word on the street? We get it the way we always do. Dress up a couple Vice guys as bums, turn a couple of the ladies into hookers. We hang out for a bit, put our ears to the ground. My guess is half the population is buzzing about Vee. In a day or two, we'll probably know not only where he's hiding, but what the kid's been eating for breakfast."

"And then there's the snitches," another cop said with more excitement. "While we got officers on the street, we can also start calling in markers. Between Vice and Gang Task Force, we gotta have thirty, forty snitches who might know something. Not everyone wants to give up the hometown hero, but for the right price, half of them will."

More enthusiastic nods now.

"We can use the family, as well," Mike drawled from the back. "We got the ID late yesterday, so we didn't have time to complete the background report. We can do a fresh interview of the sister this morning, then talk to the mother this afternoon. They oughta be able to give us a list of Toby's known haunts. If the boy is truly scared, chances are he isn't drifting too far from the familiar.''

"We should maintain watch at the house," a new officer mentioned.

"School, too," a second officer said.

"And the hospital where the mother is," a third cop concluded, and earned a fresh round of approval.

"Okay," Sandra said eagerly. "So here's what we got. Vice detectives go undercover. Gang and Vice start calling on the snitches. Detectives Rawlins and Koontz finish the background report on Toby Watkins while the patrol officers keep watch on Vee's house, school and mom. That's a lot of manpower, but I doubt the mayor is going to complain. I'll get going on the requisition paperwork. Anything else?''

Everyone looked at one another, interested and curious. Finally the lieutenants signaled that that was everything. They had a plan, and they liked it.

Sandra smiled brightly. "Wonderful. Excellent work. I'll be holding a press conference with the mayor in the east side at two o'clock, urging community reconciliation. As part of that, I'll make a plea for Vee to turn himself in. I doubt that will magically produce Toby Watkins on our doorstep, but it can't hurt to try.''

Lieutenant Hopkins tentatively raised his hand in the front. For once, the lieutenant appeared worried instead of confrontational. "Uh, Chief, holding a speech in the east side seems like asking for trouble. If we haven't found Vee yet…''

"We will be asking for a security detail," Sandra said. "Perhaps, you could put together that list of men. But the

mayor wants the conference at the scene of the shooting.
The crisis started there, so it must end there as well.''

Sandra adjourned the meeting. She was not surprised
when Mike followed her straight from the debriefing room
into her office. He shut the door hard.

''Why the hell didn't you tell me about the press conference?''

''I didn't know myself until twenty minutes ago.''

''It's too dangerous! *Mon Dieu,* what's the mayor thinking these days? Kid's still gonna be running loose and the
chief of police will make one helluva target!''

''Mike, please.'' Sandra made the mistake of placing a
hand on his chest. That only reminded her of how strong
he was, how warm, how appealing. Just twelve hours ago
they'd been in bed, having a wonderful conversation. She
already missed him.

Sandra reluctantly drew her hand back. She saw from
Mike's face he felt the loss as acutely as she did.

''Quite a night, wasn't it?'' she said ruefully. ''So much
for being able to wake up in each other's arms.''

''Yeah,'' he said more calmly, looking worn now himself. ''You picked one helluva job, *ma chère.* Sure you
don't want to back out now?''

''Can't. Turned down the final job offer with my
daddy's firm this morning. You're stuck with me now.''

''Your parents have given up on changing your mind?''

''My father has. My mom's going to need more time.
By the way, you're officially invited over for a barbecue.
Family only. They promised to be on their best behavior.''

Her big, strong ex-husband smiled feebly. He said
bravely, ''Great! Looking forward to it.''

''Liar.''

''Okay.''

Sandra smiled. He tried and that meant a great deal to

her. Perhaps one of the greatest secrets of marriage was merely focusing on all the things your spouse did do, instead of the things he didn't.

"I wish we could steal a minute alone," she said softly.

"Me too, *ma chère.*"

"I liked having you naked. Have I ever told you just how much your body turns me on? Getting to run my hands across your chest, down your strong rippling arms…"

Mike's gaze had gone dark. He said lowly, "Shut up, Sandy, or I'm going to make love to you on your desk."

For a moment, she honestly considered it. A desk in a police station was about the only place they hadn't made love. Of course, she was the chief of police, he was a detective, and the whole thing spelled trouble. She sighed instead, and did her best to drag her mind back to business. It had been a long night, focus came hard.

"I'm sorry. I suppose I should get ready for the press conference now."

"Sandy…" Mike's tone was immediately frustrated again. "Don't do this. Call the mayor. Explain it to him. Two key city officials, right in Vee's backyard. You're asking for another major incident."

"He's not a sophisticated assassin, Mike. As long as the security detail does their job right, we'll be fine."

"It's too risky!"

"But it's my job. Please, you asked me to give you the space to do your work. Now give me the space to do mine."

He scowled. "It's not the same thing."

"Why not?"

"Because you're mine!" he growled. "You're my woman, and I have the right to protect my woman. Ask any caveman. That's the way it works. You tend fire, I go kill woolly mammoth."

Sandra raised a brow. Then she lost her fierce composure to a smile. Damn, Mike was sexy when he was overprotective. And cute. And she had to admit, it made her feel special. For the first time, they were interacting as allies and friends outside of the bedroom.

Then, in the way their relationship often worked, it made her want to strip him naked again.

She sighed longingly and got herself back under control. Her ex-husband was gazing at her curiously, a scowl still marring his features.

"Go away," she ordered. "Find your partner, and get some work done."

"I'll only come back at one-thirty."

"Then come back at one-thirty. I suppose I could use someone willing to club a woolly mammoth."

"Promise?"

"Cross my heart."

Mike finally looked mollified. He didn't walk away, however. Instead, he glanced quickly at the closed door, then enfolded her in his arms. Her body immediately decompressed into his. She hadn't realized just how tense she'd been this morning. Now she could feel the knots loosen in her shoulders, feel some of the weight of the world slip away. Sandra closed her eyes and focused on the reassuring rhythm of Mike's strong, beating heart. He felt so good against her. Sometimes it was hard to believe they had ever drifted apart. But they had, and in spite of her bold words to her parents, Sandra was still afraid. Right now things were going well, but what about six months from now or one year from now? How did you know when you were truly ready for "better or for worse"?

"I don't want anything to happen to you," Mike said abruptly, his voice low.

"I'll be fine," she murmured. His arms tightened.

"I have a bad feeling, Sandy. I just do."

"That's not surprising. You haven't slept in twenty-four hours."

"I know." He reluctantly drew back. Sandra could still read concern carved into the strong planes of his face. She gently traced the lines with her fingertips.

"We're all working together now, Mike. The whole department. Things are finally beginning to click."

"The department is pulling together," he agreed, though he still sounded troubled. "You should be proud, *ma chère*. None of this would've happened without you."

"Thanks."

Mike pulled all the way back now. A frown still marred his brow.

"I'll find Koontz," he said. "We'll get the background report done."

"I'll see you at one-thirty. And Mike—I am nervous. I really would like you up there at my side. Thanks."

"*Ma chère,* be *careful.*"

"Of course."

By one-thirty, the security detail had conducted a clean sweep of the buildings located around the hastily constructed speaking pavilion. Press vans had arrived, speaker systems were being wired and microphones installed. Cars were beginning to appear, from white news vans to black stretch limousines. City council was present, as well as several prominent black leaders. Then there were the east-side civilians, from store owners to retired citizens to several noticeable groups of teens.

Officers were tense. So was the crowd.

And back in the police station, Sandra was finally beginning to sweat. Lieutenant Hopkins personally brought her a bullet-proof vest. He instructed her to wear it over a T-shirt for comfort, then cover it with her blouse. Standing in front of the mirror, she looked thicker than usual, but professional.

Sandra didn't feel normal, however. She was unbearably conscious of the weight of the vest on her body. The stifling heat. The sweat trickling down between her shoulder blades. This was how she had sent her officers into duty every day for nearly a week. No wonder their nerves had been on edge.

At one forty-five, Sandra assembled her notes. Lieutenant Hopkins was waiting for her outside her office. Strange how she'd come to see him as an ally today. In the midst of a crisis, many things had changed.

Mike came running up just as she and Lieutenant Hopkins entered the parking garage. He'd obviously been working up to the last minute and was out of breath.

"Sorry I'm late."

"That's okay. How did the background reports go?"

"Got it." He held up a list of places Toby Watkins was known to favor. "Will pass it on to the sergeant at the press conference. Any news?"

"Nothing yet. It's only been four hours, though. Where's Koontz?"

Mike's expression faltered. "He, um, he got held up."

Sandra stopped walking long enough to give Mike a look. She knew what he meant. "I'm going to have to discipline him," she said softly.

"Let me talk to him first—"

"Mike, this matter is too serious for a partner-to-partner chat. Times like this, officers have to be willing to put their personal feelings aside. I'm sorry, I'm going to have to put him on probation. It's the only option I have left.''

Mike's face fell. He knew as well as she did, however, that Koontz had crossed the line. Officers did not bug out when their city had just suffered a riot.

''Did you get to talk to him at all?'' she asked.

He shook his head. ''He's not at home. I don't know where the hell he went. Sometimes…man, what goes through his head?''

Sandra sighed. ''We'll have to deal with it. Just not right now.'' She rubbed her temples, feeling anxious and tense again. She could tell by the look on Mike's face that he felt the same. And for a moment she was tired of Koontz and the strain he'd put on her and Mike's marriage. She wished Rusty would just go away.

Something must have shown on her face, for Mike's expression immediately shuttered closed.

''Later,'' she murmured.

''Yeah, later.''

Sandra climbed into the police sedan. She did her best to pull herself together. She was the chief of police. Besides, she had all of Alexandria's police force working to protect her. Oh, God…

She was breathing hard by the time they arrived on the scene. Mike also appeared subdued.

''Security team?'' he asked Lieutenant Hopkins.

''Went over every rooftop and building with a fine-tooth comb. Area is secure.''

''From Vee,'' Mike muttered, and Sandra immediately saw his point. Several large groups of teenagers loitered at the edge of the news vans. They were geared up in gang colors and wore belligerent expressions as they stared at Sandra.

Lieutenant Hopkins and Mike exchanged looks. ''Keep

calm, keep cool,'' Mike instructed Sandra under his breath. ''First sign of trouble, we'll hustle you right outta here. Got it?''

The clock hit two. Camera lights came on, and the mayor stepped out of his car, flanked by two bodyguards. Show time.

Mayor Peterson approached the podium first. He thanked the news crews and community leaders for attending the afternoon's news conference. He spoke regretfully of the ''tragic chain of events'' that occurred last night and sent his heartfelt condolences to the families of Officer Brody and Charles Smith.

Then he stepped aside, and Sandra found herself in the middle of a circle of lights. For one moment, staring out at the sea of faces, some curious, some skeptical, some openly hostile, she lost her train of thought. She wondered if Toby Watkins was out there. She wondered if he was listening. She wondered if he was still scared, because she understood him better now. She was standing in the middle of this scrutiny, wearing a bullet-proof vest, and she was scared, too.

She said to the assembled crowd, ''Alexandria's police force has failed you.''

A small gasp rose up. The press, electrified by such a bold statement, started scribbling furiously. Mayor Peterson stared at Sandra as if she had lost her mind. Mike and Lieutenant Hopkins appeared to agree with him.

Sandra continued smoothly, ''And you, the people of Alexandria, have failed us.''

Another shocked murmur. People shifted self-consciously on their feet. Sandra leaned forward and got into it.

''The mayor is right. Alexandria is in a state of crisis. We fear one another. In some cases, we hate one another.

We look around and we see only our differences—white or black, rich or poor, cop or civilian. No one tries to look beyond that anymore.

"Ironically, I understand what happened. Economic differences began to divide the community, while standard policing procedure divided citizens from cops. There was a time when common wisdom held that police officers should be removed from the community in order to maintain their objectivity. But when officers only interact with citizens to make arrests, they come to see the entire community as criminals waiting to happen. When citizens only encounter officers when they come to take away their sons or deliver bad news about their daughters, they begin to see the entire police force as an unjust power to be avoided. So these practices bred distrust instead. That was our fault, an honest mistake, and now, we must move beyond that. Now, we must start looking at each other as neighbors again.

"Already, when I gaze out upon this crowd, I see similarities. I see community members who are worried about their town. I see kids who want to feel they have the same opportunities as other kids in other cities in other parts of America. I see lots of people, white, black, rich, poor, cop, civilian, who have been touched by letters written by a thirteen-year-old named Vee. How many of you out there have read those letters to the editor?"

A collective murmur arose. People nodded and seemed encouraged to find their neighbors nodding, too.

Sandra said quietly, "I'd like to tell you the rest of Vee's story, what we've been able to learn. His story is our children's story, and we must never let it happen again."

Sandra glanced down at Mike's background report. Then she slowly spun the tale of a thirteen-year-old boy

growing up on the east side without a father, without a
brother. A shy, quiet boy surrounded by gang activity. A
boy growing up under so much pressure, his own mother
collapsed beneath the strain. And she talked about his at-
tempt to reach out and how, in the end, it sent events
spiraling further from his control.

"We have reason to believe that Vee shot Officer Brody
last night," Sandra said finally, as the reporters continued
to take notes. "We also have reason to believe he was
acting under extraordinary circumstances. Speaking for the
Alexandria police department, we are willing to take that
into account. We are willing to do everything in our power
to help Vee get the assistance he needs. Now it's time to
find out if Vee is willing to do his part by coming forward.
It's time to find out if you, out there, are willing to do
your part by working with us to insure that other children
don't have to grow up like Vee. Are we willing to work
together yet? Are we willing to be citizens of Alexandria,
and not of the east or west side?"

Silence. People glanced uncertainly at one another. Still
confusion and mistrust. Sandra leaned forward and continued almost fervently.

"Please, it's not that hard. There are so many opportunities for us to join forces to improve our lives. Citizens
can work with police officers in community policing. Police officers can work with citizens to clean up graffiti and
reclaim the streets. We can come together on weekends
and holidays, plant shrubs to brighten parks, sweep discarded needles off the sidewalks. We can make this city
better and stronger. Help us try. We all desire peace."

The reporters had questions. They drilled Sandra for
more details about the shooting between Officer Brody and
the teen. She told them, "No comment." They demanded
more information about this "community policing" stuff

She gave them as much as they could take. They asked her if she was being too optimistic. She said no. They asked her if the police were truly willing to cut a deal with a kid who had allegedly shot a police officer. Sandra ignored her officers and said yes.

It took until three-thirty to wrap things up. In the aftermath, Sandra discovered she was suddenly brutally tired. But then she looked around. The crowd had not immediately dispersed. Instead community members were lingering, seeming to look officers up and down. For a change, her men were not glaring back. They seemed to be regarding the citizens with fresh interest, as well.

People were considering her words. They were not convinced, but they were considering.

Beside her, Mike's police radio crackled to life. He stepped aside and put the receiver to his ear.

Sandra took a seat next to Lieutenant Hopkins while she waited.

"Not bad," he grunted.

"Thank you."

"It'll never work," he assured her. "But it makes good PR."

Sandra smiled wanly. Then she noticed Mike. Standing at the back of the speakers' pavilion, he had gone pale. And suddenly, Sandra had a horrible chill.

Slowly she rose to her feet. Slowly she crossed to him.

"Vee?" she whispered.

He shook his head. "Koontz."

"What?"

His arm dropped to his side. His dark eyes were hollow and bleak. "Some officers found his car abandoned six blocks over. It was smashed up and rolled behind a Dumpster. They think it's been there since last night. They think he was probably attacked by a group of rioters when he tried to head home. I shouldn't have let him leave like that. I should've made him wait for me. Oh, God, Sandy, there's blood all over the front seat.''

Chapter 13

Vee stood in a side alley, stubbing his toe on the ground. He'd been running for so long, he didn't know where he was. In gangland turf that was a dangerous thing.

Cops had poured in last night. Black brothers gathering. Vee had read the signs and gotten the hell out of there. Ain't nothing good gonna happen when homeys strap on their colors. Later he heard windows breaking. He heard sirens and car alarms and store alarms as everything busted loose.

He kept on truckin', his head ducked low. Even if he had BGF money in his pocket and two hand guns beneath his shirt, he still be a homey without a hood. No telling what some gang do to him.

Now he was alone and unsure. He be a straight shooter now. He kept waiting to feel different. He didn't.

Mostly his stomach hurt. He wanted to go home.

He guessed he wouldn't be doing that no more. Man like him had to take care of himself. He had money. He could sell a gun for good dough. Live like a king in some junked-out building. No one to answer to but him.

He slouched against the alley wall. He closed his eyes, and he saw his mama in his mind. His big, strong mama, yelling at him to grow up straight.

Vee pressed the heels of his hands hard against his eyes to make the tears go away. Then he heard a noise.

Big kids approaching. Five or six. They be decked out in thick down vests and low-slung jeans. Vee looked around. Had to find some place to hide. Bigger, older homeys be the most dangerous kind. They'd beat the crap out of a small brother like him just for lookin'.

Then Vee noticed something else. Kids be walkin' funny, like they pullin' weight. And they had a half-mad, scary-funny gleam in their eyes. They be laughing and pushing each other around. They be looking mean.

Vee heard a moan. He finally understood. The homeboys had themselves a toy.

White guy. Punked-up good. Bangers be dragging him along by the collar of his shirt. Dude's face was covered in blood. He had that green look people got when punched too much in the stomach. Red froth foamed at his mouth.

Now the brothers be discussin' the best way to kill their cop. They'd been playin' all night and it had gotten old. Time to send a message, the lead banger said.

They came upon Vee. Gave him the stare. He faded into the background, like the little black kid he be, and finally they trudged on, still talking about what to do with their catch.

Cop woke up. Eyes fluttered opened as the brothers dragged him by.

Vee stared at the beaten-up white man and it was too late to turn away. He saw bitterness. He saw rage. He saw a need to fight. Bound and beaten, the man was still prepared to war. He be the kind that go down hard. Like Vee's brother, before he became a white coffin with eighteen bullet holes in his back.

Vee looked at the older kids. He thought of his mama, his sister. He thought of how much they'd cry when they knew what he'd done last night…what he would probably still do. Ain't no going back. His brother had taught him that, too. Ain't no going back.

Least not until ashes to ashes, dust to dust.

Vee stepped back out of the shadows. He said, "Yo. I be Vee."

The other kids stopped. The other kids turned and stared. Leader finally said, "Righteous."

Vee could come over to play.

Three hours later, Mike and Sandra were back at the police station. Mike was pacing the debriefing room with a raw, savage energy that had everyone on edge, especially Sandra. They had gone straight to Koontz's car after receiving the call. CSU was already there, piecing through the wreckage and diligently documenting the scene.

Nothing had been good enough for Mike. He wanted to know exactly when the car had been attacked and exactly when Koontz had been kidnapped. Why hadn't he radioed for assistance? How many kids would it take to roll a car behind a Dumpster? Couldn't they identify any tracks leading away from the wreckage?

After one hour on the scene, CSU hadn't had many ready answers. They believed the blood was old, maybe twenty-four hours old. Preliminary theories were that Koontz had been ambushed, beaten, then led away from his vehicle.

Vice was still working the streets. The Gang Task Force had been making the rounds. No one had heard talk of anyone kidnapping a police officer, though. Twenty-four hours later, they were just discovering that Koontz was gone. Everyone knew that as each hour passed, so did their chances of finding him alive.

Officers were mad again. Mike could see the resentment building in their eyes as they studied broken buildings and pothole-ridden streets. Mike didn't care anymore. He was angry himself and tired of feel-good speeches about everyone playing nice. He'd given those speeches to Koontz and look what had happened to him.

Koontz had been right to be wary. Koontz had been right to be afraid. When all was said and done, Koontz was probably going to die at the hands of some black gangbanger.

And it was Mike's fault. He had let his partner leave alone. He'd been too consumed with taking care of Sandy. Blacks might kill Rusty, but it was his white partner who'd failed him first.

Sandra finally approached him from across the room. Mike read wariness on her face. He wished she'd listen to her own emotions and leave him alone. Now was not a good time. Especially with a room full of fellow officers watching.

"How are you holding up?" she asked quietly.

"Just dandy."

"Mike...it's time to go home—"

"No."

"You haven't slept in nearly thirty-six hours."

"Don't care."

"You are useless in this condition!"

"Sandy, get the hell away from me."

"I can't, Mike. Lieutenant Banks just ordered me to get you out of here. He wants you gone."

Mike promptly looked over at the lieutenant and snarled. Banks didn't care.

Sandy tentatively brushed Mike's arms. The concern was still bright in her eyes. "We have nearly fifty patrols working the streets, Mike. There is nothing we can do now but wait. Come on, Mike, get some sleep."

Mike shook his head, shoving his way forward. But then the room started swimming before his eyes and he had to put out a hand to steady himself. Sandy was looking at him sympathetically. He had pushed himself too hard, and they both knew it. It all just made him angrier. Koontz was his partner. Koontz was his friend.

"Okay, Mike. Here we go."

Sandra led Mike out to his car. He tried to protest, but his exhausted mind was no longer functioning clearly. He didn't even remember the drive to her house. The next thing he knew, she was leading him into her bedroom, and all he could think was he'd made his bed and now he would have to lie in it.

Koontz all alone. *How could you fail your partner like that? How could you put Sandy ahead of Rusty? How could you not? What was a man supposed to do?*

"Sandy, I can't do this anymore. You, me—it's not going to work. We're just going to destroy each other...." Then, as sleep overcame him, he could hear Sandy crying quietly. And he couldn't do anything. He had nothing left to give.

Hours later, he became aware of Sandra lying beside him, her fingers brushing back his hair. In his dreams, he had traveled someplace far away from him, leaving him empty. But now his eyes were open. Reality had returned. He was here. His partner was missing and probably dead.

"We're going to find Koontz," Sandra murmured as he shifted edgily. "It's going to be okay."

"He was my partner and I left him alone with a mob."

"Shh."

"I can't be a good husband and a good partner. Koontz was right."

"No. We're going to get through this, Mike. You, me, and Koontz—"

"Will we?" He rolled over, feeling harsh. Too many images were raw in his mind. Sandra in a peach-colored teddy. Koontz's car, covered in blood. He no longer knew how to make sense of them. "Tell me the truth, Sandy. Your life would be better without Koontz. _Our_ lives would be easier. No more Mike belonging too much to his work. No more Mike hanging out with his partner at the Code Blue. It could be everything you ever wanted."

"No," she protested. "That isn't what I wanted. Not us together like this."

"Yes," he insisted stubbornly.

"No! _Dammit._" She sat up, grabbing his face and looking fierce, the way she always looked when they fought. "Four years ago, Mike," she said sternly, "four years ago I would've said yes. Let Koontz rot in hell. Let me get my husband as far away from the police department as I can. But _I was wrong._ Do you hear me? I was wrong. I wasn't listening to my wedding vows. I wasn't understanding what it really meant to say for better or for worse. Instead I wanted to love you only on my terms, if you'd live where I wanted you to live and work how I wanted you to work and speak to me when I wanted you to speak with me. I loved you without understanding what it meant to really love someone. And for my arrogance, I got to spend four years without you, Mike. We both had to pay our dues.

"Well, I don't want to do that again. As far as I can

tell, this is it. We love each other, we were meant to be together. Together we may fight, but boy, do we make love. Together may involve sacrifice, but apart is so much more lonely. Face it, we challenge each other and understand each other and drive each other nuts. And we're going to grow old together. This time around, we're not going to quit. I won't, and if that means I'm spending the rest of my days with Rusty Koontz as well, then by God, let the man start whittling his rocking chair. Because I'm not letting you go, Mike. I'm not!''

"I can't be both a good husband and a good cop!"

"You can! We were the ones tearing you apart, Mike. It was our fault, not yours."

"He's my best friend, and I failed him. What kind of man does that make me?"

"One who is learning."

"I gotta get back out there." He rolled over, still feeling edgy and undeterred.

"I know. I'll go, too."

Mike immediately shook his head. "You do what you gotta do, Sandy, as chief of police. But I have business out there as a partner. I have some of my own places to go."

"You mean you're going out on your own?" she asked sharply.

He simply nodded.

Sandra inhaled deeply. Her lips parted. He could tell argument was on the tip of her tongue. Then slowly, carefully, her shoulders relaxed.

"I trust you, Mike," she said simply. "You do what you need to do."

The phone rang. Sandra swiped up the receiver. She said hello, then nodded twice, hung up and bolted out of bed. Mike eyed her warily, already steeled for the blow.

"That was Lieutenant Banks," she said simply. "We're supposed to go look at the news."

They both moved into the living room, and a minute later, sat stunned

Alexandria's citizens were flooding the site where Sandra and Mayor Peterson had given their speeches. They were bringing search lanterns and flashlights and jugs of hot coffee. They were bundled up in warm coats and they were all offering their assistance to find Detective Rusty Koontz.

Smithy Jones, with his tattoos and leather jacket, stood on the speaker platform coordinating the scene. He had implored his neighbors to take a stand for justice on the east side, to pull together as a community, and they had responded. Young and old, black and white, they were all convening upon the square.

"Store owners, retirees, working moms, kids. They're being matched up with cops and given a search grid," Sandra observed. "Then they're going door-to-door. Hundreds and hundreds of people, Mike. All looking for Koontz. Isn't it the most beautiful sight you have ever seen?"

It was. Mike put his arms around Sandra. For a few moments, they simply sat beside each other on the carpet, holding each other close.

The news clip ended. Sandra and Mike rose together. No need for words anymore. They grabbed their heaviest jackets, two flashlights and headed for the speaking pavilion.

The night was cold and dark, but the crowd of people lit the way and warmed the air.

Hang in there, Koontz, Mike kept thinking. Hang in there.

* * *

In some house now. Vee didn't know where. Probably belonged to somebody's O.G.B. House reeked. All sweat and urine. Fridge held nothing but beer.

Couple of homeys be sleeping. Collapsed on sofas and snoring to wake the dead. Brothers had been drinking all night, Vee heard. Some wanted to sleep it off. He knew the type. Three others still be awake. Dark looks in their eyes. Crazy drunks. Vee be afraid of them.

Still didn't know what to do. White cop awake now. He be propped up in a corner, shoulders slumped against the wall and legs straight out in front of him. Vee could see the dead man's gaze patrol the room. Watching, waiting. Watching, waiting. White cop never moved, though. His breathing had gained a wheeze. Man not gonna make it much longer. Seemed to know it, too.

The three crazy drunks sat in the kitchen. One of them was bored now. He kept saying, "Let's kill the dude and be done." He had the cop's two guns. He twirled them around and around on both his index fingers.

Other two crazy drunks weren't sure. They were waiting for some other homeboys to arrive. Maybe they shoot the cop then and go dump his body in rival turf. Bring the heat down on the BGFs.

First banger laughed. He thought that was a righteous idea.

Vee roamed the living room, feeling the white cop's gaze. Gotta do something. Didn't know what. Still had two hand guns strapped beneath his shirt. Against a bunch of straight shooters, that meant squat.

Vee stopped in front of the white cop. Guy be staring right at him. He looked mad. Vee finally realized the poor dude was trying to gather enough saliva to spit.

Vee shook his head. "Don't draw attention. Maybe they pass out soon."

Man looked confused.

"I say, F-you mister," Vee said more loudly. He stomped the floor. At the same time, he dropped a gun and quickly kicked it beneath the dead man's leg. Cop's whole body twitched.

Two homeys came into the living room. They looked at Vee, standing over the white cop, then laughed.

"Look, Vee's talking trash to the Man. Ah, just don't kill him too soon, baby dude."

Vee faked a smile.

The white cop spit up blood.

And in the kitchen, the third banger said, "Hey, come here quick. Look what's on TV!"

At the speaking pavilion, a rustic command center was quickly and efficiently coming together. Sandra commandeered a dozen phones from the police station and miles of telephone cord. She sent word out that card tables would be great and the next thing she knew, she had five grandmothers, two grandfathers and three gargantuan great-aunts standing in front of her with card tables and folding chairs. They announced they would man the phones. Sandra obediently set them up.

Shortly thereafter, a small contingency of kids ran underfoot, maintaining a steady pipeline of hot coffee to the tables. Sandra was offered four cups in three minutes, while ten pairs of old black eyes gazed on. She accepted each cup, thanked each child and downed the potent brew. She finally, reluctantly, received a stiff nod of approval.

Sandra decided the phone lines were definitely in good hands and she pitied the first crank caller.

She moved on to where Mike stood next to Lieutenant Banks and Smithy Jones, poring over maps of the city. Lieutenant Banks had sectioned off the city blocks into search quadrants. Smithy Jones was supplying local reconnaissance. This area fell under this gang's control. This area belonged to this group. Drug dealers here, working girls there. If you're going to send people down to that area, make sure they're heavily armed.

Police officers, of course, were taking the most dangerous areas. Lieutenant Banks was also doing his best to assign at least one officer to each patrol group. The officer would give his members general instructions on technique and safety. In the worst-case scenario, the officer would also be present to advise his group on how to preserve the crime scene.

People were trying not to think about that, however. Two hours into the organized effort, the mood was optimistic and almost festive. Citizens were pleased to be part of a greater cause, while police officers were clearly touched. A few veteran cops were even spotted discreetly wiping tears from their eyes. Of course, search efforts generally started on a high note. Surely with so many people coming together they would get the job done.

The mood would slip later, when hours passed without result. When the hot coffee ran out and hope began to dim and the dark night turned into an even more daunting morning. People would stop thinking they were searching for a man and would start thinking they were looking for a body. Then the mood would be entirely different.

For now, Sandra shook Smithy Jones's hand and thanked him for his part in getting this effort going. Smithy blushed and appeared almost giddy.

''Ma'am, that was some speech you gave this afternoon. I've been waiting years for someone to give a speech like that. Gotta say I can't wait to see some things change around here and am just happy to finally have an excuse to act.''

"So I can count you in for community policing? Maybe you'd like to be a block leader?"

"Tell me where to sign."

"You're a great man, Smithy."

The ex-marine blushed again. "Save that for when we find your detective, ma'am. Still got a little work to do here."

He leaned back over the map. Mike tapped a new section and inquired about information.

From what Sandra could tell, it appeared regular patrol officers had thoroughly examined BGF territory during the daylight hours. Ironically, Koontz's car had been found at the apex of three different gangland turfs, making it tricky to judge who might have grabbed him. Mike and Lieutenant Banks were still convinced he could not be held too far away from the automobile. They couldn't imagine Koontz willingly walking anywhere. Rusty knew the rules: Never go anyplace with a captor, not even if the other person had a gun. Odds were always better in a public location than once you'd been led somewhere private.

Chances were, the attackers had knocked Koontz unconscious. Then they'd dragged him somewhere close. A full-grown man was a lot of dead weight to be lugging around a city. Mike promptly paled again at Lieutenant Banks's unfortunate choice of words.

The area around Koontz's abandoned car contained a lot of houses, nearly eight or ten each on a block all nestled shoulder to shoulder. Officers could request to search the premises, but home owners didn't have to let them in. It made matters trickier and time-consuming and the men were clearly not optimistic about results.

"What if we went back to the TV stations?" Sandra asked. "We could offer a reward for Koontz's release."

Lieutenant Banks immediately shook his head. "Oh, no.

We don't want people thinking they can make money by snatching a cop. Then we'd never get through the streets.''

Sandra nodded. She hadn't thought of that.

''We could appeal for his safe return,'' she tried.

This time Mike shook his head. ''The more importance you place on Koontz, the more thoughts you risk putting in the rioters' heads. Then they might think of making ransom demands or a very public statement. It's better for them to turn on the news and see community pressure. Whoever has him has got to live here. If they think their actions are now unpopular, they may quickly change their minds and turn him loose.''

''Okay.'' Sandra rubbed her hands together for warmth. ''I just keep thinking there ought to be more we can do.''

''I know,'' Mike said. He was still studying the map, his expression dark and intent. Finally he pulled away and rubbed the back of his neck. ''I keep thinking there's something we're missing. This is Rusty. If he was conscious at all he'd drop something, try to leave a trail, anything to help us out. So why does it seem as if he vanished into thin air?''

Sandra could only squeeze his hand.

Just then, a little boy came running up, his eyes nearly bursting out of his head. ''Mrs. Chief, Mrs. Chief, phone for you.''

Surprised, Sandra followed him over to the folding tables where one of the great-aunts sat guard, arms folded over her massive chest. Sandra picked up the receiver. The voice was low and rushed, and not who Sandra expected at all. Moments later, she was furiously waving her arms at Mike and Lieutenant Banks.

''I got a lead. Someone grab me a radio. *Now!*''

In the back room, Vee hung up the phone just as a brother appeared.

"What you doin'?" the boy demanded to know.

"Nothin'."

"You were on the phone."

"Called my sister."

The big kid grabbed Vee's ear, hard, and dragged him into the kitchen. All five homeboys were awake again. They'd opened the beer but still carried a mean, hungover edge.

"Hey. I found the little dude on the phone."

The lead banger shrugged. "Who's he gonna call?"

"He said his sister."

Kid shrugged again. "What's he gonna say? Vee don't know where he is, do you, little creep?"

Vee shook his head. He had no idea where he be. He just a long way from home.

"Come on," the lead homey said. "Time to rock."

Everyone moved into the living room. They'd been watching news of the search efforts on TV, hot-line number scrolling across the bottom of the screen. Then the lead brother had kicked the TV onto the floor. All those people working together had ticked him off. Now he said time was up. They had to kill the white cop. Things were getting too hot.

Vee's hands were shaking. It was going down fast. He didn't even know if the pretty chief of police had believed him. Had to speak so quickly. Quiet, too. And he be a cop-killing dude now. Maybe the pretty chief of police didn't even like him no more.

This need not end in violence.

Lady, lady, lady, you gotta come now. Please, please, please. Somebody help me.

But no one knocked down the doors. The crazy drunks moved in on the cop.

White cop's eyes opened. Man, he looked ticked. Anger

burning so bright. White guy's arm swung around. He held Vee's gun.

White cop slurred, "Po—leeese."

And the lead banger kicked the gun outta the man's limp hand. Man didn't have the strength left to swear. He was a goner, and they all knew it. The brother slapped him across the face.

"Come on, crew. Join the fun."

The homeboys moved in for the kill. Most of them were laughing.

Vee knew there was nothing he could do. Boys would kill him, too, or beat him so bad he'd wish he be dead. That's just the way it be. He'd tried to tell everyone that just the way it be. Especially for a stupid, cop-killing baby dude like him.

Vee didn't know what he was doing until he did it. He pulled out his gun. He said, "Halt."

The bangers turned. They looked surprised. Then the lead kid suddenly laughed and his eyes turned ferocious. "Ah, look, the baby dude thinks we're cops. Come on, baby dude. Show us what you got. You draw down on me, you better open fire."

The brother moved in fast. Vee tried to pull the trigger. He wanted to be tough. He wanted to be an O.G.B. Big S Sammy, buried with two guns so he could keep on killin' even up in heaven.

Vee couldn't do it. Not in cold blood.

The kid knocked the gun out of Vee's hand. His crazy gaze now be clear.

And Vee knew what would happen next. His turn to go down. Just like his father. Just like his brother. Another black dude, dying in the hood, and it don't mean a thing.

When the first blow landed, it still hurt more than he thought.

This need not end in violence.…
Poor pretty lady, Vee thought as the metal-toed shoes
*found his head. Poor pretty lady to care about a loser little
kid like me.*

"I see it, I see it," the first volunteer yelled. "Fourth
house in, on the left."

Weasel moved in close, glanced at the front window and
nodded excitedly. He spoke into the radio. "Team F reporting, Team F reporting. We have the house in view.
Requesting backup and EMTs."

Orders followed, curt and quiet. Weasel moved his civilians back. A dark van came to a screeching halt two
blocks over and released a stream of black-clothed men.
The SWAT team poured into Weasel's block and formed
a tight perimeter around the house. Moments later, a sedan
pulled up and Sandra and Mike came running out.

The SWAT team leader assumed command. Orders
came in the form of hand signals. Men in position. Shields
up, battering ram in place. One, two, three.

Four men crashed the wooden ram through the front
door and everything happened at once. Shots fired. Windows breaking. The sound of someone screaming.

"The back, the back," one officer yelled. Two teens
came racing out a side door and were promptly tossed to
the ground. Another tried to come back out the front. He
encountered Mike's enormous build, running up the front
steps to find Koontz. The kid promptly put his hands in
the air.

Mike left the subdued teen for other officers to process.
He burst into the house with Sandra on his heels and only
one thought in his head. And he found himself face to face
with a wild-eyed gangbanger wielding a .45 Colt Magnum.
Mike had just raised his hands in a placating manner when

Sandy stumbled in on his heels. The kid jerked his hand-gun toward her and she promptly froze.

"Easy," Mike said.

They all stood stock-still. The kid was breathing hard, the heavy pistol beginning to tremble in his hands. Around them came shouts as the last few teens surrendered to other police officers. But inside this now tiny space, the Magnum loomed large and the kid's face was growing cruel.

The barrel still rested on Sandy. Mike hated that most of all.

Then a groan came from the corner of the room. Koontz.

"Mike," Sandy said quietly.

"I know."

"Shuddup!"

"Your call," Sandy said. "Whatever you say…"

"Shuddup, dammit!"

"Sandy, duck."

Sandra promptly flattened to the floor. The kid jerked, his gaze automatically dipping down to follow her move-ment. Mike didn't need a second invitation. He stormed forward, catching the kid in the gut with the full force of his shoulder. The teen yelped. Mike wrenched the gun from the boy's hand and pushed the offender to the floor. The boy had no fight left. Robbed of his weapon, he curled up sullenly.

Sandra rose up, dusting off her clothes. The look she gave Mike was grateful and warm and made him feel ten feet tall.

Then a movement in the far corner of the room caught his eye. Mike saw Koontz.

Curled up. Hand holding his belly. Eyes swollen shut. Frothy blood foaming at his lips.

Oh, God.

Mike bolted across the space. He tried to figure out where to touch, how to help. It was beyond him. Vaguely he was aware of Sandy calling frantically for the EMTs. Vaguely he was aware of her own cry as she looked into the adjacent room and discovered Vee. But mostly he just saw Koontz, proud, arrogant Koontz, beaten into a bloody mass on the floor.

"Don't move," he whispered thickly. "I'm here now, partner. Don't move."

Rusty's eyes fluttered open to thin slits. He looked at Mike dimly. His lips curved. Maybe a grimace, maybe a faint smile. Then he coughed violently, his shoulders wracking hard. He said, "Vee...first."

"The EMTs are coming for both of you, buddy. Hang on. Hang on."

"Vee...first."

"Shhh, don't speak. Save your strength."

"Kid...gave me...gun. Too weak." Koontz grimaced. Fresh blood flecked his lips. "Sandy...was right. Damn smart woman. Keep...her."

"I know, I know. Enough talking now, Rusty. You just rest, save your strength. Then you can heckle Sandy yourself. I swear."

Koontz's body suddenly shook. Mike tried to hold his partner together with his hands until the spasm passed. Dammit, where were the EMTs?

Koontz was whispering again. "How?"

"Vee called the hot line. We came as fast as we could."

"Thought...didn't know...place."

"He made a sign for the search parties. He taped two pens to the front window, in the shape of a V."

Koontz smiled roughly. He said, "Good kid."

Then his eyes rolled back in his head.

"Dammit!"

The EMTs were clattering through the front door. They hastily pushed Mike aside, then strapped Rusty to a gurney and administered immediate emergency care.

"Looks like internal bleeding," one EMT said sharply. "Get him stabilized and to the OR. Stat, stat, stat."

They rushed Koontz back down the front stairs into the waiting ambulance. Mike was left all alone, feeling helpless with his partner's blood still smeared across his cheek.

A moment later, Sandra was at his side. She knelt down beside him and put her arms around his shoulders.

"Toby Watkins?" he asked.

"Not good. They loaded him up first."

Mike closed his eyes. "You were right about him, Sandy. He really is a brave kid."

They looked around the room. The V was still taped to the window. Blood spotted the floor.

"Lord, Mike," Sandra said after a moment. "They're supposed to be children. Just children."

Mike didn't say anything. He wasn't sure he could. After a moment, he pressed his face against Sandra's hair. They held each other more tightly. And together, they got through.

Epilogue

The day of the dedication ceremony dawned beautiful and bright. Multicolored helium balloons waved cheerfully in the breeze while newly planted trees showed off a fresh dress of leaves. Sandra, who had spent most evenings for the past four months working on the site, thought it had never looked so lovely.

Of course there had been a lot of help. One of Alexandria's top nurseries had donated the trees and flowerpots now lining the street where her press conference had once been held and a community search effort had been organized. A leading architecture firm, friends of Sandra's family, had agreed to draft a plan for rehabilitating the abandoned warehouse where Vee had fired on Officer Brody. Then, a lumber company had shown up the first day with all the timber and building supplies a community crew could desire. Four carpenters had arrived. An electrician had agreed to do the wiring for free. A plumber decided to do the same. Over long days and longer weekends, the building slowly and surely took shape and community excitement increased.

The next thing anyone knew, a local sporting goods store decided the new community center needed at least four Ping-Pong tables and two pool tables. Their parent company liked the idea so much, it paid to have a basketball court installed in back. A home goods store threw in free carpeting. Their main competitor, not to be outdone, installed a kitchen.

Now three stories of formerly abandoned warehouse gleamed in the morning sun. Windows had been washed, the outside facade freshly painted. All that remained was the ribbon-cutting ceremony, which would formally open the new center to the community.

Outside, the press gathered eagerly. Local citizens were also out in force. Sandra recognized many of her hot-line volunteers seated prominently in their folding chairs. Smithy Jones was also present with his wife Bess. Sandra waved at them both merrily. Smithy's patrol block—Main Street—officially boasted the highest drop in crime the city had ever seen. He'd recently taken over four more blocks and other community volunteers were now training with him. Sandra also liked to start her rookie officers with Smithy's community policing team. More than one cop had grudgingly confessed he learned more from one week with Smithy Jones than one year at the academy.

In the front row, of course, sat the guests of honor. Toby Watkins's mother, doing better these days, and his sister, Opal, who had finally scheduled an appointment with Dr. Morgan. Mayor Peterson was also present, of course. He never missed an opportunity for good press. So were Sandra's parents. She had finagled them a seat next to Mike's parents. She and Mike had a bet over who would draw first blood. So far, Mike's mom was winning, but Sandra's mom was beginning to come up to speed.

Mike and Sandra didn't request that their families mix often. Mostly, they'd found a nice balance by asking their parents over to their house from time to time; that way they could control the atmosphere and the guest list. Plus Sandra and Mike had a new home perfect for entertaining—a nice, sprawling rancher set out on three acres of land. Beautiful back deck, big yard for barbecues. They sported a European country look now, each piece of furniture picked out together for the start of their new life. Lots of old wood and painted pine. It was sophisticated enough for Sandra and comfortable enough for Mike.

She thought it was the first place they'd had both of them considered home.

There'd been other adjustments as well. Right after the beatings, Sandra and Mike had both spent a lot of time at the hospital, Mike with Koontz and Sandra with Vee. That had ended up being good for them. Mike needed quality time alone with his partner, and Sandra also preferred her own interests. She discovered that the less she begrudged Mike time alone with his cop friends, the more open and sharing he became when they finally had time together. They talked more now. They relaxed and laughed outside of the bedroom.

Sandra thought they appreciated and respected each other more. Two months ago, they'd even gone running off all by themselves and had a second wedding. Just the two of them and some little old lady they'd dragged in off the street to be a witness. It was the most wonderfully romantic moment of Sandra's life. And not a bad wedding night…

Things were definitely going well these days. Sandra rested her hand lightly on her stomach. Then she saw the time and hastily returned to her seat. Mike was already there, grinning.

"Think he can get through it without breaking into a sweat?" he asked.

"Not a chance."

"Department pool is giving only one-to-one odds that he cracks."

"Department pool is smart."

The mayor stepped up to the microphone and they obediently quieted down. Mike took Sandra's hand. She squeezed his fingers. She knew he was secretly proud of his partner and Koontz deserved it. The gruff detective was now the number-one proponent of community policing in the department. He'd also spent a number of his weekends working on the community center. Somehow or another, he was never that far away from Toby Watkins. Recently he had even joined the Big Brother program. Twenty guesses on who he'd chosen to be his little brother. The two were good for each other.

The mayor gave his spiel. He talked about the "momentous" events of last spring, when the city had almost gone to war. He recapped Vee's letters, the shooting, and then Vee's life on the run. Standing beside Koontz in front of the crowd, the fourteen-year-old wiggled self-consciously. Then the mayor started talking about the capture of Detective Rusty Koontz, who had worked heroically to stem the riots. Koontz, beaten within an inch of his life, held hostage by five drunken teens.

Koontz turned bright red and looked as if he wished the ground would swallow him whole. Vee punched him playfully in the arm, happy to have the spotlight off him, and the crowd laughed.

Mayor Peterson revved up for the grand finale. Everyone coming together to find the captured detective and the kid named Vee. African-Americans working with Caucasians, civilians working with cops, old working with young. The power of community.

Everyone nodded. Most had become involved in various efforts and they liked to feel good about it.

Finally, the conclusion. For his heroic efforts in aiding Detective Koontz, Toby Watkins received a limited sentence for shooting at police officers. In addition to community services, Toby took weekly anger management classes and reported to a juvenile parole officer to make sure he stayed on track. Now, in order to reach out to other youths, Alexandria was officially opening this new community center, named the Toby H. Watkins Building. East side's children would now have a safe place to hang out after school. They could blow off steam playing games and sports. They could receive tutoring or join mentoring programs. The community center was even trying to get its hands on a number of computers. Soon east-side kids could be exploring the Internet.

The potential was boundless, the way it should be for children. And now, Mayor Peterson officially declared the building open.

Together, Koontz and Vee held up the oversize scissors. At the last minute, however, Koontz backed up and let Toby do the honors alone.

Vee snipped the yellow ribbon. Lightbulbs flashed and everyone cheered.

"Koontz did well," Mike said approvingly, clapping away.

"He wimped out."

"He was showing respect for Toby."

"He was scared out of his mind."

"Ha. My kid's better than yours," Mike teased.

"In your dreams." But Sandra was laughing, too. She

drew down her husband's head for a kiss that lingered, then grew. Second chances, Sandra thought, had never tasted so sweet.

* * * * *

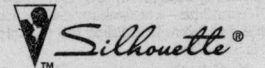

SILHOUETTE'S 20TH ANNIVERSARY CONTEST
OFFICIAL RULES
NO PURCHASE NECESSARY TO ENTER

1. To enter, follow directions published in the offer to which you are responding. Contest begins 1/1/00 and ends on 8/24/00 (the "Promotion Period"). Method of entry may vary. Mailed entries must be postmarked by 8/24/00, and received by 8/31/00.

2. During the Promotion Period, the Contest may be presented via the Internet. Entry via the Internet may be restricted to residents of certain geographic areas that are disclosed on the Web site. To enter via the Internet, if you are a resident of a geographic area in which Internet entry is permissible, follow the directions displayed on-line, including typing your essay of 100 words or fewer telling us "Where In The World Your Love Will Come Alive." On-line entries must be received by 11:59 p.m. Eastern Standard time on 8/24/00. Limit one e-mail entry per person, household and e-mail address per day, per presentation. If you are a resident of a geographic area in which entry via the Internet is permissible, you may, in lieu of submitting an entry on-line, enter by mail, by hand-printing your name, address, telephone number and contest number/name on an 8"x 11" plain piece of paper and telling us in 100 words or fewer "Where In The World Your Love Will Come Alive," and mailing via first-class mail to: Silhouette 20th Anniversary Contest, (in the U.S.) P.O. Box 9069, Buffalo, NY 14269-9069; (In Canada) P.O. Box 637, Fort Erie, Ontario, Canada L2A 5X3. Limit one 8"x 11" mailed entry per person, household and e-mail address per day. On-line and/or 8"x 11" mailed entries received from persons residing in geographic areas in which Internet entry is not permissible will be disqualified. No liability is assumed for lost, late, incomplete, inaccurate, nondelivered or misdirected mail, or misdirected e-mail, for technical, hardware or software failures of any kind, lost or unavailable network connection, or failed, incomplete, garbled or delayed computer transmission or any human error which may occur in the receipt or processing of the entries in the contest.

3. Essays will be judged by a panel of members of the Silhouette editorial and marketing staff based on the following criteria:

   Sincerity (believability, credibility)—50%

   Originality (freshness, creativity)—30%

   Aptness (appropriateness to contest ideas)—20%

   Purchase or acceptance of a product offer does not improve your chances of winning. In the event of a tie, duplicate prizes will be awarded.

4. All entries become the property of Harlequin Enterprises Ltd., and will not be returned. Winner will be determined no later than 10/31/00 and will be notified by mail. Grand Prize winner will be required to sign and return Affidavit of Eligibility within 15 days of receipt of notification. Noncompliance within the time period may result in disqualification and an alternative winner may be selected. All municipal, provincial, federal, state and local laws and regulations apply. Contest open only to residents of the U.S. and Canada who are 18 years of age or older, and is void wherever prohibited by law. Internet entry is restricted solely to residents of those geographical areas in which Internet entry is permissible. Employees of Torstar Corp., their affiliates, agents and members of their immediate families are not eligible. Taxes on the prizes are the sole responsibility of winners. Entry and acceptance of any prize offered constitutes permission to use winner's name, photograph or other likeness for the purposes of advertising, trade and promotion on behalf of Torstar Corp. without further compensation to the winner, unless prohibited by law. Torstar Corp and D.L. Blair, Inc., their parents, affiliates and subsidiaries, are not responsible for errors in printing or electronic presentation of contest or entries. In the event of printing or other errors which may result in unintended prize values or duplication of prizes, all affected contest materials or entries shall be null and void. If for any reason the Internet portion of the contest is not capable of running as planned, including infection by computer virus, bugs, tampering, unauthorized intervention, fraud, technical failures, or any other causes beyond the control of Torstar Corp. which corrupt or affect the administration, secrecy, fairness, integrity or proper conduct of the contest, Torstar Corp. reserves the right, at its sole discretion, to disqualify any individual who tampers with the entry process and to cancel, terminate, modify or suspend the contest or the Internet portion thereof. In the event of a dispute regarding an on-line entry, the entry will be deemed submitted by the authorized holder of the e-mail account submitted at the time of entry. Authorized account holder is defined as the natural person who is assigned to an e-mail address by an Internet access provider, on-line service provider or other organization that is responsible for arranging e-mail address for the domain associated with the submitted e-mail address.

5. Prizes: Grand Prize—a $10,000 vacation to anywhere in the world. Travelers (at least one must be 18 years of age or older) or parent or guardian if one traveler is a minor, must sign and return a Release of Liability prior to departure. Travel must be completed by December 31, 2001, and is subject to space and accommodations availability. Two hundred (200) Second Prizes—a two-book limited edition autographed collector set from one of the Silhouette Anniversary authors: Nora Roberts, Diana Palmer, Linda Howard or Annette Broadrick (value $10.00 each set). All prizes are valued in U.S. dollars.

6. For a list of winners (available after 10/31/00), send a self-addressed, stamped envelope to: Harlequin Silhouette 20th Anniversary Winners, P.O. Box 4200, Blair, NE 68009-4200.

Contest sponsored by Torstar Corp., P.O. Box 9042, Buffalo, NY 14269-9042.

PS20RULES

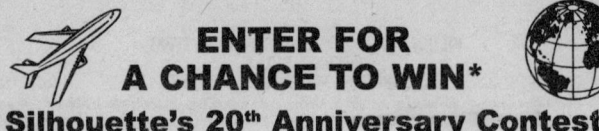
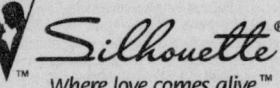